I0823119

PRAISE FOR *NARROW THE ROAD*

"A born storyteller and a joy to discover, James Wade is one of, if not *the* finest novelists in Texas. Filled with engrossing characters and a young man's need to do what he thinks is right and necessary, *Narrow the Road* is a heartfelt coming-of-age tale that will sweep you away."
—REAVIS Z. WORTHAM, AUTHOR OF THE TEXAS RED RIVER MYSTERIES

"This is a haunting and lyrical journey down an uncertain path, where dangers lurk in the shadows, but friendship and courage will help us survive in a broken world."
—WES FERGUSON, JOURNALIST, PODCASTER, AND AUTHOR OF *RUNNING THE RIVER*

"A saga that could be likened to other master storytellers, but Wade's voice is his own…A soulful, thoughtful, and wise story I didn't want to end."
—DONNA EVERHART, AUTHOR OF *WOMEN OF A PROMISCUOUS NATURE*

"One of the best journey novels I've read in a long time. You can feel the sting of sweat in your eyes and smell the foulness of Texas's Big Thicket. James Wade is the Western's heir apparent to Cormac McCarthy."
—JOHNNY D. BOGGS, TEN-TIME SPUR AWARD WINNER

"Mythic and sweeping yet intimate and humble…James Wade summons a storm of words and emotions and masters it like a prophet in the eye of his own hurricane. One of America's greatest storytellers, he has delivered yet another memorable masterpiece."
—RUDY RUIZ, AUTHOR OF *THE BORDER BETWEEN US*

NARROW THE ROAD

BOOKS BY JAMES WADE

NOVELS

Narrow the Road

Hollow Out the Dark

Beasts of the Earth

River, Sing Out

All Things Left Wild

NARROW THE ROAD

A NOVEL

JAMES WADE

Published in 2025 by Blackstone Publishing
Cover and book design by Kathryn Galloway English
Gorilla illustration by Turaev/Adobe Stock Images

Printed in the United States of America

First edition: 2025
ISBN 978-1-6650-2413-6
Fiction / Literary

Version 1

Blackstone Publishing
31 Mistletoe Rd.
Ashland, OR 97520

www.BlackstonePublishing.com

For my children

Thou spurnest the hollows and trees
That offer thee refuge of peace,
And findest within the sky
No safety or respite

Clark Ashton Smith, "The Mad Wind"

But small is the gate and narrow the road that leads to life, and only a few find it.

Matthew 7:14

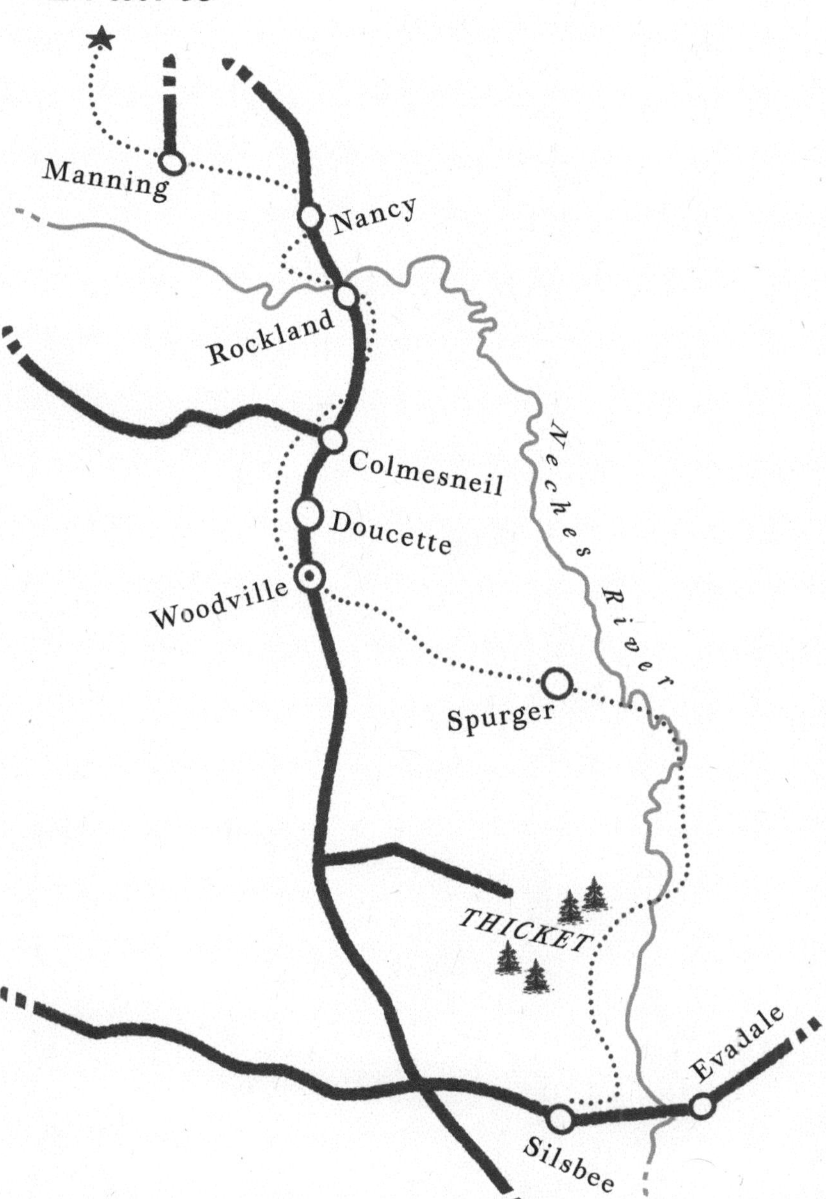
Highway
William's Path
Shawnee Prairie
Manning
Nancy
Rockland
Colmesneil
Doucette
Woodville
Neches River
Spurger
THICKET
Evadale
Silsbee

PROLOGUE

Here he comes, this boy. And what to make of him?

A gawky, spindle-shanked creature. Fair hair and fair skin—set about with freckles—and knobbed knees and big green doe eyes, and at least the young fella has boots. Endicott Johnson, by the looks of them. Good, strong leather. A much finer wear than his ragtag jeans and soiled cotton shirt. Canvas sack tied to a cane pole and resting there on his sharp bone of a shoulder.

Wayward young wanderer, alone against the enormity of being.

But on he comes, ever forward through the trees. Through blue and blackjack oaks, over grasses and forbs, and beneath great willows in their eternal weeping. On he comes.

A young person in a dying land. A dying time. War and rumors of war. Pandemics and economic woes, and what option is left to him but to keep at the path, unforgiving though it may be?

Here he is, this boy. Made up, like the rest of us, from that first whit of calcium what came spilling forth from the cosmos, fleeing the last gasps of dying stars in that time before time—abandoning their elemental hosts so that a new form might come barreling into existence. Vestiges of forgotten galaxies turned energy ripe for creation.

And what does he want if not some answer for it all? Some reckoning for the pain.

He wouldn't mind the hurt. No. Wouldn't hold it against the hand that engenders infinity, so long as it's purposed. So long as it's just.

And where might he turn to quiet the great dread? Fear rattling bone and spirit alike.

Might he pray? Seek out some temporary stillness bought by viridity and superstition?

Well. Bless him, then. Bless us all. Because it won't be silenced. It can't be—such terror. Such wonder.

And there now, he passes. One and the same.

Look at him. Closer.

There might be something to him yet. Some sort of grit. And he'll need it, won't he? Traveler upon this cursed and thankless path. Pilgrim of the one true passage. Ever forward.

Listen close, friend. Can you hear it?

You know that rhythm.

You can feel it beating.

Withered and worn, but still this boy's heart beats as if it were your own.

Even as you shake your head, his heart is your own.

I

LEAVING

September 1932
Shawnee Prairie, Texas

1

He woke to her wailing.

What dreams his consciousness chased from his mind, the boy could not say. Something that happened long ago. Perhaps a thing that never happened at all.

He lay awake in the hot dark and stared out the open window and a lizard passed along the sill and he watched it come and go and waited for it to return again but it did not.

"Thomas," she cried from the other room. "Take it away. It's in my head."

He closed his eyes and held them shut tight as if he were a small child hiding from ghosts. As if only the things he looked upon would be made real.

Then low moans and he could hear her turning in the sheets. Crying.

"Take it away."

He'd gone to her twice in the night. Twice every night. He made sure she had water though she rarely drank. Made sure she had food though she rarely ate.

"That's about all you can do, if she's gonna keep refusing the morphine," Doc had told him.

Time passed. She settled. The house was quiet again. Quiet and hot.

He kept his eyes closed for a good while, but sleep had fled and the dreams with it and eventually the boy stood and pulled on his clothes, all but the shoes, and went barefoot into the kitchen and lit the fire and put the coffee on to boil. He could feel the dawn, inching ever upward.

He drank his coffee in the near dark of the morning and watched from the porch as the car's headlights made shadows of the forest where it came out from the trees and alongside the scarce field of cotton. It was a Chevy Confederate with a stove-bolt engine and the boy knew the car and knew the man and what he wanted. He pitched the last of his coffee into the yard and let the car come closer before turning and walking into the little house and leaving the door open behind him.

He grabbed a rag and used it to pick up the metal pot by the handle and he filled his empty cup halfway and took down another cup from the shelf and filled it as well. Then he took both cups and set them on the table and sat himself in a fiddleback chair.

There was a brass beveled mirror hung on the adjacent wall and the boy looked at himself through the layers of dust and grime and he straightened his back and tried to make himself taller while he waited for the bank man to knock on the door.

Mr. Roth sat across the table, sweating in a three-piece suit. Frowning. He pushed back at the trace of hair left atop his head and leaned forward.

"Do you understand what foreclosure means, son?"

The boy looked out the kitchen window at the pale dawn as it gave shape to a bank of rolling thunderheads. Flycatchers with yellow bellies and thick gray necks dotted the various lengths of barbed-wire fence meant to keep the neighboring cattle away from the cotton. But there was little cotton to speak of and the boy had not seen a cow in months.

"He built this house," the boy said without looking away from the window. "It's his."

"He might've built the house, but the land it's sitting on belongs to the bank. I've held off as long as I can, but they've sent these fellas down from Dallas and it's about to be out of my hands."

"The land," the boy repeated, and the light now throwing the shapes of the fence posts along the ground—umbra and penumbra alike, reaching out over old rusting saw disks, piles of scrap wood, and the much-traveled Parlin plow.

"They won't even wait until harvest?" he asked, turning to stare at the man for the first time.

"You might could put them off that long. But speaking plainly, it won't matter much," Mr. Roth said, his eyes affixed to his ledger book. "Do you know what cotton's at, as of this morning?"

"Six or seven a pound?"

"Try five and a quarter. Besides, I've seen your crop, William. Even if these were the old days, how much do you really think you're going to cull out there?"

The boy nodded.

"It's been tough," he mumbled. "Just me and Clara. Still, there might be some late bloomers."

"Clara? That the mule? You could sell her," Roth said, shrugging. "Wouldn't stop the bank, but it might keep you in groceries for another month or two."

Roth looked to the darkness of the hallway where the morning light had not yet reached.

"How's she doing?" he asked.

The boy didn't look and didn't answer.

"You ought to get her down to Jefferson Davis in Houston," Roth said.

"Hospitals cost money, don't they?"

"They do, sure. But there's some doctors now that'll accept installment plans or—" Roth stared at the boy with a certain pity. "What about Thomas? Any word?"

William stayed quiet.

"You know, if he were to talk to these fellas, there might be a way to buy some time," Roth went on. "With his history, I mean. They'd probably feel a little more squeamish tossing a veteran out of his house."

"I heard Lonnie Stone and them boys talking at the exchange," William said. "They say help's coming once Hoover gets the boot."

"Won't matter," Roth told him, shaking his head. "Roosevelt will win, there's no doubting that. But he won't take office until next year. And it'll be a good long while before all those promises make their way down here. If at all. Do you know where he is? Your father? I know things didn't go well for him in DC. I was pulling for him. For all of them. It ain't right that the government won't pay their own soldiers what they're owed."

"What about the mill?" the boy asked.

Roth sighed and leaned back and took a rag from his pocket and dabbed at his forehead in a hurried manner, as if he'd lost something up there and was feeling around for it.

"You're what, thirteen?" he asked.

"Fifteen."

"Well, that would be old enough if the mill was hiring. But I'm afraid they're going the opposite direction. And even if they were to have something come open, there's grown men chomping at the bit for an opportunity. I can't imagine them passing over half the county just to hire a boy. Not to mention the bank wants the money now. Today. Hell, yesterday. They ain't gonna sit around and wait on a year's worth of paychecks."

"There's got to be something," the boy said, but his voice betrayed the words.

"Listen, William, you're my first stop this morning, but you won't be my last. People are hurting, and all of them are looking for ways out. Just like you. Sometimes there's nothing left to do but let go. And without your daddy here to speak on his own behalf . . . well."

"He's on his way back," the boy lied. "He ought to be home any day now."

Roth looked at his watch. Looked around the small, plain house. Puncheon logs along the floor. Crochet doilies on the table. A small stack of books in the corner. The boy seemed thin. Seemed tired.

"That's good," Roth told him. "The sooner the better. I know these jackasses from the Dallas branch. When the time comes, they'll have an auction. Try to sell off the farm and recoup some of what Thomas owes them."

The boy shook his head.

"How long?"

"There's paperwork. Postings. I'd guess end of this month. Early October at the latest," Roth said. "There's places you could go. Dallas. Houston. They have some camps down that way where I heard you—"

"Shantytowns," the boy cut him off. "She wouldn't last a day. Even if she could make the trip."

Roth closed his eyes and took a deep breath.

"I wish I had something else to tell you," he said.

"But you don't."

"No."

"Well. I guess that's it then."

"I guess so," Roth said, standing.

He nodded and shoved the rag back into his pocket and picked up his ledger and walked across the small cabin to the door. He stopped with his hand on the knob and turned back. The boy was still sitting at the table, his back to the door. Streaks of penciled light fell across him and across the room and captured small motes of dust therein, and Roth let his head drop as if he would speak some sacred word.

"I'm too old to believe there's any sort of fairness in life," Roth said. "But the things the Lord has seen fit to put on your plate—and with Thomas not being here—well, it just don't set right. I don't know. I don't know what I'm trying to say. I'm sorry is all. For whatever that's worth."

The boy turned in the chair and looked up at him.

"It's worth less than cotton."

2

Soon the light burned golden orange beyond the reefs of clouds, as if the storm would bring with it a great fire upon this blighted domain.

William waited until the sound of the car's motor had faded into the morning and then stood and walked down the short hall to the bedroom and took off his hat and waited again outside the door.

It was slightly ajar and he peered through the slivered gap like a voyeur. She was laying there and her eyes were closed and he wondered if she'd heard any of what was said.

He pushed the door open. Its modest creaking abrupt in the quiet house and so too his footsteps on the wood floor as he crossed the room, and so too the ever-clicking pendulum of the wall clock as it swings back and forth in a morose and merciless rhythm.

Sepia photographs with curled edges were scattered on top of the dresser across from the bed and medals hung from the long oval mirror above it. In the corner of the room under a small table there was a shave kit and an old pocketknife that had been tossed on top of a wadded army jacket, and next to them a pair of black, mud-crusted boots. His father had worn brown boots the day he left.

The wooden desk chair stood vigil at her bedside where the boy had moved it weeks ago. Weeks that felt like years. He went slowly to the chair and pulled it forward a half inch and sat with his hat on his knee.

He studied her. The linen that covered her body was threadbare and faded and it rose and fell with each breath. Short and shallow breath.

He leaned over and felt the sheets and found they were soaked in her sweat.

He took her hand and held it in his own and brought it up to his face and kissed it and touched it to his cheek.

She stirred awake. Her eyes opened green and for a moment he thought he saw the old fire burning therein. Something left of the woman he remembered—a fraction of soul untouched by disease and the decline that follows.

She blinked and the flame was gone.

"C'mon, Momma," he said, and he gathered her up in his arms, small and bent and clinging to his neck, and sat her in the chair next to the bed and pulled the sheets off and tossed them through the doorway and into the den. He took a folded set of sage-colored sheets from the closet and stretched them over the bed. They were almost twice the size of the mattress and he tucked them underneath until they were pulled taut across the top.

"Your father bought those sheets," she said, her head lolling to one side as she slumped in the chair. "It was a flea market in Diboll. He said he'd never seen green sheets before. Said one day we would have a bed big enough to fit them."

William picked her back up and laid her on the flea market sheets.

"I think they were the only thing he ever bought at that market that wasn't a book," she said. "We'd come home with an apple box full."

She was looking past him at something too far away to see.

"The smartest man I ever met," she said. "Your father."

He stood for a while and watched her.

"I'm cold, William," she said after a time, her eyes still holding their distance.

He covered her with a quilt his great-grandmother had made.

"Give me another one, won't you?" she said.

"You'll get too hot, sweat through the sheets again. Let's just start with one."

He wiped down the chair with an old towel and pitched the towel into the den with the wet sheets.

She was mumbling now. Her lips purple, her face impossibly pale.

"I told him not to go," she said, soft. "I told him to stay here with me."

"Daddy?" the boy asked, and the word felt strange and he was embarrassed for saying it.

"He wouldn't listen," she continued. "He said everybody else was going. Homer Renfro, Dee Allen, Jonas Compton. He said they would think he was a coward if he didn't go too. I said that wasn't true, but he just wouldn't listen."

William frowned. The memory was as old as he was. Born just before the war.

"Momma, that was—"

"My head," she screamed, her body wrenching in a sudden pain. "It's in my head."

Her hands gripped at the mattress. Knuckles white. Face twisted up in an agony all her own.

The boy moved quickly and slid a bucket out from under the bed frame. There was an inch of water in the bottom and a tattered rag draped over the side. He soaked the rag and wrung it out and laid it over his mother's forehead. She recoiled from the dampness but he held the rag on her and then he held his hands on either side of her face and told her it was alright and told her he loved her and told her the pain would go away and in time it did.

He kept his hands on her while her breathing steadied.

"Better?" he asked.

She nodded.

"Doc says you don't have to hurt like this," William told her. "If you'd just let him give you something for the pain."

"I rejoice in my suffering," she said. "I share in it with Christ my Savior, for He suffered as well—suffered beyond anything you or me could ever imagine."

The boy's shoulders fell. He looked away.

"There's been something wrong with the coffee," she said, rolling onto her side with her back toward him. "I can't taste it."

"There's nothing wrong with it."

"I think I'd like some orange juice," she said.

"We don't have any oranges."

"What about those great big oranges we picked from Miriam Quinn's orchard?"

"That was two years ago," he said, but she wasn't listening.

"I've always liked Miriam. A godly woman. Maybe she can help look after you."

"What?"

"Once I'm gone, I mean," his mother said, and her tone was neither sad nor fearful.

"We don't have to worry about that for a long time yet," he told her. "Not until you're an old woman."

She ignored him still.

"I heard you and Mr. Roth," she said.

"You did?"

"Don't let anyone take me to Houston."

"Why not?"

"This is my home, William," she said, and now she turned toward him so that he might see the finality in her face. "This is where I belong."

"Might be that there's doctors in Houston who could save you."

"I'm already saved, child," she said. "Besides, I want to be here when your father gets back."

William chewed at the inside of his cheek.

"It's been months," he said, almost a whisper. "What if he doesn't come back?"

"He'll come back."

"How do you know?"

"I saw it," she told him. "In a dream. I was cold and it was raining. He brought me Lenten roses—a great big bouquet."

William shook his head. He wasn't sure if it was her unshakable faith that bothered him or the lack of his own.

He saw the hurt in her every movement but still she reached out and took his hand.

"William," she said, reading the consternation on his face. "Don't turn your heart from him. There is a reason for this. And a reason for everything. One day you'll understand."

He resented the way she looked at him—like it was *she* who pitied *him*.

He was too young to remember the first time his father left. Thomas had gone to Washington to help Robert Marx fight for the rights and care of disabled veterans. Together they'd helped establish the Disabled American Veterans and started chapters across the country. William was six when his father returned in 1923 but he was gone again soon after—called away to testify before committees or lobby on behalf of veterans. Then there were the funerals. Dozens of men who Thomas had served with and who had survived the war only to return home and find they could not survive themselves. But he would return for the planting and harvest, and in those days William considered the excitement of receiving letters or postcards bearing his own name as nearly being worth his father's absence.

As time passed, Thomas was away more frequently. Field hands were hired out to help with the crops. The letters that William had so looked forward to were now fewer and further between and when they did come they were only reminders that he did indeed have a father, even if only one whose image he'd conjured in his head. Memories and brief conversations like projections of an incomplete puzzle that William was trying to solve.

Then the market fell.

Some cared. Others did not. Few in Texas saw it as the panic-inducing event that the eastern newspapers claimed. It won't spread, they said, and yet spread it did. A black shadow. A cold truth.

In the three years that followed, the boy's father spent his days at his desk, penning letters until his hands turned dark with ink stains and at night he'd travel to Manning or Diboll to speak at town meetings or rally mill workers to unionize. But his primary allegiance was to those he'd fought alongside and he began working tirelessly to demand veterans' war bonds be released to them.

Sometimes there were meetings held in their own home and the boy would press his ear to his bedroom door and try to understand what was being talked about. As if in understanding words like *depression* and *revolution* he might thereby understand something of his father.

"Our brothers across the country are starving. Half of these men will be in the bread lines by spring," he'd hear his father say. "That's if they survive the winter. The government has turned its back. We must march on Washington. Form ranks."

"It's a terrible thing, Thomas," someone said. "And I will pray for them day and night but we have our own families to think about, do we not?"

"Besides," another man added, "the Manning mill is still open. They've only furloughed the coloreds."

There was silence and William could hear his father's boots as he paced.

"Would that Christ had been so lucky as to share your selfish nature, gentlemen," Thomas said at last. There were a few groans.

"Love thy neighbor as thyself," he said, "but only until they're worse off."

"Nobody's saying that, Thomas. But there's got to be some priority, don't there?"

"Justice is the priority. If Congress won't release the bond money then families will starve and children will die and there is no other priority than preventing that from happening."

"I'm with you on this," another said. "But who's to say Hoover or anybody else won't just run us off. I'm not looking to get shot at ever again unless it's my brother-in-law returning fire."

A few chuckles.

"That's why it ought to be a great demonstration," Thomas said. "Thousands. Tens of thousands. For all the failures of the United States government, it does respect its veterans. It owes us a debt. And I believe we can convince our representatives to make good on that debt."

When all the men had gone, the boy's father sat drinking by the wood-burning stove. The boy had not heard his mother's footsteps, soft as they must have been, but now she was talking and he strained to hear her quiet voice.

"Please," he heard her say.

His father spoke too now in hushed tone.

"Have I lied to them?" he said. "Is there any hope left?"

"Turn to the Lord, Thomas. As you've always done."

"He has abandoned me," Thomas said, his voice rising.

"Hush—you'll wake him."

Footsteps. Then the front door opened.

"Stay with me, tonight," she said. "Please, Thomas."

The door slammed and the boy went to the window and peered out as his father walked out to the barn like a man condemned. The night was cold and dark and empty. Even the most industrious insects had long gone to ground for the winter.

The boy could hear his father's boots crunching into the frozen ground with each step and could see the smoke from his breath and halfway across the yard the man stopped and leaned his head back, staring up at the heavens as if they'd just called his name.

There were bands of moonlight loosely held by the clouds that covered them but mostly there was darkness and past the door of the barn it was darker still. The boy watched his father walk alone into the black of it all, himself but a shadow returning home.

Thomas left in early February on the coldest day of the year. The air was drugged with burning pine as smoke rose from chimneys, and orchards in the throes of winter lay bare along the countryside which itself was covered in wheatgrass and wild rye and covered also in winter grass whose spears and awn-tipped seeds had been long foraged by turkey and deer so that only great seas of glume remained in those golden-brown pastures. Pastures, William thought, that must roll on forever. Though he'd heard of mountains and oceans and deserts that stretched further than any man might venture, he still saw the world with his eyes, and his eyes knew there was not but field and forest. River and stream. And while his mother had repeated exhaustively that his father was doing what was best, William's eyes saw not but the train departing. He wanted to ask how long he might be gone, but he knew not to—in that same way he knew not to ask about money or taking the day off or what his sister's middle name had been. And so he watched the train leave and watched his mother smile and wave as if she were happy to see it go.

He felt the same way now, sitting at her bedside. His mother in denial and himself a child on a platform, being left behind. He looked at her laying there, frail and thin and fading.

"He abandoned us," he whispered, and when his mother hushed him his voice only grew louder.

"He abandoned us," he said again.

His mother closed her eyes as if she would deny even seeing his words.

"There are others who need his help more than us," she said. "We have to be strong in his absence."

He wondered if she believed that truly—or if it had simply become a tool she used to comfort herself.

"There is salvation in sacrifice," she told him. "What he does, he does for the greater good. There are so few men who can bear the weight of this world and still strive to help others. You ought to be proud your father is one of them."

"But how can anybody matter more than his own family?" he challenged her. "How could he just leave us?"

"I'm not gonna talk to you when you're acting this way."

He was tired and angry and near to shaking.

"Fine," he said, and he left the room and left her there with her eyes closed.

"Don't go off like this, William," she said softly, and the door slammed and she heard his boots on the porch and then she heard nothing at all. "Not like this."

3

William went out back to the barn and already the promising rain clouds had cleared with nary a drop. The barn door was open and Clara lay on her side in the shaded entryway. She rose at the boy's approach and walked and stood next to the tack wall.

"Not today," William told her as she stamped at the dirt floor. "I just come to check on the cotton."

William heard something in the shadows. They quieted, boy and mule.

A white-faced owl came barreling down from the rafters and William ducked and raised his hands as it passed overhead. It swung low across the field from north to south and landed on the top rim of the well and looked back at the boy and screamed and then took again to the sky and was gone beyond the trees.

He watched it disappear and turned back to Clara who was watching it also.

"Been in here with you all night?" he asked the mule.

"Come in around eleven thirty," a voice said, and William turned and there was a boy about his age emerging from a pile of hay like some strange farm golem. He wore brown breeches with unclipped suspenders dangling and a once-white shirt with stalks of straw still clinging to it.

"Jesus Christ, Ollie," William said.

"Them ones with white faces is bad luck," the boy replied.

"What are you doing?" William asked him.

"I slept here."

"I can see what you did, bud. I was more on the trail of why you did it."

"My aunt and her whole brood showed up at the house yesterday," Ollie said, brushing at his sleeve. "Six squawking kids and a wagonload of shit from their place in Weatherford. Husband out of work these last six months. Momma said it's the Christian thing to do."

Ollie looked around and spied his boots near the hay and reached down and pulled them on.

"She'd better hope five loaves can feed five thousand," he added.

"Y'all ain't got but two bedrooms in that house," William said.

"And here now, my good buddy comes to the *why* of the matter—like a horse not realizing he's been led to water until he's standing three hands deep in the middle of the stream," Ollie said, clapping William on the back. "I seen Herbert Roth's car this morning. What'd he have to say about the way of things?"

"Says they're crooked and liable to stay as such. You working today?"

Ollie had walked out of the barn and unbuttoned his pants.

"You know I am," he said, and commenced urinating on the dry dirt. "The old man has me prepping Mrs. Spivey this morning."

"Mrs. Spivey died?"

"Day before yesterday," Ollie said.

William leaned, cross-armed, against the open door.

"She used to beat me red with a hickory switch if I talked during Sunday school," he said.

"You ain't telling me nothing. I imagine there's half of Angelina County with scars across their ass on account of that old woman."

"Well. Good luck getting the wrinkles out of her."

Ollie fastened his suspenders and bent backward at the waist and stretched.

"Daddy says I ought to call them acquired facial markings. Says it gives the decedent some sort of dignity."

"Yeah? What's he say about the dignity of sleeping in barns?"

"Don't piss in the oat bucket and always lock up behind you," Ollie said, grabbing an old hat from a tack wall peg and centering it atop his head. "But seeing as you're here and I'm late, I'll just leave everything to you."

"That was my great-grandfather's hat," William told him, amused.

"I do believe he'd have wanted me to have it," Ollie said without hesitating. "You know your cotton looks like shit?"

"I know it."

"More rain than I've ever seen this past winter, then the spigots shut off."

"Yep."

"What a shame."

"Sure is."

"Tough time to be growing anything at all, really," Ollie went on. "I mean even the jackrabbits are carrying canteens. You know I bet there ain't a half dozen farms in the whole county that won't lose a good bit of their—"

"Ollie," William said.

"Right. Sorry, bud."

"It don't matter much," William told him. "Roth said the bank's getting ready to auction this place off anyway."

The two of them looked out at the sparse, heat-worn field. Beyond the ragged rows of cotton there was a brown grassy knoll and at its peak stood a line of trees like sentries to some darker world where even the sun has no authority.

"Shit, son," Ollie shook his head and then turned and looked up at the house. "You might as well tear your robe and shave your head. Just don't seem right."

"That appears to be the agreed refrain. But there ain't nothing to be done about any of it," William told him. "I guess I could talk to your momma about renting a room, seeing as y'all got so much free space to fill."

"That ain't funny. Them little bastards will eat us out of house and home and ask for seconds. You watch."

"I wouldn't fret too much on it. Long as folks keep dying, you'll never be out of business."

"Daddy says if Roosevelt don't turn things around, there won't be nobody who can pay for a plot, let alone a box to put in it. Too broke to die, he says. Imagine that."

"Get on from here," William told him, "'fore that old woman hops off the cooling board and starts looking for a hickory tree."

Ollie sighed and went on and stuck up his hand as he went.

William stroked Clara's neck. The sun and the day moon now both in the sky, circling like celestial sovereigns warring over some lesser planet.

A juvenile cardinal, its beak still black, darted past the barn and landed at the base of the cotton field and twisted its head up as if in disapproval and then flew on.

"You too, huh?" the boy asked.

He walked the dozen or so yards to the first row of plants and knelt and took one of the stems between his fingers and examined it.

The stem was covered in black and brown leaves and black pericarp bolls riddled through with blighted splotches of bacteria. He took his shears and started to cut away at the infected areas, but for every pruned leaf there were a half dozen more to take its place. A nation of wilt and rot. He moved from plant to plant, each one seemingly worse off than the last.

He'd known the risk of sowing the cotton seeds so close together, but he'd done it anyway. Without his father there, he'd taken the gamble. Closer rows meant more plants. More plants meant more yield. Maybe enough to save this place for another season. He'd imagined his father returning to a bumper crop of cotton, astonished and smiling. But none of it had gone like he hoped and now the budworms crawled silent along the stalks and leaves of the plants, and they were visible to the boy's naked eye, such were their robust numbers, and he knew before he reached the end of the first row that the harvest was lost.

He let the shears drop into the traitorous dirt and walked back to the head of the row and picked up the ridging hoe and stood there in the first true heat of the day. He felt the sun's gaze, autarkic and uncaring, and would that it might scorch everything around him. The land. The field. The barn. Burn the house. Burn it all and the bugs too.

Caterpillars and worms come up from the planted soil to take his meager crop and in the boy's mind they waited, greedy and insatiable—maggots by the tens of millions—searching for their next frenzied feeding. The next thing to destroy. He could see them waiting there for a new crop to consume, devouring the essence and leaving the dead gray roots like old bones. Like his mother's bones.

The boy raised the hoe over his head and brought it down atop a withered stalk and the blade cut clean through and made a metallic thud in the ground. He jerked it back up and brought it down again, and then again, and now in a flailing and frenetic repetition for there is rage in the boy. It is the blind and righteous rage of the young who have yet to accept the way of things—who perhaps and hopefully never will.

He hacked at the plants and at the dirt and if he thought he spotted an insect he hacked at that too, such was the fury of his indignation. After a particularly ferocious blow, the wood handle of the hoe broke apart from the head and the blade stayed stuck there in the soil of that merciless country, and he threw down the splintered wood and walked with raw and bloodied hands to the barn and stood there for a while yet and listened to the pattern of his own breathing.

The mule watched him with a certain resignation, as if she knew all men were destined to madness and this was simply the boy's fated end.

But William steadied himself. He thought of his mother. The anger dissipated and was replaced now by guilt. He shook his head and vowed to act less like a child and more like a man. He started back toward the cabin then stopped and headed instead for the road.

4

Not nine o'clock and already a searing-type heat. Autumn yet a rumor. Something that happens someplace else.

He didn't go far down the dirt road. A half mile and he came to the gate and he unlatched it and swung it open and went through and then closed it again and returned the latch.

Up the gravel drive, sun-stained rocks riddled with bitterweed and broomstraw, until he reached the top of the hill where the house had been built in the relative shade of an ancient oak grove. Like the country it belonged to, the old plantation home stood haggard but still proud. Warped siding, pillars of peeling paint, and a large front porch where the old man sat rocking and having his morning coffee.

"What say, young Carter?" he called down to the boy.

"Mr. Quinn."

"What's the news from down the road? My cows ain't in your field, are they?"

"Nossir. I hadn't seen the first cow since the start of summer."

"They've been shaded up in the north woods ever since this heat set in. I thought we might be gonna get some rain this morning."

"Yessir. I thought the same."

"Well. I put my farm in the Lord's hands years ago. If he wants to run grasshoppers on it, that's his business."

"I come to see about buying a couple oranges off of you."

"Oranges?"

"Yessir. My mother says she's got a craving for some orange juice in particular."

"Del Childers don't sell oranges at his place?" The old man leaned forward and gave the boy a suspicious eye.

"Well, yessir, I imagine he does, but I thought I might save myself the trip to town if'n you all had some you could part with. I got money."

Mr. Quinn crossed his arms and contemplated the situation.

"I guess I'd take two dollars an orange," he announced.

"Two dollars? Mr. Childers sells them for ten cents at the commissary."

"Take your ass on down to the commissary then," the old man said, shrugging.

William started to protest further but Mrs. Quinn was already out the door and hollering.

"You don't listen to him for one second, William, you hear me? Not one," she said and swatted at her husband with the dishrag she carried. "You can have as many oranges as you need, darling."

The old man laughed until it turned into a cough.

"Keep your money," he said, collecting himself. "Come on inside and drink you a cup of coffee. Miriam'll get you a mess of oranges."

"Two dollars," Mrs. Quinn mumbled, shaking her head. "Why, I never."

"I really can't stay," William said. "I told her I'd be back shortly."

The old man stood and raised an eyebrow.

"If you want free produce, you can come inside and visit a minute. Let Miriam dote on you."

"Yessir."

They sat in leather chairs in the windowless den at the center of the house. Whitetail mounts on the walls, their shadows small and straining in what little natural light escaped the foyer. The room smelled of wax and pine and wet tobacco. It was hot.

"You'll have some breakfast, won't you, William?" the woman called from the kitchen. "We done et, but we got sausage left and some biscuits wrapped up. Oh, and I can make you some fresh eggs. I would make those silver-dollar pancakes like how you used to like but we hadn't had no sugar around here since Imperial started trying to process figs. Can you believe that? And that was what, January? Or was it February? I think it must have been January because Cheryl Calhoun was the one who told me, and I'd run into her at the town meeting, which was in January. Or was it February?"

"I really can't stay, Mrs. Quinn. I'll just take the coffee and the oranges."

If she heard him, she didn't respond.

"Where's Thomas at these days?" the old man asked. "Seems like I ain't seen him around since the first of the year."

"He's been in Washington," William said. "Up there with the Bonus Army."

"From everything I heard, the government run them off more than a month ago."

"I guess they didn't run him off."

The old man laughed.

"That don't surprise me none. Ole Thomas. Never would give up on a thing. As determined a man as I've ever seen, your father."

The boy stayed quiet and Quinn reared back and squinted his eyes like he was about to sneeze but didn't. He coughed. Shook his head.

"Anyhow," he said. "I couldn't never make much sense of why they went up there in the first place."

"They can't cash out their war certificates until 1945," William told him.

"I thought it was '44."

"It's '45. Not that '44 would make any difference."

"When are they calling for them?"

"Now. They want them now."

"Good a time as any, ain't it?"

"That's what they want. Government says no."

"You can't hardly trust the government to plan a picnic," Mr. Quinn said, shaking his head. "They keep sending some prissy fella from College Station out here to tell me about my cows. Says the price of cattle is too low. They're gonna start slaughtering whole herds so to lower the supply. You ever hear of such a thing? I told that sonofabitch to just raise the price and leave me and mine alone. He said it don't work that way."

The old man leaned to one side of the chair and reached in his back pocket and produced from it a small sack of Red Man and pinched out a healthy plug and stuffed it in his cheek. He rolled up the sack and put it back in his pocket and flicked his fingers to rid them of the residue and then leaned back and stared at William.

"You know, when Arthur died they buried him over there. A place called Rimaucourt. They said it was an American cemetery. What that means, I don't know. How can a cemetery in France be American? After the war was over they sent us a little postcard asking should they dig him up. Send him home. There was plenty of folks checked 'yes' on them cards. Howard and Susan Henderson did. You know the Hendersons. Their boy, Cal. Had him dug up over there and brung home. Buried again, right up yonder in the Shawnee Prairie Cemetery. But there was something about the whole thing that didn't set right with me. Disturbing the dead like that. I'd spent so long telling myself my son was at peace, it didn't seem right to go in and trouble him like that. I don't know that Miriam has ever truthfully forgive me."

The boy was quiet.

"Anyhow," Mr. Quinn said. "I'm glad Thomas is giving them hell. There's been too many good boys give up on a decent life and head off into the Thicket these last few years, I was hoping Thomas weren't one of 'em. You know Homer Renfro is down there in Spurger, running shine and whatever else."

He peered toward the kitchen and then dropped his voice an octave.

"Miriam said there was word going around that Homer killed a man down there. Stabbed him to death with a pair of scissors, if you can believe that. Said the man spoke poorly of Homer's dog."

"His dog?"

"That's what they say."

"Now you hush that talk," the old woman said, sweeping into the room with a tray full of food.

She set the tray on the table and patted William's leg. In front of him was a mug of coffee, a glass of milk, a plate of biscuits, two pieces of pattied deer sausage, and boats full up of honey and jam each.

"I can't eat all this," William protested.

"Go on and just eat what you want of it," she said, gesturing with her head.

"Goddamnit, the boy said he ain't hungry," the old man raised his voice so that it caused his head to shake. "He's done said it when he first come in."

The old woman crossed her arms, hurt.

"I don't see why you got to use such ugly talk. Just plum ugly, taking the Lord's name like that."

Mr. Quinn scoffed.

"The Lord ought to have more on his mind than how I talk," he said.

"Can't even have a nice visit from William without you going and ruining it," she said.

"How 'bout you wrap me up a couple of sausage biscuits to go?" William asked.

This seemed to satisfy her.

"I can sure do that," she said, and William just barely had time to pick up the mug of coffee before she was yanking the tray away and retreating back to the kitchen.

"She's getting about as crazy as the country," the old man said. "And me, one step closer to death each day."

"Ain't that everybody?" William asked, sipping the coffee.

"It ain't everybody that concerns me," Mr. Quinn told him.

William sat his coffee mug on the table and adjusted it slightly, turning it to where the handle was just so, to his liking.

"I saw Herbert Roth's car come down the road this morning," the old man said. "I can put two and two together."

"Yessir."

"I bet you anything when Thomas gets home he'll clear this whole mess up," Mr. Quinn shook his head. "You ought not have to be bearing this burden on your own."

"Yessir," William repeated. "I know that would make Momma happy. For him to be home, I mean."

Mr. Quinn fished around under the coffee table and produced an empty fruit can with the label peeled away. He spit into it.

"But not you?" he asked.

William thought for a minute and somewhere in the foyer there was a clock ticking.

"He's not in Washington," the boy said. "I lied."

He looked down at the wood floor and the oval rug, a deep maroon, thin and brittle.

The old man raised his eyebrow but other than that made no reaction.

"He sent a letter last week," the boy went on. "From Doucette."

Now Mr. Quinn leaned forward.

"Doucette?"

"Yessir."

"What'd the letter say?"

"Not much that I could understand. But it didn't sound like he was headed this way anytime soon."

"Doucette?" the old man asked again.

"Yessir. And Roth says, and Doc too, that I ought to take Momma to Houston," William went on unburdening himself, "but she don't want to go. Not until Daddy gets back."

"But she hadn't seen the letter," Mr. Quinn said. "And you don't know if he's coming back."

"That's right," the boy said, and he was talking faster now. "And if I was to try going after him—that don't set right. Leaving her like she is. And who's to say I'd find him, or if I did find him, if I could get him to come home."

"I guess you're right there at the nip then, ain't you?" Mr. Quinn offered.

"I don't know what that means."

"No? And here I had you figured for a hand."

"Guess not."

"In the mill"—the old man lifted his spit can and used it to point east—"the nip is the spot when all things converge—when the belt carrying the wet sheets, and the pulp that's been treated and pressed and vacuum-dried, and all the other little parts and processes, they all meet at the start of them great big granite rollers. That's where they get pressed into paper. A transformation like. That's the nip. The moment of truth. That thing you've been forever working towards."

"I hadn't been working towards nothing."

Mr. Quinn nodded.

"Yeah, well, neither has the paper," he said. "But something's been sending it along, pushing it forward. You too, I'd imagine. Except, unlike the paper, you got some say in what comes next."

"I wish I didn't," William said. "I wish somebody would just tell me what I'm supposed to do. Tell me how to fix all this."

"Fix it?" the old man said, spitting into the can and wiping his chin. "Oh, son, you're more lost than I realized."

Mrs. Quinn came into the room with a sack of oranges, sausage biscuits wrapped and pressed in a towel, and a thermos of coffee. The boy smiled and nodded and took the towel and opened the sack and set the towel and its contents gently atop the oranges and closed the sack and carried it and the coffee out of the den and through the foyer and out of the house.

The old woman followed him and stood in the open doorway and watched him descend the porch and disappear down the road. Once he was gone she stood there some more and she felt very much like crying but couldn't say why.

"Close the goddamn door," her husband called. "You're letting in every fly in Shawnee Prairie."

5

He didn't want to go home yet. The thought of clearing the diseased field made him shudder. But it seemed a poor idea to wander aimlessly in the oppressive heat, so for a while he just stood at the bottom of the hill looking up and down the road like a child lost. *Was* a child lost.

He might well have stood there until the trumpet sounded were it not for a wagon of women that came over the hill and jostling toward him.

The lady driver whoa'd the horse and the horse stopped.

The boy looked up at the folks in the wagon and raised one hand in greeting and the other to shield the sun.

In the back were two girls from his class. They were both named Katherine, but one was called Katy and the other Kathy. He recognized the stout woman driving but could not remember which of the Katherines she was mother to.

"William," the two girls said in unison, as if they'd been rehearsing it for the stage.

The boy nodded.

"What are you doing just standing out here?" Katy asked.

"It's hot enough, ain't it," Kathy added.

"It is," he said, "and I ain't real sure."

"We're going into town to get more ice," Katy told him.

"So hot we need extra," Kathy added.

"Alright then."

"How's your momma?" asked the woman.

"She's alright."

The woman eyed him, suspicious.

"I ain't seen her in church in what seems a month of Sundays."

"She hadn't been feeling too good lately," he said and didn't say anything else.

"Hadn't seen you in church either," she said, staring down at him from high in the wagon.

William looked at the ground.

"You going to the Labor Sunday dance?" Katy asked.

"Everybody else is going," Kathy said before he could answer.

The boy shrugged.

"You ought to go cool off somewheres," Katy said. "You know Carl Platt up and passed out in the middle of his daddy's watermelon patch the other day."

"On account of how hot it was," Kathy said, nodding.

"Vernon said Carl was out there doing unseemly things to the produce," Katy said, raising her eyebrows. "But you can't believe anything Vernon says."

"List of lies longer than a well rope," Kathy confirmed.

"Girls," the woman snapped, disapproving.

"Still," Katy shrugged. "Vernon says he was making that melon juice fly sure enough."

"Hush that talk," the woman said. "It ain't ladylike. Or Christlike to boot."

She gathered up the reins and popped them and the horses started on and William watched the girls grab hold of the wagon to steady themselves. The dust kicked up behind them as they went and he gave thought to following, to telling Katy he was going to the dance and asking if she wanted to go with him.

Instead he went home and called out an apology before he'd even said hello. He went to the kitchen and cut open the oranges one by one and squeezed the juice into a glass. He took a sausage biscuit from the cloth and pulled off the top of the biscuit and took down a jar of mayhaw jelly and spooned some onto the top of the sausage and then put the biscuit back together and put it on a plate.

He took the plate and the glass and went into the bedroom.

"Mrs. Quinn sent some oranges and a little breakfast," he said, and he stood there holding the plate in one hand and the glass in the other and when he saw the truth of it he was, for the briefest of moments, immobilized.

She was sprawled out across the floor between the bed and the doorway, and he couldn't tell if she'd fallen from the bed, but it didn't look like it. It looked like she'd been trying to walk across the room.

He looked around the room as if he'd never been in it before, desperately seeking a surface to set the food where it wouldn't spill. Where she could still eat it later.

"Hold on, Momma," he said, putting the plate and the glass on the desktop and kneeling beside her.

She was breathing, but that was it. Eyes closed, body limp.

The doc was a young man. Not yet thirty years. He hovered above the woman, using various instruments to conduct tests or make determinations which the boy could hardly guess at. At one point William's mother came awake with a low haunting moan and the doctor soothed her back down as if she were a startled child.

William thought he looked like some modern-day sorcerer readying his latest devilkin. He half expected the doc to start speaking in tongues or chanting incantations—either of which the boy would have readily accepted had it helped in the healing of his mother.

He watched with worried eyes as the young doctor went methodically about his work and the boy watched also the ticking of the clock—the measuring of time and its rigid ascertaining of every second.

"William," his mother said, her voice strained to the point of whispers on the wind.

The boy was at her side in an instant. On his knees. Holding her hand.

"Thank you," she managed, "for the orange juice."

William kissed her hand.

"You need to rest," he told her.

"Mrs. Carter," the doctor said, slow and deliberate, "I'm going to borrow your son to help get my things to the car. He will be right back."

They walked out of the bedroom and the doc was shaking his head even before he spoke.

"I can't say what it is," he told the boy. "Not without getting her down to Houston. There's hospitals there where folks are doing good work on these sorts of mysteries. They may be able to tell you what's what."

"She won't go down there," William said. "I need *you* to tell me."

"I can't," the doctor repeated. "Not with any degree of certainty."

"Well what about with uncertainty?" William asked, agitated. "I won't hold you to it if it turns out errant."

The doc passed his fingers through his hair and sighed.

"I thought," he hesitated. "I thought, initially, it was some sort of intracranial lesion. I'd hoped it might be something that had swelled and would go back down on its own. But at this point my guess would be that it's a tumor. And that the tumor is growing. It could be pressing against her temporal or parietal lobe. That can cause all kinds of complications—not unlike what your mother experienced today. Fainting. Disorientation. Fatigue. There's been cases where patients with cancer of the brain will fall into a coma if the pressure is great enough."

"Is that what you think is gonna happen?" William asked.

"Like I said, I can't say with any degree of—"

"*Doc.*"

"Yes. I think if left untreated the tumor will continue to grow and eventually your mother will fall into a coma and from that point will have only a few days left. If that."

William didn't react for a time and when he did he just nodded.

"I need another guess from you, Doc, and I hate to put you on the spot again," the boy said. "But if I did find a way to get her to Houston, what are the chances she might live?"

In his dreams the boy wandered lost in the blackness of a subaltern cave. He could hear a voice somewhere in the dark but could neither discern the words nor the direction from which they originated.

Another voice. Whispers. The dripping of stalactites—colloids of sinter and sand suspended sharp there in the damp cold. Now, gone. Now, nothing.

He struck flint rocks together.

Where or how the flint materialized was a secret known only to the dream and not the dreamer.

The rocks gave off sparks of quick-dying light and in such brief flashes were illuminated each collected horror of the boy's subconscious. Fear unmasked. Faces coming forth out of the gloom and hands with long drawn fingers curling toward him. And then away. Banished to that tenebrous realm where no light yet touches.

In the dream he stood, rocks in hand, his chest rising and falling with cold heavy breath. He could feel them there in the dark, circling. Ever lurking. Waiting for the boy to give the light another try.

He woke from the dream and the feeling it left was sick and empty.

He sat up and looked to the window and the lizard was there again, watching. He stood and went quietly from the house and onto the porch and looked out at the yard that had once seemed so big.

He came down the wooden steps in his boxers and stood before the barren field and the forest beyond. Black of night, and the trees blacker still, inked against the twilight sky. A nocturnal orchestra of katydids and crickets rose up around him and the rim of the cratered moon hung there in the dark like a pale horn that would blazon the victory of night.

He was a long time standing. The sky shifting soundless above him.

And further still, somewhere beyond the firmament, the whole of creation expanded at the edges. Heavenly bodies yet uncoiled, fleeing the savage force from which they were birthed.

Would that he could make sense of it all. Or any one piece of it. Any single thing. Perhaps then he could set it all right.

Instead he went back inside and pulled off his boots and left them by the door and went into her room and crawled into bed beside her and wept.

6

The morning that followed, he was up and dressed and sitting at the rolltop desk while she slept. He had read in late July of the Bonus Army's defeat in Washington, DC, and while he knew the outcome was a bad thing, he could not help but feel relief that it was over. His mother's first fainting spell was the first day of August and he spent each day thereafter awaiting his father's return. When the letter arrived, he stopped waiting.

He debated showing it to her. In the end he did not. Could not. He worried it would break whatever will she had left.

He took the envelope from his pocket and laid it flat on the desk. He took out the letter and unfolded it with a delicate touch, like he'd been charged with the handling of some rare artifact. Everything slow. Everything measured. He smoothed it open with his palm and felt the creases and pressed down gently upon them, then moved his hand away and looked at his father's words.

Dear Laurie,

My faith fails me. It turns away from me. Or I from it. I have declared war on God and he has refused to fight. In his absence, I war with myself. Please give my love to William, as I know he will not understand. He is a smart boy. And because of this I fear he will be an angry boy. But I cannot return home. Not yet. Not while the battle rages. I must atone for it. For everything. Until I do, I know that my presence would only serve to corrupt the both of you. To darken your days. To wear at your souls.

I fear the world is not but an oyster without a pearl.

My love and endless apology,
Thomas

When he folded it back up, he did so tenderly, as if too harsh a movement might somehow shift the contents. Erase the words he'd read so carefully and so often in the weeks prior. His father often spoke in ways the boy found difficult to understand and the letter was no different but he understood enough for the words to sting. Though not nearly so much as the return address which originated from Doucette, Texas—a town not forty miles from their home.

He'd sent his own letter in reply. Scrawled on a torn sheet of paper the same day.

Momma is sick. Come home.

He received no response.

Might be that he's coming so quick he didn't want to waste the time with a letter, the boy thought, but after another week there were no lies left to tell himself.

He tucked the envelope safely away in his back pocket and then began rifling through the desk drawers as if there might be some single discovery that would stay the pending journey. He looked inside old cookie tins full up with knickknacks and pencils and rubber bands and thumbed idly through the pages of his father's ledger books wherein he kept sums and figures related to cotton and feed and fertilizer. He didn't know what he was looking for. A satchel filled with money, maybe. To such ends he found only a few French coins in a small satin pouch. He held one and turned it over in his hand. On one side was the image of a woman throwing seeds. An olive branch on the other.

His father had not been one to regale him with tales of war. William knew he fought in France. He knew many men died. But such things—the war, fascism, the horrors of men—were yet foreign to the boy. He knew more of the desk itself than the things it held.

It had been carved by his great-grandfather's uncle somewhere in the hills of Eastern Europe. Loaded onto a hay wagon some three score and two years prior, along with what little else the boy's paternal ancestors owned, and carried then across the whole of the continent to the English Channel, where it was unloaded and loaded again, this time following the family onto a single-screw steamship bound for the Port of Galveston and a place called Texas.

The boy's grandfather, the first William Carter, had been born aboard the steamer in the middle of the night. He had, tragically, traded places in the world with the woman who birthed him, leaving him a motherless child of no country.

The boy looked at his own mother. He knew less of her lineage. Only that her father had been a minister and her mother a minister's wife. Both early to the grave.

He placed the coin pouch back in the drawer next to an old tintype of his mother and father. Young and smiling and standing in front of the little house. He wondered if his mother was pregnant with Gwen. He wondered if either of them could have guessed the trouble to come. And if so, would it have mattered? How do you go about changing a future that's always and only one moment away?

He ran his finger across the metal plate and their faces unmoving and the image all but colorless—brown and rust, like tea stains. Like the ghost of an image.

William looked at his father's boots. They had sat there for nearly seven months. He looked again at his mother as if to make sure she was asleep and then he slipped first one foot and then the other into the boots and moved some to feel their fit and then bent and pulled the laces tight.

He stood at the bedside and looked down at her and anything he could have said would have been a lie and the only truth was a thing he could not bring himself to say. He took the tintype from the desk drawer and put it in her hand and folded her fingers soft around it. He bent and gently kissed her forehead and then he left the room and closed the door and stood with his back against it.

William came from the house with a canvas satchel slung over his shoulder and his father's 30.06 rifle balanced in his hand.

He went to the barn and saddled the mule but didn't ride her.

"You ain't gonna like this one bit," he said, patting her side. "Not one bit at all."

He found a long leather scabbard and tied its latigo straps to the D rings on the saddle and once it was attached to his liking he slipped the rifle in the sheath with the stock facing up and back. He'd filled the canvas bag with a couple changes of socks and a jug of water and a quilted blanket to sleep on and he tied the bag to the saddle horn and off they went, laboring along the road in the unabated heat. What little wind there was came faint and episodic. Grasshoppers fled before them in waves—their great numbers going forth in a lightsome series of aerial matrices.

There was a makeshift ballfield without any fences and some boys he recognized were in the middle of a game, hollering insults at one another in between pitches. William could see they were a few positions short.

He passed along crusted fields of switchgrass and yankeeweed and he passed men ahorseback and a few cars whose tires threw at him rocks and dust and just before he reached the crossroads he passed the Shawnee Prairie Baptist Church. Its main chapel was set back from the road and he could see the reverend hunched in the doorway, sweeping dirt out beyond the threshold.

He made the turn for Manning, which was only a half mile further, but the boy was drenched in sweat by the time they hit town, such was the stifling humidity of early September.

On the far side of the street, where the houses began, there was a waist-high picket fence that ran continuous from one yard to the next and when the wind gusted up behind him the boy could hear with a great clarity the little chimes hung from the porches as they clanged and tolled like halfhearted bells in an old graveyard where the dead grow restless.

At the railroad trestle they stopped.

The SH&G was on the track and men from the commissary had climbed into an insulated boxcar and were unloading giant ice blocks, each weighing around two hundred and fifty pounds.

The boy watched as the crew pushed and grunted, sliding the great frozen blocks to an affixed chute that led from the boxcar straight into the icehouse. The thick, double-shiplap doors were drawn open and the big blocks were turned loose to the chute whereon they went glissading down and into the icehouse, their momentum carrying them across the sawdust floor to thud hard against the back wall. With each successive block, the entire structure shook and rattled as if it were tasked with containing some small seismic episode within.

He stood there a minute and marveled, but the sun was growing hotter and he found that looking at the ice was not enough to cool him. He walked the mule alongside the tracks until they reached the engine car and the two of them passed in front of it and down the other side to a red dirt path.

The short trail gave out at the mill pond and the boy and his mule traced a quarter mile along its edge to the colored side of town. Tom Coleman was coming out from the first alleyway with an old bay horse toting the honey wagon.

William touched his hat and Tom did the same and the animals, horse and mule, appeared to nod at one another in passing.

The colored neighborhood was full up with clapboard houses left unpainted. Like on the white side of town, there was a pool hall, a church, a school, and a barbershop, though each of these buildings—and the houses as well—were slightly smaller structures. A not-so-subtle reminder from the mill owners who'd built the town.

Hampton Jones ran a mule barn on this side of the pond and he sat on a stool whittling a piece of basswood when the boy and the mule walked up, one beside the other.

"What say, Ham?" William asked.

"Having a conversation," the man said.

"With who?"

"Myself."

"What about?"

"Can't say," Hampton told the boy. "I ain't much of a listener."

The boy smiled, but Hampton did not. Instead he used the blade to point over his shoulder.

"I expect you're needing a mule," he said.

"What makes you say that?"

"'Cause this is a mule barn," Hampton told him.

"I already have a mule," William said, looking over his own shoulder at Clara.

"Might be that you need two," Hampton said.

"I don't. I need to sell this one."

Hampton shook his head. "I rent mules. I don't buy them."

"I know that," the boy said. "But I thought you might know of somebody looking to buy one."

Hampton frowned. He stood and folded the knife away and put it in his pocket and arched his back.

"Now, if I was to know somebody needing a mule, they'd come down here and rent one from me. But if they was to buy a mule, well, then they wouldn't have no business renting one, would they? You see the pickle you're putting me in here, son?"

"Alright, well, what if you *were* to buy a mule?" William asked. "Surely you got to get new ones every so often. And I'd let her go cheap."

Hampton thought about it.

"I might could take her on," he said, relenting. "Ruby's looking her age these days and don't nobody want to pay full price to rent an old mule. How old is your girl there?"

"Twelve years, I believe."

"Ain't no spring chicken herself then."

"Nossir."

Hampton thought about it.

"Sorry, son," he said. "I can't do it."

"I'll buy her back for more than you pay. Just give me a little time."

"Oh, so now I'm running a pawn shop for mules?"

"Fine. How about I throw in a rifle and scope."

Hampton raised his eyebrows.

"That's a fine looking ought six," he said, scratching the back of his head. "I'll tell you what, I'll give you sixty-five dollars for the mule and the gun. You can buy the mule back for fifty after one week. Two-dollars-a-week after that. And I keep the gun."

"That's my daddy's rifle."

"That's your daddy's mule. Maybe I ought to be dealing with him."

"Alright. Sixty-five dollars then."

He led the mule just outside an old iron catch pen and looped her lead rope over the top rung and collected his money and started to leave. Then he stopped and turned back and Hampton watched him and the boy went to the mule and whispered in her ear and gave her a pat.

"What'd you say to her?" Hampton asked.

"I told her I loved her. That I'd always love her. And that if we never see each other again, it's not her fault."

7

The Manning mortuary was in between the coffin house and the picture show. It was a long, narrow building with a small shopfront. There were no front windows—barely room for the door—but inside there was a skylight of sorts that lit the receiving area and the front desk. Ollie had said his father hoped it would mimic the light from heaven that became visible upon one's death.

When William opened the door, Mr. Leek was standing beneath this light, nodding solemnly to a middle-aged couple who whispered to him between their soft sobs.

"And you know she was just the nicest woman," the man said.

"The nicest," the woman confirmed.

"And the children. Oh, how she loved the little children."

"Loved them more than anything 'cept the Lord, I'd say."

"I'd say it too. More than anything."

Mr. Leek continued his nodding. He spotted William and motioned for him to go on back.

William held up his hand and went past the front desk and through the door and down a long hallway to the last door on the left and he opened it and went inside without knocking.

Ollie was hunched over a cooling board that held the dead body of an elderly woman. There was a thin trocar stuck into her arm and connected by a rubber tube to a glass jar on one end and a vacuum pump on the other. Ollie was working the pump and watching intently as the fluid drained from the old woman's body.

The room had the burnt-plastic smell of formaldehyde.

William pulled the door shut behind him and Ollie looked up.

"Howdy, bud."

"Ollie," William said, his face solemn.

"What are you doing coming in here looking so forlorn?" he asked.

This made William smile.

"Where'd you learn a word like that?"

"Aw, hell, you pick up all sorts of things at the funeral parlor," Ollie said.

"What things?" William asked, doubtful.

Ollie thought a minute.

"You know," he said, "forlorn things. Anyway, if you want some cheering up you can take a few cheap shots at the old bag. I'll hold her."

"I thought you was dressing up Mrs. Spivey *yesterday*."

"Them two out front are her spawn," Ollie said. "Called up here yesterday morning and told us not to touch her until they could get down from Longview and confirm her dead. You believe that? Daddy told them he'd been in the mortuary business going on thirty years and hadn't had nobody ring a bell on him yet. But what can you do?"

Ollie bent back over the corpse and gave the trocar a couple of thumps before sliding it out.

"I come by to ask a favor off you," William said.

"Whatever you need," Ollie said without looking up. He had dumped blood and fluid from the glass jar into a mop bucket and was now dabbing some sort of wax onto the small incision left by the tube.

William frowned. How many jars would his mother fill? How many buckets?

"I need you to look in on Momma for me," he said, shaking away the thought. "Just for the next two or three days. You can sleep in my room if you need to. It ain't as swanky as the barn but it smells a little better."

Ollie straightened.

"What?"

"She won't get better unless she goes to Houston," William told him. "And she won't go to Houston without my daddy. So I'm going to fetch him and bring him back. I got fifty dollars here. You sit with her, and if she needs anything—or if the doc says she needs anything—you get it or send somebody to get it. Whatever's left, you can keep."

"Where in the good hell did you get fifty dollars?"

"Can you do it or not?" William asked.

Ollie looked concerned.

"I can do it, I just—"

"You don't think it's a good idea?" William asked.

Ollie pulled off his gloves and sighed, thoughtful.

"I don't imagine a fella can call an idea good or bad until he lets things play out a bit," he said. "What kind of fool judges something at the beginning? You read the first few pages and it's all grapes in the garden, but it ends with a seven-headed beast and lakes of fire."

William stared at him.

"Just saying." Ollie shrugged. "There ain't no telling the future, except for the one thing we all got coming. So, you got a decision to make, you make it. You keep on going. You can look back at every place you turned right when you should've gone left, but you still end up on the board, same as the rest."

William crossed his arms and sighed.

"You don't think it's a good idea," he said.

"No, not particularly I don't."

"Well, that makes two of us. But I don't know what else I'm supposed to do about any of it."

"Washington DC's a big place, bud," Ollie said. "You think you'll really find him?"

"I'm not going to Washington."

William pulled the folded envelope from his pocket and handed it to Ollie, who looked it over.

"Doucette?"

"Got this a couple weeks back."

"What'n the hell is he doing in Doucette?" Ollie asked.

"That's what I aim to find out."

"He didn't say in the letter?"

William shook his head.

"He didn't say much of anything."

"Well, shit," Ollie said. He crossed his arms and then quickly uncrossed them and wiped some blood off the back of his hand. "You know the train don't go through Doucette."

"I know it. I'm going to try to make Nancy by nightfall and hitch a ride in the morning."

"And it ain't fixing to get no cooler out there neither."

"I know that too," William said. "I ain't asking you to come with me. I'm asking you to go look after Momma for a few days."

"But see, that's the thing. You're my best friend."

"So?"

"So you shouldn't have to ask, I'm supposed to just insist on going with you. But as it stands, I've already let you down—on the insisting part, that is. And not helping matters none is the fact that my aunt was a nurse during the war. And here now she's just happened to show up in town. So if I was to try convincing myself that nobody could do as good a job as me when it comes to looking after Ms. Laurie, then I'd be telling a bald-faced lie to myself. And I ain't real big on liars. You see the predicament you've gone and put me in?"

"I think you've put yourself there, bud. But let me help you out of it by telling you right here in front of Mrs. Spivey and anybody else: You don't need to come with me."

William gave Ollie a stern look and Ollie nodded and held up the dead woman's hand and waved it as the boy left.

8

William toted his satchel back toward the center of town. The sun was white hot and climbing. There were few folks about, with most either at the mill or waiting to attend their business until the relative cool of the evening. He walked along the thoroughfare and into the commissary and walked the half-empty aisles, filling the satchel with provisions. Canned ham, fruit tins, a box of matches, and the like. Del Childers took the boy's money and gave a sleepy nod and returned to his paper.

The town was half of what William remembered. Already dying. One hotel, where once there were three. Shops shuttered. The picture house was long abandoned with cigarette butts and bits of trash collecting in the alcoves beneath the marquee. On his ninth birthday William's mother had taken him to see *The Gold Rush*, the latest Charlie Chaplin film, and he had marveled not just at the expanse of the screen or the live musical accompaniment but also the attendees in their finery and furs. Such had been the decade for mill towns. But those days were gone and gone for good. The boy stood outside the picture show and strained that he might hear the clicks and slides of the projector. Any indication that the magic within had yet survived. There was sulfur in the air when the breeze turned westerly across the mill and a paper sack kicked up against the brick footing of the ticket box and held there for a moment and then glided back down. It was hot and the air was heavy and William looked toward the road that would take him back to Shawnee Prairie. Back home. He bit the inside of his lip.

If I did find a way . . . what are the chances she might live?

He thought of the young doctor's face. He turned to the trees and whatever awaited him within that deep dark. He thought of Mr. Quinn and the nip and the moment of truth. He hesitated.

His resolve was wavering when Ollie came up the sidewalk at a near sprint.

"Alright then," he said, grinning and panting as he reached William.

"Alright then *what*?"

"I'll go with you."

"I thought you said it was a bad idea."

"All the more reason not to do it alone," Ollie said. "Besides, I've been cooped up too long in this place. I need to spread my wings some. Have me an adventure."

"An adventure?" William looked doubtful.

"Sure," Ollie clapped his hands on his knees. "Just two old boys headed west like in the songs."

"We're headed southeast."

"You're hung up on particulars," Ollie said with no loss of enthusiasm. "Still, let's go on and get this rat killing started before I talk any sense into myself."

"What about Momma?" William reminded him.

"I took care of it," Ollie said. "Talked to my aunt. The Leek clan is fixing to stay at your place in shifts until we get back."

"They don't mind?"

"Not if you don't. Lord knows they need some extra room. And fifty dollars never hurt nobody."

"They're alright with you being gone a couple days?"

Ollie shrugged off the question.

"We'll be back before they miss me," he said.

II

THE ROAD

9

The expanse of country before them was inundated with southern pine of every imaginable order. A glut of hardwoods and scrub brush that had, since the last great tectonic dividing, found purchase and constancy in the red clay hills and low leached river bottoms.

There was no road from Manning to Nancy. Only dirt paths. Trails and shades of trails.

The boys steered southeast as best they could by compass. As Ollie had forewarned, the sun showed them no charity. It was strangely militant in its onslaught, as if it would seek them out no matter the depth of shade beneath which they sheltered. In the deepest woods, when the sun was well and blockaded by the overgrowth, the heat would then seem to rise, coming up out of the ground, and there trapped by the canopy of trees and bearing down on the boys as they went. And they went further still, their shadows walked alongside them, holding back the light.

Even in the dense forest they were never alone.

Swamp rabbits, possums, and pocket gophers sprang up as they passed, and their path was ever attended by birdsong and bullfrogs and though it was hot and the air thick, soon they were at the big creek and William was surprised at how quickly the time had passed.

Piney Creek gathered up from various drainage spots around Kennard and flowed southeast, bending every which way but straight until at last it hit the Neches River at the three-county junction south of Manning.

They stood on the bank and looked down at the low, roiling water.

There was little of it. Two feet at most. Moss-green as it flowed over small river rocks and swirled beneath low-hung branches from cypress trees what grew direct from the creek bank like great aquatic pillars. That the water flowed at all was naught but miraculous and yet flow it did—verdant and trickling some four hundred miles from its headwater.

"How many snakes you figure are in there right this minute?" Ollie asked.

"That don't help," William told him.

"In any given five-by-five area," Ollie said, ignoring him, "you think there's a half dozen water moccasins? More?"

"You want to go fifteen miles down and find a bridge?" William asked. "A rope swing maybe?"

"I'm just saying it's an ugly way to die."

"Compared to all them pretty ones?"

William shook his head and braced himself on the lip of the bank and slid down into the shallow water and held the bag up around waist level and crossed.

"There you go," he said. "Not a snake, one."

"They were probably too surprised to make a move," Ollie said. "But they're ready now. I imagine you got them good and stirred up."

"Get your ass over here."

Ollie unshouldered his bag and swung it across the creek to William and then slid down the bank and went whooping and splashing through the water and up the other side.

"To hell with you, snakes, you no-good, slithering bastards," he called, and then they were off again along a narrow and bedraggled path, bowered on either side by willows and pine and wandering oaks.

And such was the travel for those not on the highways. Dirt roads and game trails. Paths marked by crushed rock or cut brush, and all of them winding through the thickets of East Texas like braided ribbons, crossing and recrossing in a matrix of tendons that held together what they could of such land. Such perilous country.

It was early evening but the sun showed no signs of letting up. The wet from the creek had long dried and crusted on the legs of their pants and both the boys were covered in sweat and pine pollen by the time they came out of the woods and into a dry grass field.

"You got an idea of where you're going?" Ollie asked, passing his arm across his forehead and letting his mouth hang open.

"Southeast to Nancy."

"That's it?"

"That's it."

"My god, bud. And if I ask you where the fish are, I guess you'd say in the water, huh?"

"There ain't but a few little logging roads out here," William told him. "We find one, it'll lead us right where we aim to go."

"Said Moses to the Israelites."

They cut through the field and back into the trees. By and by they hit an old game trail and followed it through the understory of goldenball and sprawling kudzu and through stands of cottonwood that would yellow in the fall.

The wind came soft through the trees and the forest let loose a shiver, and from somewhere a wood duck called, though the boys could see no water.

In time the trail spilled out onto a dirt road. Reddish dirt sloping away into black sand.

"This ought to take us right into town," William said.

A half mile later and the road had curved and doubled back and was heading west into the setting sun at a steep incline.

"I'm hardly an expert in the complex ways of navigation," Ollie said, panting. "But I do believe we're pointed in the dead-wrong direction."

"It'll bend back," William said, unsure. "Let's just keep going. Every road leads to something."

"Hold on," Ollie said and stopped and William stopped too.

They could hear a string of curse words coming from over the hill.

"Good-for-nothing sonofabitch," a man was saying and it sounded like he was wrestling with something and losing.

They pushed on at a trot and little plumes of dust puffed up beneath their boots and when they topped the hill they looked twenty yards down the road and saw the man hunched over in the bar ditch with both hands on either side of a wooden barrel. He was swearing and panting. Near him was a large pile of brown blankets.

"Might be trouble," William whispered to Ollie.

"Might be somebody who knows the quickest way to Nancy."

"What say, fella," Ollie called, shuffling down the hill. William followed.

"Don't never trust a drunk monk," the man hollered. "That's what I say."

The man did not wear a hat and sweat poured from his head and his short-cropped hair.

Ollie turned back to William.

"Did he say *monk*?"

"You're goddamned right, he did," the man responded, louder this time. "'Help me get this whiskey down the road, Cyrus. Little speak just outside of town. I know a back way where there ain't no revenuers. All the free hooch you want, Cyrus.' And then there's me with the faith and foolishness of a small child. Could I have believed him had he told me of treasure buried fifty feet beneath the ground, if only I would but dig for it? Who's to say? Fool that I am."

"Are you Cyrus," Ollie asked, hesitant.

"Of course I am, boy. And yonder lies the castaway Carmelite, if indeed he still draws breath."

"He does." The pile of blankets shifted and the boys could see now that it was a large robe and the man wearing it tried to sit up and then collapsed back into the dirt. "By the grace of infinite truth, he does."

"Grace my ass," Cyrus spit. "Drunk by noon. Stumbling ever after.

Leaves me to drag this thing right out here in the open, and does he offer to help? Twenty-three gallons and does he offer?"

"No?" Ollie said.

"No, of course not, by god. 'Another mile,' he says, 'and then we'll be there.' Be there, hell. Ain't nothing here but deer ticks and cottonmouth snakes."

"See there, I told you," Ollie said to William, crossing his arms. "Cottonmouths."

William looked down at the inebriated monk and then back up at Cyrus. The latter was a large man with great bulging muscles that threatened the stretch of his cotton shirt. He was older. Forty, if William had to put a number to it. And his skin was tan and leathered with roped veins running the length of his arms. Still, the barrel seemed to have gotten the best of him.

"Do you know where it is y'all are trying to get?" he asked.

"A little cabin out here in the woods somewheres is what was told to me. The only thing keeping me from turning back is the fleeting hope that I'm closer now to something moving forward than I could possibly be to those places left behind."

The monk was now staring up at the sun and laughing.

They watched him.

Cyrus shook his head and used the back of his arm to wipe sweat from his forehead though it was replaced instantly with another wave.

"Sonofabitch came into Nancy last night in that same set of robes and riding a donkey to go with it. Looked like something out of the goddamn Bible. The donkey had a little cart to it and there was two barrels settin' on the cart. Well, here I am, bit of a drinker, so I ask if that's what I think it is in them there barrels. 'Why sure,' says he. 'Aw hell,' says I. And off we go. Next thing I know, the morning star is risen and I'm dipping my head in a water trough in the middle of town and here's this Bethlehem-looking bastard standing there beside me like he ain't got a care in the world. Said if I was done baptizing myself, he had a way for me to pay my debt. 'What debt,' says I. 'For all the whiskey you drunk,' says he. 'Help me haul the barrel to a speakeasy. Ain't far. Just right down the road. I'll even pay you two dollars on top of everything.'"

"Where's the donkey and the cart?" William asked.

"Where's the other barrel?" Ollie added.

"Questions I had myself," the man said. "Turns out I weren't the only one with a debt. He sold the lot of it for thirty pieces—minus a bottle's worth from the second barrel, which he's done and guzzled down while I do all the work."

"How far to Nancy?" William asked.

"How far to the speak?" Ollie countered.

"Supposed to be right here or right back there or who can even understand the sonofabitch at this point. 'Burden of the breath,' he says. 'Temporal truths.' Rambling on about stars and men. He ain't nothing but a drunk in a habit. And I done checked his pockets. He ain't got a cent on him, let alone the two dollars he owes me."

"The Lord will provide," the monk mumbled and chuckled as buzzards circled above the four of them. "They both burn out. Stars and men."

William turned and looked back down the road.

"There's a cabin about a quarter mile down on the left," he said.

"There is?" Ollie asked.

"Might be the place you're looking for," William said, then turned to Ollie. "You were looking at your feet."

"Whether it is or it ain't, that's where I'm fixing to leave this bastard," Cyrus said. "I need to save my strength. Come up from Colmesneil last night. I'm fixing to box me a monkey."

"You say Nancy ain't far?" William asked again.

"Fixing to what?" Ollie asked.

"If you keep on down this road, it'll bend back east and you'll come up behind the livery in about an hour. Maybe less. But I'll tell you, I sure could use some help with this heavy sonofabitch. And with this barrel too."

"We gotta get going," William said. "We're trying to make town while it's still light out."

"Going to see the medicine show too, are you?"

"Don't know anything about that," William told him. "Just looking for somebody. A man named Thomas Carter. You know him?"

Cyrus shook his head.

"Can't say that I do."

"I know him." The monk sat up in the trail with his feet out in front of him. He looked dazed but still grinning.

Cyrus gave him a hard scowl.

"Don't listen to anything he says," he told the boys. "I imagine he don't know his own name at this point, let alone the fella you're hunting after."

The monk blinked, squinted again at the sun. He was short, swallowed up by the robes. He had small dark eyes and small features, and the top of his head was shaved but for a ring of hair that encircled it. Like something from a storybook William had once seen.

"I'm Travis Bowie Crockett," he said. "Descendant of the brave men who fought and died at the Alamo. Fine soldiers, all of them. Though their mission was not God's."

Cyrus threw up his hands.

"You see what I've been listening to all goddamn day?"

"And Thomas Carter," the monk continued. "Another fine soldier."

William stepped forward. "What did you say?"

"I need a drink, Cyrus," the monk announced. "Where's that bottle?"

"There hadn't been nothing left in the bottle for the past hour. You want a drink, your best bet is to get up off your ass and help me haul this barrel to whatever cabin these young folks seen."

The monk struggled to stand.

"Do you know Thomas Carter?" William repeated, pulling him up by the sleeve of his robe.

"He don't know him," Cyrus said again.

"I know what I know," the monk challenged. "And *who* I know. Ask Merle. He'll tell you."

"Who's Merle?" William asked.

"The embattled gentleman who spends his days at the speakeasy."

"What speakeasy?"

The monk looked confused.

"The one we're going to, of course," he said. "It's in the cabin, not a quarter mile up the road there. I was under the impression we'd just said as much."

The monk suddenly looked spooked.

"Or did I only hear the words in my mind?" he asked himself.

"Where else would you hear them?" Ollie said.

The monk considered this a moment and then gasped. He grabbed Ollie by the shoulders and gazed strangely at the boy.

"My goodness," he said. "What a thought."

"For god's sake," Cyrus spit.

"We'll help you," William said to Cyrus.

"We will?" Ollie asked.

"If Daddy's there, we might not have to go all the way to Nancy, let alone Doucette. And if he's not, maybe somebody there knows something."

"We'll help you," Ollie confirmed to Cyrus, and he and William helped the man lift the barrel and together they carried it back the way the boys had come.

10

There was the thinnest of deer runs that disappeared into the woods, and the cabin beyond was near camouflaged by the forest that surrounded it. But there it stood, and it was there they went.

Cyrus stepped up onto the porch and knocked on the door while William and Ollie stood back, breathing heavy overtop the barrel.

The boys watched Cyrus pacing on the porch, scowling at the monk.

"Did he say he was fixing to box up a monkey?" Ollie whispered.

Before William could answer, a woman flung the door open and looked at Cyrus and then down at the boys. She wore a red-patterned flour sack that was tied at the waist with thin rope and if she was expecting anyone to patronize her place of business, she did not show it.

William could barely make out the dark room behind her, but there were a few small tables with chairs and short candles and a short bar along the back wall.

"Got whiskey for you," Cyrus said.

"And who the hell are you?" she asked, taking a step back and putting her hands on her hips.

"I'm the dumb sonofabitch that trusted this here monk," he said and moved out the way so that she could get a good look at the man grinning from behind his robes.

The woman's eyes lit up.

"Travis," she called and stepped past Cyrus and threw her arms around the monk. "I wondered what had happened to you. I thought you was gonna be here yesterday."

In her presence the monk put his head down and looked up, bashful.

"I was delayed in Enoch," he said, almost singing. "By a charming dog and a pawnshop owner who wouldn't stop humping my leg. Or was it the other way around?"

The woman looked at Cyrus and the boys and then back to the monk.

"And?"

"No, no," he said, "unfortunately that's the extent of it. Speaking of lost loves, where's Delilah?"

"She went into town to get a new shovel. The handle snapped off ours last week. Dadgum dirt has gone to cement on us. Can't you pray for rain or something?"

"I can pray for anything you'd like," he said. "Though I admit the returns are often uneven."

"I was promised two dollars and some free drinks," Cyrus interrupted.

The woman stopped smiling but told them to come inside and they did. She went around behind the bar and counted out two dollars in quarters and stacked them next to a glass and filled the glass with whiskey and sat the bottle down hard.

"Why is it you keep looking at me like you wanna carve my liver up and laugh while you do it?" Cyrus asked.

The woman scoffed and walked away without answering.

"Don't take it personally, dear Cyrus," the monk told him. "You just remind her of someone."

"Who?"

"Every man she's ever met."

Cyrus grunted and saddled a bar stool and drank his whiskey and helped himself to the bottle and poured another glass. Ollie lingered near the bar like a dog waiting for someone to drop a piece of steak.

The monk put his hand on William's shoulder and moved closer to him and William could smell the alcohol on his breath and in his sweat.

"You have the look of a lost child in search of his father," the monk said. "I know such a look. I've worn it many times myself. Perhaps I wear it still. Alas, I don't know where he's at."

"Who?" William asked. "Your old man or mine?"

"Yes," the monk said and spun away from the boy.

"Who are you looking for, kid?" the woman said, coming back down the bar.

"Thomas Carter."

She nodded.

"I know him," she said. "You're William?"

"Yes ma'am."

"He talked a lot about you," she said, fishing about in her apron for a cigarette and finding one.

"He was here?"

"Sure," she said, the cigarette in her mouth and now searching for the matches to go with it. "He come in a half dozen times to talk to Merle."

She motioned with her head and William looked toward the corner of the small room and there was a man with his arms splayed out on one of the small tables and his head was resting there on the wood and the candle flickering just above him.

"Do you know where he's at now?" Ollie asked her, but she shook her head.

"He come by when he got back from DC but that was more than a month ago."

"What a fickle and unseemly mistress time can be," the monk said.

Cyrus shook his head and downed his glass for the second time.

"You know where he might've been headed?" William asked the woman.

"Doucette," she told him and popped a match. "Said something about seeing a woman down there. Making sure she was alright."

"He's married," William said before he could stop himself.

The woman shrugged and blew out smoke.

"Well, I guess this'll be the first time in all the long history of the world where a married man has himself another woman in another town."

The boy felt foolish. His anger like that of a child stomping their feet.

He thought of his mother's arched and writhing body and the veins in her neck pressing against the skin as she flung her head back in agony. All she wanted was her husband by her side. But even in the midst of such torturous happenings and alongside the vast and vacuous space that was his absence, she would not betray him. Not by word. Not even, the boy imagined, by thought.

I'll find the sonofabitch, he told himself. And I'll drag him back to Shawnee Prairie if I have to.

William forced a neutral face. He pulled out the envelope and pressed it smooth against his stomach and then held it out to the barmaid.

"Do you know this address?" he asked.

She shook her head.

"Sorry, honey," she told him. "I imagine it's the woman's house."

William took a long breath.

"Alright then," he said. "Thank y'all for your help. We'd better get on."

"Whoa, hold on a minute," Cyrus said then turned to the woman. "These boys toted this whiskey barrel a pretty good piece down the road after I'd done and give out on account of this here no-helping bastard. I think they're owed something for their troubles."

"That's alright," William said. "We're in a sort of hurry."

"How about a beer for the road?" the woman asked.

"A beer sounds good to me," Ollie said quickly.

"We ain't but fifteen, ma'am," William told her.

"Whiskey then?" She winked.

"I'll take a whiskey," Ollie told her.

"No he won't," William said.

"Yes he by god will," Ollie said. "I've been walking half a day through the hellfire forest out there. It ain't gonna slow us down for me to have one drink."

The woman poured him a glass and Ollie threw it back and slammed it down on the bar top and motioned for her to fill it up again.

"For me to have two drinks," he said.

William went into his pocket and pulled out his watch and looked at the time.

"In a hurry you say, young pilgrim?" the monk asked.

"Yessir. I'd like to see done the thing I set out to do. The quicker the better."

"A poor outlook for a young man," the monk said. "For any man. Certainly not the attitude to take with a lover. Best to just recede into the current of the all-around."

William gave him a dismissive nod and started toward the bar to grab Ollie.

"I'm not as crazy as you think I am," the monk said, and he sighed and smiled and William thought he looked sad. Perhaps just tired.

"But I've lost my faith," he told the boy. "Or it has abandoned me. Or it went out for cigarettes. I can't say."

William thought of his father's letter. He turned back and regarded the man. He'd never seen anyone in real robes like that. It looked equal parts sacred and ridiculous.

"What happened?" the boy asked. "For you to lose it, I mean."

The monk shrugged.

"I heard a story once," he said, "where a boy was born and lived the whole of his life inside a room with no windows and one small door. And cut into the door was a slot and through this slot food and water would be given to him each day. So, in time, the boy grew to be a man. Of course, he couldn't talk because no one had ever talked to him and he didn't know what a face looked like because he'd never seen one—not even his own. And perhaps most tragic of all, he didn't know what a door was because he'd never seen one open. So he crouched and hunched near the door and paced the room back and forth in front of it, and even slept with his head next to it. Inches from freedom, and yet he had no understanding of his own confinement. That is until one day when he awoke to find the door slightly ajar. Naturally the man was curious, though not overly so—after all, what curiosities might a man have when he hasn't the perspective to even imagine—and so he pushed the door and the door opened and he walked out of the room."

"What was on the other side of the door?" William asked.

"Everything else."

The boy shook his head. "What's that have to do with your faith?" he asked.

"What does Gilgamesh have to do with Noah," the monk said, toying at the locket around his neck. "Perhaps everything. Perhaps nothing."

He opened the locket and closed it and opened it again, and each time William tried to get a look at what was inside, the chain turned this way or that and he never saw it, and finally the monk snapped it shut and tucked it under the collar of his robes which were far too large on him, the ends frayed and dust-painted and dragging behind him.

"Are you really a Carmelite?" William asked.

"I'm not really much of anything at all," the monk said. "I think I'll have a piss."

William watched him retire to the back door and again the boy started toward the bar to collect Ollie and again he was thwarted.

He had neither seen nor heard the man get up from the table and cross the room but he was now at the boy's side, staring at him through red, drunk eyes. Glassed eyes that reflected the dim room and the light from the room and they settled on William and considered him and the man seemed not to know what to say.

"I'm Merle Trout," he announced at last, his head quaking a bit as he spoke. "Did your old man ever talk about the Meuse?"

William saw that the right half of his face had been badly burned and was now scarred over with pink poxed skin. His right shoulder hung lower than his left.

"Nossir. He didn't talk about much."

Merle nodded and the boy was not sure if he was disappointed or relieved.

"Well. Probably for the best."

"Were you there?" William asked.

"Yes," Merle said. "I was. It's where I got my beauty marks."

He turned his head sideways and craned his neck so that the boy might see the extent of his scarring.

"And it would have been the place where I died, if it weren't for Thomas."

"He saved you?" William asked.

"He saved all of us. Him and Roger, and that goddamned Homer Renfro. Come charging into the thick of it, screaming and hollering. I don't believe the Krauts had ever seen anything like it—band of Texans going up and over the trenches like they was charging the Eastern Gate. Crazy bastards."

Merle shook his head.

"I guess there's none of it that don't seem crazy now."

"He would come here," William asked, "to visit with you?"

"He would," Merle nodded. "Ask am I doing alright, do I have enough money—things like that. He didn't much care for me drinking like I do, but he understood it. He'd even get himself a pull every now and again. Maybe just to make me feel better. That's the way he is, your father—always looking out for everybody else."

The reverence with which the man spoke of Thomas disarmed the boy. It reminded him of his mother. Her unyielding faith. He looked at his watch.

"That's why we elected him to lead us in the first place," Merle said. "But I've heard they quit all that—letting the boys choose their own lieutenants. They won't even let fellas go join up and serve together no more. Don't want to lose a whole generation from the same place, they say. Wipe out the future of one town or another. Government talk. All it is. They talk like they never fought a war, because they hadn't. Don't know the first thing about it."

The man went on at length about the woes of war and William tried to imagine it but could not. Even in his darkest depictions he knew it was somehow worse.

There was a sconce on the wall near the door and a candle stub burning down to the last inch and William watched the trailing wax and the dance of the flame.

Merle quieted and then leaned in close to William's face.

"You ever hear a horse scream?" he asked.

William looked up.

"I gotta go, sir," he told the man and went and tugged Ollie away from the bar.

"I've had a few twitchers, is all I'm saying," Ollie said, slurping at the last of his drink. "'Bout scared me out of my damn skin."

William was all but dragging him toward the door.

"Thank you ma'am," he called. "I'll be sure to come back."

The boys left the cabin and rejoined the road and William tried his best not to think of his father with another woman, and he tried to think of what he would say to his mother—if he would say anything at all.

Ollie meanwhile had seen a marked improvement in demeanor.

"What a great place," he said. "And Emily? My goodness, what a woman."

"Who's Emily?" William asked.

"She runs the joint," Ollie said, laughing as if this were a fact known unto the wider world in full. "Her and Delilah. They're lavenders from Lovelady. Moved out here to be by themselves but then they realized there were all sorts of folks around who needed a place to go and just be who they are. So they turned the cabin into a speak. Still sleep right there in the back and everything."

"You found all this out in fifteen minutes?"

"I'm a people person, bud," Ollie said. "And a helluva listener."

"You spend your days with dead bodies."

"That's how come me to be a purveyor of details. Speaking of, Cyrus *did* say monkey. But he meant *box* like *fight*. I thought it might be code talk or something but it ain't. Apparently that medicine show he was talking about has a big-ass gorilla they tote around and folks can fight it for a chance to win money."

"Christ," William said.

"But don't worry about ole Cyrus. He used to be a professional boxer. Highest he ever got in the rankings was losing to a fella that lost to Jack Johnson, but that still makes him the toughest man in the county by a pretty good distance."

William just stared at him.

Ollie pointed to his ears.

"We'll get a room in Nancy and see if we can't catch a ride down highway forty to Doucette in the morning," William told him.

"What about the medicine show?" Ollie asked.

"What about it?"

"You got something against monkeys?"

"I ain't got no grievance with monkeys, Ollie, I just think we ought to bed down and get a good start in the morning. It got hotter than hell today, and if we leave early enough, we might make Doucette before our hair catches fire."

"Blair went to a show in Zavalla this past spring and said they had some type of love potion what would make a gal crazy about you."

"And you believe Blair?"

"I know Vicky Hughes followed him around all summer. And her about twice as good-looking as he is."

William considered the evidence.

"Girls don't always go for looks like how boys do," he said.

"Tell me more, oh wise and wonderous lover of ladies."

"Shut up."

"We're going to that show," Ollie told him.

"We ain't going."

"We're going."

"Nope."

11

They reached Nancy just in time for the show.

It was the end of the day's business and the town was full of motion.

The lamplighters went forth with their turpentine torches and the lanterns came alive around the square and flames erupted from barrel fires casting light and shadow—the town now aglow in the lessening eventide air.

The butcher in his stained and bloody apron sat smoking on a stool outside his shop and the postman locked his door and the barber and the dentist and the grocer and all came out into the street where gathered a few dozen townsfolk and more coming up the way.

To the west a merciful sunset. Pink of sky. Dusk and sounds of dusk rising up from the forest as cicadas trilled and crickets and frogs, and here the boys came forward into town with sun-stained necks and sun-dried denim.

"You catch a piece of that breeze, it's almost nice out," Ollie said, still slightly drunk.

They made their way along the street and stopped at the edge of the gathered crowd and rose up on their toes to see. Great canvas tents lined the square, covering the lawn like some sort of carnival. There were men and women setting out their wares on tables and old blankets and atop apple crates, and when the wind did blow, the tent sides rippled and the torch flames danced and there was an electric feel to the air.

In front of the row of tents was a low platform stage and the show's featured wagon, the likes of which the boy had only seen in picture books. It was long and squat and painted black with a gold trim that ran along its side in looping laces. On each corner was a pilaster, jutting out, and atop each post was carved the dueling Athenian muses of Melpomene and Thalia, which gave to the wagon a look of something from another place or time or world entire. The hull was solid save for a glass cutout in which pyrite-colored curtains had been hung and drawn back to reveal a sign in the window. In fine red script was written *Doctor Downtain's Mount Zaphon Medicine Show.*

"Looks fancy," Ollie said, peering around a group of men who stood in front of the boys and passed a tobacco pouch between them.

"I don't see a monkey," William said.

"Well, I doubt if they'd just have it right out front for everybody to stare at the whole time," Ollie said, shaking his head. "Anticipation is the secret to showmanship. Hell, everybody knows that."

The men in front of them were laughing and one of them looked upset.

"I don't give a damn if y'all believe it or not," he told the others. "I'm telling you I know the sonofabitch. He used to run a whorehouse in Joplin, Missouri."

"Yeah? And what was you doing in a whorehouse in Missouri?"

"There's things I ain't proud of," the man answered, defiant. "But it was all before I met Sarah."

"I bet you hadn't told her about them things you ain't proud of," another man teased.

"Y'all ought to be careful casting them stones."

"Don't sull up on us, Harry, hell."

"And I'll tell you another thing," Harry said, arms crossed. "They come and arrested him in Missouri on account of some of his girls was too young."

"Well, I'll say this for him—if any of that is true," one of the men spit. "It's probably a damn sight harder to sell pills and potions than it is to sell pussy."

The men laughed again but they were interrupted by a drumroll and a flash-bang and there was a thin pillar of smoke on the stage and Doctor Downtain himself stepped through it. He was a thin man in a black suit despite the heat and a black high hat to match. He had auburn hair and his orange mustache was waxed and curled and he wore a pair of black pointed boots fashioned from snakeskin.

"Let's move closer," Ollie said, and William nodded and they pushed their way forward as Downtain greeted the audience and began his spiel.

"Good people of the Nancy township, what I offer you here this evening are products and provisions sourced from around the world. From the Arabian deserts to the jungles of Africa. You will not find such wonders in catalogs or corner stores," Downtain paused and removed his hat for effect. "With all due respect to the upstanding merchants of your fine town."

His cadence reminded William of a preacher he'd heard once at a traveling revival. He was ten years old and his mother had insisted they attend and for hours they'd stood alongside other believers in a muddy field and listened to the preacher share the word and every so often someone would cry out and the preacher would call the person to the front and lay hands upon them and whatever ailment they suffered from would be removed—or at least the seed of removal planted, as sometimes God's miracles need a day or two to take root. Others would pray with him and then go to a holding area off to the side where they would put on liverish-colored robes that had once been white and wait to be baptized at day's end.

William knew all good men were eventually baptized but he had always thought of it in terms of a future endeavor. Still, he could see his mother looking to him expectantly each time someone went forward and he began to feel the burden of inaction. She could do that to him, his mother—make him feel guilt with only a look—such was his desire to make her happy. And it was that longing, not some eternal belief, that led him to go up front and pray with the preacher and don a stained robe with the rest of the candidates for salvation. And as the sun set beyond the pines, the congregation and its robed contingent went singing into the dark waters of the Neches River, where the sinners were, one after another, submerged and washed clean. His mother had smiled in a way that he had never forgotten.

Now, he thought, his goal was not so different as it had been. If he could find his father and bring him home, surely she would smile in such a way again.

"So at your leisure you can visit any of the four tents, two to my left, two here to my right," Downtain was saying, and he pointed to each side of the wagon where the large canopy tents were erected. "And my agreeable associates will be happy to sell you any of the items we feature here this evening, as well as other products and prizes that we won't get to on the main stage but that you're more than welcome to inspect and inquire after in the aforementioned areas. Now, ladies and gentlemen, if you all are ready to begin, you need but give a rousing round of applause and we shall proceed."

There was a weak smattering of claps.

The doctor smiled, undeterred.

"Alright then, first off I'd like to tell you about our newest product. Straight from India. From India, ladies and gentlemen, directly to our man at the docks in the port of San Francisco and delivered personally then into my hands, the very hands which show you now a revolutionary new medicine to combat sickness. Revolutionary, folks. What sickness, you may ask. And to you I'd say name one." The doctor spoke in tones ranging from hushed to boisterous and he spoke with animated hands as if he were plucking invisible words from one spot and depositing them in another. "This miracle elixir is only found in the jungles of India, where in the Talle Valley near the fertile banks of the Brahmaputra River grows a never-before-cultivated plant. A plant unknown to all but a single tribe.

And from this rare and beautiful plant a purple flower blooms but once a year, and during its blooming it releases the very smallest amount of nectar. Truly the most rare droplets. These droplets are collected, ever so carefully, to be used by the tribe's shaman on the sick and the suffering. Men with bad backs, women with awful, agitating headaches. The elderly with aching joints or stiff bones. This incredible plant potion alleviates it all. It's even been known to cure cancers."

William felt himself stiffen. But only a fool would believe such things, he thought.

"For years the British government has tried to obtain the plant," Downtain went on, "but it is so remarkably rare that the tribe has been able to keep it hidden. Until, ladies and gentlemen, in my extensive travels across this wide world of ours I came to that very village in India and met that very tribe. Now, I'd like to tell you fine folks that the shaman saw something worthy in me, something special, and because of that he bestowed upon me the lifesaving nectar of his people. But that would be a lie, and I'm not here to lie to you this evening. No, I offered the old shaman the only thing I believed worthy of such a magical mixture—money."

There were a few chuckles.

"That's right, American dollars. And so folks, when I say this is an expensive elixir, I mean it. I know personally just how expensive it is. To cultivate, to harvest, to bottle and ship and transport. It took a great deal to get this here for you wonderful people but get it here I have. I'm proud—no, honored—to say we have ten vials available here this evening. Ten vials. And if you say that's not enough, I wouldn't call you wrong. Surely, I wouldn't. I wish we had more. We started off with two hundred. Two hundred of these vials we started out with, but they've been gobbled up by folks all over the country and until I get word from my friends across the ocean, I can't say when there might be more. For all I know, these may very well be the last ten vials ever in existence. And I say that sincerely."

"How much?" a man called out.

"What's that, my friend?"

"Enough with the silly stories," he said. "How much for the medicine?"

"Ah, a straightforward man. I can certainly respect that. Well, it only takes one drop to cure what ails you, and each vial contains twenty drops, so the fair price—and I do mean fair, my friends—is set and unmoved at five dollars per unit. Five dollars can get you a guaranteed cure for whatever pain is troubling you or your loved one, and my associates in the tents are standing by to take your orders."

A few people wandered off toward the tents. The man who asked the price stayed put.

The doctor continued on with his script, introducing one tincture after another and then artifacts and relics, each with its own incredible story. The crowd was growing restless.

"Alright, alright, you've suffered me long enough," the doctor said, ever smiling. "I know what you're all here for. But allow us a brief interval to set the stage. Visit the tents. Enjoy the reprieve. I shall see you back here in twenty minutes' time."

The night was on them now and the lamplight made silhouettes of men as they passed before it.

The boys moved with the herd, wandering the tents. A phonograph played an Eddie Lang tune and lanterns were hung on tentpoles and sat atop tables and there were rows of glass bottles with foreign markings, and old leatherbound books said to contain various spells and manifestations, and decks of cards painted with strange figures, and great bins of bayonets and rusted swords.

"Got one of the knives they used to stab Caesar himself," said a bald man with blue dots painted in a line beneath both eyes.

He sat on a stool behind a bin and there were a dozen other men and women from the medicine show spread out amongst the wares. Many of them wore odd costume-like clothing—mummer's suits or elaborate wigs. And others had markings or drawings all about their skin. Gypsies from some other order of men entirely.

"Et tu, Brute?" the blue-dotted man asked.

William nodded, unsure, and kept walking.

There were cups made from molded clay and lined up on a wooden slab that lay across the top of two vinegar barrels and the town's sheriff stood drinking from one of the cups and when it was empty a large-chested woman filled it again and the sheriff grinned at her and burped.

A boy in a newsie cap slid in front of William and Ollie and pulled a flask halfway out of his pants pocket.

"Got some bourbon whiskey left this ole boy give me in Leesville," he said, glancing behind him. "If you got a nickel, I'll give you both a fair splash."

"We ain't going nowhere until the morning," Ollie told William.

"You're bound and determined to get rip-roaring ain't you?"

"Who the hell gets drunk from one nip of whiskey?" he asked, handing the boy a dime. "Or two."

A few minutes later Ollie was a blushing bride. Warm and lovely.

"They ought to be starting the show back up here pretty quick," William said.

Ollie didn't answer.

"I'm fixin' to go hunt me a love potion to use on Kathy Thurgood," he announced instead and William watched him work through the traffic toward the far side of the tent.

William went on without him.

There were stereopticons with three-dimensional views of places the boy had never been or even heard of. Plant elixirs that were said to keep a man awake for days, and others to keep him asleep. Potions that could make you a better lover or cure you of melancholia.

There was a man who snapped his fingers and made fire come out while a few folks oohed and aahed. William stood for a moment and watched as the man set flame to various things and twirled them about, extinguishing them under a fire cloth.

"Careful now," he told a woman who leaned too close. "This here is ferrocerium. Comes from Austria. More flammable than a mother-in-law. Buy a jar of it and you won't ever have to wait to get warm this winter."

William walked on. At length he came to the case where the Indian plant extract was housed and there he stood with a few others.

"You think there's anything to it?" a man next to him asked.

"I kindly doubt it," the boy said. "Fella's story don't make much sense. If all it took was money, seems like other folks would've been able to get ahold of it before now."

"Who said all it took was money?" The question was low and hissed-like in William's ear.

The boy flinched and turned and the doctor from the stage now stood in front of him. The other man moved quickly away.

"I said money was what was offered," Downtain slid his cane tip across the length of the case. "I never said it was accepted."

"What'd you give for it, then?" William asked.

Downtain smirked.

"I've given more than you could ever know, boy," he said. "And in return, I was shown where true power lies. Not in dollars or deities or some ancient wisdom from above, but here, where we stand—here, with the sons of disobedience and the children of wrath."

William frowned.

"So you're saying this really cures anything?" he asked. "Even a tumor?"

"I'm saying there's only one way to find out."

Downtain touched William with his cane and then touched it to his hat and slipped away into the crowd.

William looked back at the case. There were five or six tinctures left and two men were standing on either end of the table haggling with prospective buyers. William watched one of the men open the case and take out two of the vials and give them to a woman with no shoes. Her hand shook as she passed him a ten-dollar bill and she looked at the money after she'd turned loose of it, watching the man open his lock-box and put the bill inside.

The boy felt uneasy and the air seemed to thicken in his throat. He shook away the discomfort and searched for Ollie but soon each step he took felt heavy, as if he was mired somehow in the well-trodden dirt. Again he sought to ignore the feeling but now the dread was moving into his lungs and he couldn't inhale. He looked for water. For a way out of the tent. His vision seemed to blur, and the sides of the world were closing in around him. The people and the noise multiplied. Someone was laughing. His knees weakened. He'd heard of men who experienced vapors—bouts of hysteria or mania—and felt as if they were dying. Was this such a malady? Or was he actually dying? His thoughts came faster than he could filter them.

"Boy," someone called, and he felt a hand on his wrist, pulling him toward a dark corner.

"Sit," said a middle-aged woman in a black-and-gold-patterned tunic, and William did and was grateful for the chair. He tried again to breathe.

The woman sat on a short stool across from him and picked up a deck of cards from a Navajo blanket that had been flung over a milk crate. She leaned forward and the tunic pressed against her chest and the boy stared and then quickly looked away. She had raven-colored hair that hung in front of one shoulder in a long black braid.

"You look sickly," she told him. Her face was tan and slightly wrinkled and she wore blue paint around her blue eyes. Golden rings and golden bars were pressed through her ears and cheeks and brows. She seemed at once gorgeous and grotesque. "Are you?"

"Am I what?" he asked, his pulse quieting in his head.

"Sickly."

"No ma'am," he said, looking at the back of his hands. "Not really. I just got a little dizzy, maybe."

"The earth turned without you."

"I guess so."

"Don't let it," she warned him. "Bad for the spirit. I'll read your cards." She was shuffling.

"No, that's alright," William told her, looking behind him at the crowd.

"I'll read your cards," she said again.

"I'm not buying, ma'am."

"And I'm not selling, boy."

The woman turned the top card and ran her fingers down the length of its face. A slender man in a blue tunic and red leggings hung from a gallows pole by one ankle. He looked at the man's expressionless face, yellow sun bursting behind his head.

The woman put the deck aside.

"You don't draw a bunch more?" the boy asked.

"Many cards mean many voices."

"What's wrong with that?"

"There is only one voice."

"What's this one say?"

"The Hanged Man."

"They don't hang 'em by the neck?"

"He is here by choice."

"He hung hisself?"

"He has his reasons. As you have yours. We are, all of us, bound to our reasoning."

"So what does it mean?"

"Upright, he would have you wait. He would tell you to have patience, to view yourself and your situation from another perspective. Perhaps you think you're doing one thing, when you are actually doing another."

William frowned.

"But reversed—upside down—the Hanged Man tells of a tale already in motion. A tale in which no satisfaction can be found."

The boy swallowed hard, pushing down the fear-choked breath in his throat. He stood and put his shoulders back.

"It's a good thing I don't believe in this shit," he said.

The woman sighed. She stared up at William while shuffling the cards with a deft hand, never looking down.

"Your belief," she told him, fanning out the deck, "is not required for a thing to be true."

She nodded at him and the boy reluctantly chose a card at random and turned it over. The Hanged Man was still affixed to the gallows, only now it seemed there might be the slightest smile on his face.

"You see?" the woman said.

William bent to look closer but she snatched the card away.

"Whatever you're searching for," she told him, "you will not find it."

The boy felt a familiar anger—a gnawing frustration with being told what he could and could not control.

"Like I said, I don't put no stock in card tricks and soothsayers," he told her. "My mother says folks like you are hellbound."

"And what do you say?" the woman asked, curious, almost laughing.

"It don't matter what I say," he told her. "My belief ain't required for a thing to be true."

"Well then," she said, and she smiled and held her hands up as if to signify some point.

William stared at her for a moment more and then walked away.

"Don't be angry, little angry boy," she called after him. "While you are busy being angry, the earth will turn without you. It will turn again and again."

The tents were clearing out and the phonograph had gone quiet. He walked off from the show and breathed the stale summer air and looked down the road to where the moon had yet to rise and there was no light but for a few fireflies that sparked and went black and then sparked again.

Lightning bugs, his mother called them.

You can always see God's light, she'd say, as the fireflies strobed about the yard. *No matter the darkness.*

"Lift your end higher, goddamnit," someone barked, and William turned to see four men carrying a five-foot cage with iron bars and a black sheet draped over the top and hanging down the sides.

The two men in the back grunted and hoisted the thing higher.

"There you go," the first man said. "Keep it steady now."

"Christ Almighty, Leslie. How much did you give him?"

"I couldn't remember if I'd done give it to him at the start, so I just went on and hit him with another round."

"He don't look right."

"You think Downtain'll notice?"

"You better hope he don't."

They passed before the boy, the iron cage jostling, and William saw a hand emerge from within. It came up from beneath the sheet and gripped at the bars, and there in the glow of the lamplight he could see the gray anthropoid fingers, lined and wrinkled as his own.

And then it was gone. The ape, and the cage that held it, delivered up onto the altar of the stage.

12

William went around to the side of the stage and scanned the crowd for Ollie but there was no sign of him.

All that fuss, he thought, and now he's gonna miss the monkey.

When the sheet was removed from the cage a few of the people gasped and Downtain grinned and rapped against the bars with his cane. The ape cowered. Black vassal. Shoulders raised high and head hung low.

"My friends," Downtain said. "You shall wait no longer."

Some of the men and women who'd all but fallen asleep on their feet suddenly began to perk up.

"Now, ladies and gentlemen, I see several stout fellows in this fine crowd. Several strong lads of the highest quality, I have no doubt. Why, what is this?" Downtain asked, hopping down off the platform with little effort. His landing turned into stride as soon as his feet touched the ground. He wove through the crowd and came to a slender man who touched his cap in greeting.

"Look here, ladies and gentlemen," Downtain said, turning his head backward to each side. "Here we stand in heat unrelenting, even under the cover of night, and yet do my eyes defy me, or does this man have not a drop of sweat about him?"

The crowd agreed, halfhearted.

"No. No. No. A fine stamina he may have, folks, but this is not the man."

He clapped the man on the shoulder and pushed past him, further into the crowd.

"Now, my goodness," he said, stopping in front of a rotund man broad about the shoulders and waist alike. "My goodness, my goodness. Here's a man with a hearty appetite to him. Tell me, sir, does strength come affixed to such girth?"

In a show of good nature, the man grabbed Downtain beneath his armpits and lifted him three feet off the ground.

The audience clapped more than before and Downtain could feel their excitement building.

"Alas, this is not our champion," he said. Some in the crowd groaned, feigning disappointment. "I know, I know. No doubt he would have made a fine one. But ladies and gentlemen, I've been at this occupation for many a year, and I've witnessed the rise and fall of heroes of all sizes. It's not the girth, but the grit that takes the day. Would you not agree?"

Heads nodded. Murmured affirmations.

"And of course nowhere is there more grit than right here in the fabled piney woods of East Texas."

Applause.

"You are the true standard-bearers of this nation."

"Hear, hear," someone yelled.

"The bankers in New York, the politicians in Washington. In the game of life they are nothing more than apes screeching at one another and shitting on the board."

"To hell with the bastards," came a voice, and others quickly joined in.

"They don't know grit," Downtain cried.

Cheers.

"They don't know hard work," he slammed the foot of his cane into the dirt.

Cheers.

"They are the ones holding this country back from being truly great."

He had worked the crowd into a lather. They followed him now and he could see he had them.

"And that is why, my friends, there can be only one choice to stand against this caged beast. There's only one man here before us with enough sand. With enough gumption."

At this point the crowd had all but parted like a biblical sea to allow him clear passage in front of a musclebound man who stood slightly over six feet and slightly drunk before them.

"Here, ladies and gentlemen, is our champion," Downtain said, raising Cyrus's veiny arm.

The townspeople roared their approval.

"I guess when a man needs to fight a monkey," Ollie said, appearing at William's side, "he by god needs to fight a monkey."

"Where you been?"

"Tell you later."

"And this," Downtain said, making his way back to the stage, "is our challenger. Ladies and gentlemen, meet Kushim."

The audience hissed and booed and laughed.

As Cyrus walked to the stage one of the handlers clipped a large carabiner to the ape's harness and from it ran a six-foot length of rope that was tied off at the wagon.

"They got him leashed," William said.

"Well shit yeah," Ollie said stretching his neck to see.

Cyrus ascended the stage and the crowd applauded as he slipped on the gloves.

"The terms are simple," Downtain said, twirling his cane. "You have one minute to knock Kushim to the ground. Do so, and you win five dollars. But beware, my friend, he lacks the civilized nature of a man such as yourself. He will show you no mercy."

The ape's gloves were on and now they were opening the cage. The congregation quieted.

Kushim moved forward, hesitant. Head down, shoulders up. He looked at the crowd and they looked at him, sneering and hooting. He stopped.

Cyrus looked back at Downtain who smiled apologetically and nodded to the handlers. One of them brought up a steel pipe from beneath the wagon and hammered it against the bars of the cage. Kushim crouched then looked behind him and the man held up the makeshift baton in a threatening manner. Kushim moved forward and stood erect and held up his gloves in front of Cyrus and the crowd gave a round of applause to indicate their approval.

Cyrus circled the ape. Kushim turned slowly to keep the man in front of him. The two were of similar height with the gorilla standing on two feet. Cyrus slid forward and landed a quick jab that snapped the ape's head back.

The crowd roared in delight.

As soon as the punch landed Cyrus stepped back out of range but Kushim never mounted a counterattack. Instead he continued holding his gloves up, staring at the man, turning slowly in a circle.

Cyrus moved in again, this time with a flurry of punches. Again he slid back and measured his opponent and again the ape did nothing. Once more, a combination of jabs and crosses and Kushim neither went down nor fought back.

Cyrus stood straight and dropped his gloves to his side.

"This monkey's doped up," he announced, and there were a few laughs. "It ain't a fair fight."

Downtain, ever smiling, stepped in front of Cyrus.

"Ladies and gentlemen, it appears as though the mighty Kushim is not himself this evening. Under the weather, no doubt."

"Sick, hell," Cyrus said. "That monkey's loaded."

"Five dollars to our champion by way of disqualification," Downtain announced.

Cyrus frowned.

"I don't want your money," he said, yanking off the gloves and letting them fall to the stage.

The crowd was quiet—only a few murmurs—as if it were deciding as a collective how to respond.

And then.

"I'll give you a quarter to let me swing at the sonofabitch," called the big man who had lifted Downtain.

A few people laughed.

"Yeah," hollered someone else. "I'd give a quarter to say I'd beat on the bastard."

More joined in, laughing and calling out. Soon the crowd began to surge forward holding up their coins.

Cyrus had walked off and only Downtain and the ape remained on stage and Downtain considered the prospect and then held up his cane.

"One quarter equals one swing," he announced, and there were yells of approval from the crowd.

The first man was hesitant. Bashful even. He looked at the ape and then turned and looked back at the crowd as if for permission. Then he swung. Kushim staggered backward.

There was a brief pause and then the crowd gave an applause and the man smiled and held up his hands, and a few more men were coming forward.

Downtain smiled and watched them come and he began to take their coins and even their dollars and now they were coming in waves. They clambered onto the stage without using the stairs and they hit the ape without gloves and they kicked him and more of them climbed up and they threw their money at Downtain's feet and together they fell upon the ape and never did he lift a hand to fight back. Some of the women turned away. Others did not—instead cheering the men as they sought to satisfy an unfulfilled bloodlust. Theirs was a primal and unrestrained violence. An ancient violence what saw their every disappointment and disillusion manifested there before them in the beating heart of this creature who was not one of their own. Kill and cleanse and be born anew.

Downtain watched all of this with an amused calm, letting it go on until at last he nodded to one of the handlers who fired a shotgun into the air and the mob backed away. The handlers dragged the broken ape back into his cage and removed his collar.

The cheers had died off and all was quiet save Kushim's ragged wheezing breaths. The crowd now found itself in a collective disbelief. Even those men who beat the animal seemed stunned at the product of their own aggression.

The creature's eyes met William's. Cousined eyes and full of sorrow. And here the ape held out its hand to the boy and he could see it there in all its complexity and fallacy and in its need for grace. And the boy mumbled the only prayer he could think of and when he was finished he heard Ollie say, "Amen," and the two of them moved away from the stage like mourners having said their goodbyes.

Downtain smiled and collected the loose money from the stage and he reminded the audience that the tents would remain open well into the night. He thanked them for their attendance and announced that this was the last show of the summer season.

"Anything you desire," he said, "must be obtained without delay. Opportunity is the result of action, my friend—not the other way around."

He then introduced a brother-sister fiddle act for which there was a light round of applause. The music began and the townsfolk seemed to slowly forget about what came before. Their faces softened and a few even smiled and soon they were clapping their hands to the rhythm. The brother sat on a stump and played the fiddle while the sister danced and fluffed her skirt at the crowd and the crowd cheered and each time she kicked up her white boots William could see blood on the soles.

13

The boys drifted to the edge of the crowd as the music continued and now some folks had gathered around the barrel fires and were drinking from flasks and laughing. William looked for Cyrus but did not see him. Ollie found a lamppost and leaned against it and belched and put his hand to his stomach.

"I don't feel so hot," Ollie said.

"Have you ever seen anything like that?" William asked, his mind still on the brutish display of violence.

"Too much whiskey on an empty stomach."

"And him just standing there, watching them do it," William continued.

"Huh?"

"Nothing," William said. "Let's get out of here. Find a hotel room."

Before Ollie could answer there were two vendors out from the tent and pointing in their direction.

"That's the little bastard right there," one of them said.

The men began running toward them.

"Well, shit," Ollie said. "Sorry bud, we gotta get."

He pushed himself away from the post and took off at a wobbly sprint.

William hesitated, confused. He looked back to the men and then followed down the street after Ollie.

They hit the edge of town and kept going. They stuck to the highway, making their way by moonlight. The men had given up the chase long ago but the boys kept running and didn't say a word between them until at last Ollie collapsed laughing into the barrow ditch.

"What did you do, you drunk damn fool," William asked, standing over him, panting.

Ollie pushed up onto his elbow. "Drunk fool?" he said, waving a small bottle of the Indian miracle elixir in front of his face. "Well. Maybe this'll be my cure."

William started to respond, but Ollie's grin shifted.

"Wait a minute," he said.

"What?"

"I think I might—"

William watched him throw up in the ditch.

"Let's just get off the road and find a place to sleep," William said, finding it difficult to be too upset while his best friend put on this most pathetic showing.

"A fine idea," Ollie said, wiping his mouth. "I suppose that hotel back in town is out of the question."

"It is now," William said. "You took care of that when you went and made us outlaws."

"So I did," Ollie said, wistful. "A drunk fool indeed."

A half hour later they were well off the road and had made camp in a small clearing, such as it was, surrounded by maple and dogwood and other understory trees. They'd brought no bedrolls but William let Ollie use his blanket as a pallet and the satchel as a pillow and William himself wadded up the grocery sack from the commissary and was trying to get comfortable.

"Say, bud?" Ollie whispered.

"Go to sleep, Ollie," William told him, annoyed, and they were both quiet for a minute and then William rolled toward him. "What?"

"You believe in hell?"

"Hell?"

"Yeah."

"You laying there thinking about that eighth commandment?"

"I might be."

"Well. Do you believe in hell?"

"I don't know," Ollie said. "That's why I'm asking."

"Alright. Do you believe in heaven?"

"Who don't believe in heaven?"

"You can't believe in one without the other," William told him.

Ollie was quiet.

"Why not?" he asked after a while.

"You just can't," William told him. "You take the good with the bad or you don't take none of it at all."

William turned onto his back and crossed one leg over the other and lay there looking up through the canopy and who can say what he saw in the night sky or what he saw in his own heart—both imposed upon, both obstructed.

After a while he closed his eyes

"No," he said. "I don't believe in hell."

William could hear Ollie snoring.

The crickets were calling. And frogs. The night was anything but quiet and the boy's own thoughts adding to the cacophony of noise that kept him from sleep.

His mother was much on his mind. When other sons were carried home from church on their father's shoulders, it had been his mother who held both of his small hands and swung him forward over mud puddles and collected him up into her arms and pressed her nose to his and first told him of love and the power that it held. The power to hold the two of them together, she told him, for all of time.

But now every step took him further away from her. And closer to what?

The decision to leave his mother was troubling enough but he'd given little thought to what he would say when he found his father. He could scarce remember the last conversation they'd had that wasn't about cotton bolls or firewood or the proper way to carry out some task.

He's gone to see about some woman.

The boy could feel it inside him—a rage that would not soon be contained.

He tried again to sleep but could not.

Sometime in the night he stood and walked a dozen or so yards into the trees and unbuttoned his trousers and pissed into the brush.

The night air was warm and after standing for a time he buttoned his pants and was making to turn when something hard pressed into the back of his neck.

"Is your pecker in your pants?" a girl asked.

William was slow to answer. He raised his hands up next to his head.

"Yes ma'am," he said, afraid but also curious.

"Anything else in there with it?"

"What?" He began to turn but the cold iron pressed harder.

"I didn't say move," the girl said. "And I mean a knife. A gun. Something you might try to reach for if I let you loose."

"No ma'am."

"Alright," she said, and he felt the gun barrel move from his neck. "Turn slow."

He did.

The girl looked to be not much older than him. They were near to the same height. She had thick hair cut straight across her shoulders. He could not see the color of her eyes in the dark of night but he could see the wildness in them all the same.

She kept the pistol trained on him.

"What about your buddy yonder?" she asked. "He carrying anything?"

"No," he said. "The burden of ignorance, maybe."

He thought he saw her smile.

"Get over there and wake him," she motioned with the gun. "Tell him what's happening."

"What *is* happening?"

"I'm robbing you two. Taking your satchel. Food. Money. Whatever else you got."

"How old are you?"

"Old enough to pull a trigger."

William walked back to the makeshift camp and nudged Ollie's shoulder with his boot.

"Wake up, bud. We're being steamed by a girl with a gun."

Ollie frowned, his eyes half-open.

"What'n the hell are you talking about?" he asked, his hands raising to rub his temples. "Christ at my head."

"Well," William said, pointing. "This is the girl. And that's her gun."

"What's she clipping *us* for?" Ollie asked, sitting up. "We ain't hardly got a damn thing to our names."

No one spoke. Finally William turned to the girl.

"He says what are you stealing from us for, we don't—"

"I heard what he said, smartass. And I don't care what you have or don't have. Take everything out of your pockets, put it in that satchel, then pass it over here."

"Let's rush her," Ollie said, rising to his feet. "She ain't gonna shoot nobody."

The girl fired the pistol into the dirt near his feet and Ollie shrieked and fell backward.

"You can rush her," William said, turning his pockets inside out. "I'm just gonna give her the ham and be done with it."

A minute later they'd laid out the bulk of their possessions on top of the blanket. One pocketknife, a short stack of tinned fruit, a slightly taller stack of canned ham, a box of matches, two changes of socks, and a half-filled jug of water—all of which glowed blue in the moonlight.

"Boy, y'all are about as destitute a pair as I've come across," the girl said.

"At least we ain't thieves," Ollie spit.

"We tried to tell you," William said.

"What the hell are y'all doing out here?" she asked.

"Running from the law," Ollie said.

"No you ain't."

"Killed two men in Lufkin."

"No you didn't."

"Why'd you ask then?"

"I guess I just ain't ever seen such a sorry situation. Almost makes me feel guilty for taking your boots."

The boys looked at each other.

"What do you need our boots for?" William asked. "They won't fit you."

"No, but they'll fit somebody. I can trade them. Or cut them up and use the leather."

The boys didn't move.

"C'mon now. Get them off before I have to waste a bullet in your knee."

"Wait," William said. "We got something better than boots. Something better than any of this."

"What?" Ollie asked, surprised.

"Don't play dumb," William told him. "Show it to her."

"Show me what?" the girl asked.

"Show her the medicine," William said, and Ollie nodded, catching on. "You mind if I light a match?"

She gave him a nod and he popped a match against the box and went and stood beside her and Ollie reached into his boot and produced the tincture and held it out.

The girl recoiled and William thought for the briefest moment that she looked scared, the small flame dancing there on her face.

"I stole it off a fella at a medicine show," Ollie said. "It's worth a bunch of money."

"I thought you weren't thieves," the girl said, taking the vial.

Ollie opened his mouth to defend himself but then closed it again.

"Where was this medicine show at?" she asked, lowering the gun to her side.

"Nancy."

"Where was it headed?"

"Shit, I don't know—wherever," Ollie said.

"They said it was the last show of the summer," William told her. "Or last one for a while."

The match went out and the girl looked to where William had been but he was already on the other side of her, yanking the gun from her hand.

"Yes," Ollie shouted. "How's that for destitute? Give me my bottle back."

The girl looked at the small glass container a moment longer then handed it over.

"Alright, girl," William told her. "It's time you went on your way."

"Let's take *her* shoes," Ollie said, excited.

"We ain't taking anything," William said. "In fact, you can go on and get a can of ham for the road."

The girl scoffed.

She crossed her arms and shook her head.

"What is it?" William asked. "That deal don't suit you?"

"Seems more than fair to me," Ollie added.

William watched her.

"Or," he said, "you could come with us."

"Huh?" the girl and Ollie asked in unison.

"I ain't going nowhere with y'all," the girl said.

William looked at her.

"Sun's fixing to be up," he said. "We ain't too far from Rockland. Why don't you come into town with us and we'll buy you breakfast. Then you can decide."

"Jesus Christ, bud," Ollie protested. "You done forgot about that time she was holding a gun on us? I know it was a while back and all."

"She don't have a gun now," William said. "Or food. Or anything else by the looks of it."

The girl seemed to be thinking it over.

"What money have you got to buy breakfast?" she asked.

William lifted his boot and tapped the barrel of the gun against it. The girl looked angry with herself.

"You like pancakes?" he asked.

14

They came into Rockland under a purple morning sky and there was little traffic about the thoroughfare but those they did encounter regarded them with concerned stares, disheveled as they were.

William watched the girl with something like fascination. In the light, he could see she had brown hair and brown, amber-like eyes and the ridge of her nose was slightly bowed in a way that suggested it had been broken but the boy felt it wrong to ask. Her face held sharp angles though she was not slim. She had womanly curves and her shoulders were broad and strong and he could see now that she was likely an inch or two taller than him.

"You want them boots shined?" a young boy asked. He leaned against the wall of the post office with his box and kit at the ready.

"Do we look like a shoeshine is high up on our list, kid?" Ollie asked.

Ollie had been in a particularly unseemly mood what with his hangover persisting and his position by William's side being potentially usurped. He could see the way his friend was staring at the girl.

"Them's army boots," the kid said, ignoring Ollie and pointing to William. "Endicott Johnson."

"What do you know about army boots?" William asked, not unkind.

"My daddy's buried in a pair just like that."

"He die in the war?"

The kid shook his head and then looked away.

"Nossir," he said. "He come home first."

"I'll take a shine," William told him. "And you don't have to call me sir."

The girl looked up and down the street.

"You expecting somebody?" Ollie asked her.

The boy had William sit on the edge of the raised post office porch and put his boots on the shine box. The boy himself sat in the dirt and started to work.

"You don't have a chair?" William asked.

"If you ain't satisfied, I'll refund you your money."

"It ain't about satisfaction. Just seems like it'd be a lot easier on you."

"Was you in the war?" the kid asked.

"He's fifteen," Ollie said. "What war do you think he was in? Other than the one against getting to breakfast on time."

William looked around at the near empty town.

"I don't think there's gonna be no line out the door, bud."

"Y'all always fight like this?" the girl asked.

"Like what?" both boys said.

When the kid had finished William gave him a dollar and asked where the best breakfast was and the kid pointed to a diner down the street and William gave him another dollar.

The girl looked at him curiously.

"You're fixing to give away all our grub money," Ollie said.

"You just worry about the eating," William told him. "I'll worry about the paying."

"Now you're making sense," Ollie said as they went off toward the diner.

They sat at a table next to the window and a woman came from around the counter and asked what they wanted and Ollie told her they wanted breakfast. She rolled her eyes.

"Y'all got pancakes?" William asked.

"We got griddle cakes."

"Give us a big ole stack of them."

"What else?" She stood with her pencil at the ready.

"Some bacon strips," William told her.

"Make them crispy," Ollie added. "Burn 'em if you have to."

She shook her head and made a note.

"What else?"

"Bowl of scrambled eggs. Three coffees."

"How do you prefer it?"

"Hot," Ollie said, and the woman closed her eyes.

William and the girl were sat one across from the other and both in full sun from the east-facing window. William thought he saw a lizard along the bottom of the glass but the glare was strong and by the time he'd shaded his eyes with his hands there was nothing to see.

The woman brought the coffee and three cups and then brought the plates and set them on the table in no discernible order and walked away without saying anything.

"I don't believe she's took to us yet," Ollie said.

"She ain't the only one," the girl told him.

"It all comes down to taste," Ollie said, biting into a charred strip of bacon. "Some folks just ain't got none."

"Who are y'all?" the girl asked.

"I'm William Carter. That there's Oliver Leek."

"And what are y'all doing living in the woods—other than you killed somebody in Lufkin."

"We don't live in the woods. We're from Shawnee Prairie. It's close to Manning."

"I know Manning," she said.

"We're fixing to hitch a ride into Doucette to fetch my father and bring him back home. My momma's sick. Might be dying."

The girl set her coffee down.

"I'm sorry," she said, then her face scrunched up. "You couldn't just borrow a phone somewhere?"

William rubbed the back of his neck.

"Well, I know he's in Doucette, but I don't know exactly where."

"And we don't know how come he's there to begin with," Ollie added, pushing bits of food back into his mouth.

"That don't make no sense," the girl said.

"You coming with us or not?" William asked.

"Now hold on a dadgum minute," Ollie said and then swallowed hard and picked up his coffee and gulped at it a few times and then set it back down. "We don't know the first thing about this girl, excepting her attempted robbery last night. We don't even know her name."

"What's your name?" William asked.

"Lena."

"Where you from?"

"Evadale."

William looked at Ollie.

"This is Lena. She's from Evadale."

"How come you ain't in Evadale now?" Ollie asked.

"I ain't got to answer any of your questions," she said, "'cause I ain't going with you."

"Where *are* you going?" William asked.

"Home," she said. "A few years ago, before whatever this depression is, we were already so poor we didn't have a pot to piss in. A man come along and gave my momma a stack of money and took me with him up to Corsicana. I was supposed to be his servant or some such. I cleaned his house and cooked his food and the like."

"You run off?"

"He died."

"Oh." William nodded.

"So I'm going home to fetch my sister. Get her out of there before our no-account momma sells her off too."

"How come there's notches in your pistol?" Ollie asked before William could respond. "This how many people you killed, or just how many you robbed?"

"Neither. I was bored is all. Now give it back."

"Do what?" Ollie laughed but William nudged him and nodded toward the girl.

"Give it to her," William said. "We can trust her."

"We? You carrying a mouse in your pocket?"

"Give it to her," William said again.

Ollie frowned but he passed the gun under the table and the girl took it and smirked at him and the two of them went back to arguing.

William was watching her. He studied her as if she might at any moment disappear and he would be then called to recreate her. To place her eyes narrow when she spoke. To raise her brows. To capture the ferocity of her being.

"Look yonder," Ollie said, nudging him from his trance.

William looked out the window and down the street and there was Downtain, in his top hat and coat despite the burn of the morning. He was speaking with the boy on the shoeshine box and the boy was pointing toward the diner.

"Surely not," Ollie said, as Downtain began walking in their direction.

"What?" William asked.

"I think that medicine peddler is hunting me."

"Who?" Lena asked, leaning toward the window to get a better look.

"The fella I stole that little bottle off of."

"He's coming this way," Lena said, and she was the first to leave her seat.

"You think he really cares that much?" William asked Ollie.

"I ain't waiting around to find out."

Ollie slid from the booth and followed the girl and William shucked a few dollars from his pocket and left them on the table. The three of them went through the kitchen where a man sat peeling potatoes. He looked up as they passed and if he was surprised there was nothing about him to suggest it. He put his head back down and went on with his work and the three fugitives fled out the back door of the building.

They splashed through the muddy seepage of grease and dish soap behind the restaurant, and they ran further still, blind into the woods, past pepperbush and joe-pye weed and great thickets of yaupon trees and around a small pond rimmed with buttonbush and all manner of aquatic shrubs. And here they jumped a big doe and her fawn, spooked them from a morning nap, and the two deer fled before them and the young people followed up a ridgeline, scrambling over pine needles until the ground sprung more rocks than brush and only then did they stop and turn and listen for anyone or anything that might be following. They heard only their own heavy breathing.

"We should keep going," Lena said.

"If anything we ought to go back," William countered. "I don't think that man would recognize us from Adam."

"Them fellas working for him sure might," Ollie said.

William scowled at him.

"Why did you have to steal anything to begin with?" he asked.

"It was one little vial," Ollie said. "Probably nothing but snake oil anyhow."

"Even more reason not to take it."

"Drunk people do drunk things," the boy answered. "There ain't always gotta be a reason. And if there is, it don't always gotta be a good one."

"Jesus Christ, Ollie."

"And I thought," Ollie started, then he looked off for a few seconds and then looked back at William. "I thought maybe—if it was real—it might help your momma."

William didn't know what to say.

"But you don't think it now?" he asked.

"I guess things look different in the sober light of day."

"We should keep going," Lena said again.

Ollie turned on her.

"Why are you here?" he snapped. "We said, against my better judgment, that we'd buy you breakfast. We bought you breakfast. Now go on and be a thief somewhere else."

"You're the only one that's stolen something," William said, his cheeks red from the running, red from the heat, red from the anger. "She don't have to go anywhere."

He turned toward the girl.

"Unless you want to."

She looked back the way they'd come and then looked up at the ridge above them and shook her head like she couldn't decide.

"Come to Doucette," William said. "It's not far, and it's one step closer to Evadale, if that's where you're trying to get back to."

Ollie threw his hands up in the air.

"We don't need some girl slowing us down, bud," he said.

"Fine," Lena said, looking at Ollie as if out of spite. "I'll go with you."

"Good," William confirmed. "We'll stay off the roads until we're five miles clear of town, just in case Downtain really is hunting us. Then we'll hitch to Doucette."

"Deal," the girl said.

They shook on it and then started walking.

Ollie stood and watched them go.

"Yeah, you know, you're right, Ollie," Ollie said. "This is a terrible idea. So let's go ahead and do it anyway."

The boy shook his head and then jogged to catch up with them.

15

They went on past the ridgeline and descended a bald hill built up from hard red dirt and then went down through black sandy washes where shadows of looming trees were cast by a seething sun. Sun raging with light. Raging with a corporeal heat what sought to vanquish them should they linger too long in the open.

Back into the forest they went. Fled into the trees. And what trees but those of every imaginable order. Hackberry and redbud and smoke-bush. Ashe juniper, post and live oak, and bald cypress. Madrone trees. And pines—lord god at the pines. Loblolly and shortleaf and southern slash. Dogwoods. Maple. And persimmon. Persimmon with its beautiful knotted bark and sweet fruit. And in tangent, this holy garden of trees, shades of gray and brown and green. Pink and red and rust.

A planet of trees.

They went on through the woods for nearly six miles and the trees only grew thicker around them.

"We gotta get back to the highway," William said. "We'll mess around and get lost in here."

"That gonna suit you, Lena from Evadale?" Ollie asked the girl.

"Leave her alone," William told him.

"He ain't bothering me," Lena said. "I learned a long time ago to ignore an ass when it gets to hawing."

"I think it's this way," William said, and they cut southeast for a while but did not come across the highway and at some point they began to hear voices coming alien through the woods and eventually they could see a turpentine camp up ahead.

The tents were scattered beneath steepled pines and there were small cookfires still smoldering from noon dinner and the air smelled like coffee and grease and smoke. There was a blue plastic barrel filled with water and small washtubs for dishes or laundry or a quick scrub. Lengths of rope were drawn up between trees and used as laundry lines—wet clothes flung and dripping. Men stood about the camp half-dressed, trying to cool off from the morning work. Some tried to catch a quick nap while others read dime books. Still others did nothing at all, drinking their coffee in quiet contemplation of the afternoon ahead or perhaps the life behind.

"Y'all wanna chance they might know the quickest way to the road?" William asked.

"I'd rather not," Ollie said. "I've heard these are some hard bastards."

"Fair enough. We'll go around."

William motioned toward the dry gulley and the three of them clambered down a short slope and went on with the camp above them to the west. They were nearly clear of it when a man started hollering from up on the ridge.

"Hey you, girl," he called. "Stop there for a second."

"Run," Lena said.

"What?"

Other men were coming over.

"That's her right there," the man pointed. "Little bitch that stole my pistol."

"Run," Lena repeated, but a shot rang out overhead and the bullet buried into a tree with a dull thunk.

"She didn't steal mine," the gunman said, and there were a few laughs.

The three of them froze and watched as a half dozen men made their way down into the gulley.

"This her, Gus?" one of them asked, nodding at Lena.

"For a certainty," Gus confirmed and spit in the dirt. "And yonder's my pistol tucked into her belt."

"That ain't your pistol, mister," Ollie said, stepping forward. "And I doubt you ever seen my sister in your whole life."

"Like hell I ain't," Gus challenged. "I seen her at a dance hall in Mount Enterprise not five days ago. Ask me if she could hold my Colt and then disappeared with it."

"She could hold my pistol," someone said. More laughs.

"It ain't funny," Gus said. "You can't just take what don't belong to you."

"My sister was in Shawnee Prairie last week. And the week before that. Hell, she ain't ever been outside Angelina County until three days ago when we left to find our pa."

"Where's your pa?" the first man asked.

"Silsbee."

"How come him to leave?"

"Looking for work."

"Well, it's tough enough to find," the man said, nodding.

"Hold on a goddamn minute," Gus interrupted. "That's my pistol, that's the girl that took it, and I—"

"It's our pa's pistol," Ollie said quickly. "It's got the notches on it from every German he killed in France."

"Toss it here, girl," the first man said.

Lena loosed the Colt from her belt and tossed it over and the man caught it.

"Right there on the heel," Ollie said, motioning, and the man turned the gun in his hand and looked at the markings.

"Your pistol have notches on it, Gus?"

Gus hesitated.

"You sop-drunk sonofabitch," the man said. "This ain't your gun.

Probably got loaded and lost the damn thing, if you ever had one at all."

"It is mine," Gus insisted. "And I've about had it with you talking like you're the boss of this outfit. You're out here chipping and tacking tin, same as me. You ain't no better."

"Your wife might have something to say on the matter," the man said, and Gus charged him and the man calmly shot him in the head and tossed the smoking, hot pistol back to Lena, who let it fall at her feet.

William staggered backward as if the man might try to rise but he did not.

Silence in the woods. Then one of the men spit.

Ollie kept opening his mouth and closing it without saying anything.

Lena stood without expression.

"Well, y'all seen him come at me," the man said, his voice unchanged. "Let's get back to dinner. You can keep the gun, girl—but I ain't never seen you before and you ain't never seen me. Got it?"

No one disagreed and the men drifted away toward their camp and left the slain body where it had fallen.

They were some distance from the camp before anyone spoke.

"Thank you," the girl said to Ollie.

"Oh, sure," he said. "It was no bother. I tell lies that get men killed every day."

"I didn't know he was gonna kill him."

"No, but you did steal his pistol, and you are a thief. Just like I said. And you're a liar. You cut them notches so it would look like a different gun."

"Then why'd you help me?"

"You think them boys would've stopped with you? We'd have all been swinging, one next to the other, from one of those big oaks. The world's saddest wind chimes."

"There must have been twenty or thirty men in that camp," William said, almost to himself.

"So?" Ollie asked.

"Nobody stood up for him. Or went to his side when he fell. Surely he had one friend—one person who cared if he died."

They were quiet again after that.

"You ever see somebody shot before?" the girl asked after a while.

"You mean before ole Gus back yonder?" Ollie asked.

"Frank Maddocks," William said.

"You seen that?" Ollie asked

William nodded.

"I'd come into town to buy church pants."

"Who's Frank Maddocks?"

"He was a sorry sonofabitch that used to beat on his wife," Ollie said. "Until her and her brother decided they was gonna get rid of him. They had this whole deal planned out to where Billy—that's the brother—was gonna take Frank hunting and make it look like an accident and everything. Problem was, when Billy showed up at the house, Frank changed his mind. Maybe he could sense something was going on, or maybe he just didn't want to go hunting. Either way, the jig was ruint. So what does Billy do? He hauls off and shoots him anyway. Right there on the front porch swing. Broad daylight. Bang."

"It was the porch," William said, "but he wasn't on the swing. He was just standing there, drinking his coffee. He was right at the top of the steps and when Billy shot him he sort of set down, like maybe he needed to think about something."

"He died?" the girl asked.

"He did."

"What happened to the brother?"

"Not much. Everybody knew Frank was a sorry bastard. And the sheriff asked his widow if she wanted to see her brother prosecuted and she said no, and most everybody was alright with it. Frank had a brother who swore he'd kill Billy but I don't guess he ever did. There's quite a bit of road between swearing something and doing it."

"Do you think it happens like that a lot?" the girl asked. "To where somebody kills a bad person and they don't get in trouble for it?"

William tilted his head, regarded her.

"I don't imagine it does," Ollie answered. "Else we'd have folks shooting each other by the dozen and saying they all got what was coming."

16

They came across clear cut acreage and stood at the edge of the tree line and looked out across it. There was no thing so unnatural as the saw-ravaged hills poxed with stumps and stretching for miles in every direction—the ground covered in fallen bark and broken branches. An industrial apocalypse, come and gone.

A hawk swooped past, heading south, then wheeled and returned overtop the barren land as if he'd assess the damage for himself.

"Strange, ain't it?" Ollie asked.

"Like somebody's took to scalping the world," William told him.

The hawk cried out and then lifted away to some other clearing.

They crossed the cutland and were back in the woods then another mile and they were at the highway. They emerged from the cover of the trees and the girl looked about nervously. She kept turning to see the road where it led north, flinching at the sound of calling birds.

Ollie walked a few paces in front of them and William wanted to talk to the girl but wasn't sure what to say.

"It's a nice thing you're doing," he said. "For your sister."

"Nice?" she asked.

He waited a while before he spoke again.

"I had a sister," he told her. "But I don't remember her."

"What happened?" she asked.

"I can't rightly say. She was a baby. Maybe only a few days alive from what I've gathered. Maybe less than that. They don't ever talk about her. Her name was Gwen. What's your sister's name?"

"Susannah."

"That's a good name."

A car passed them by and then stopped and they thought it might reverse but it didn't. It set there until they'd caught up with it and there was a young man driving and a woman all but sitting in his lap and they were kissing one another and giggling and when the three of them got to the window the couple stopped.

"Y'all going through Doucette?" William asked.

"We're going all the way down, brother," the man said, reaching across the woman to pop the handle on the door.

"Warren's taking me to the ocean," the woman squealed and kissed the man's cheek.

The three of them filed in and sat shoulder to shoulder in the back seat. Ollie leaned forward and pulled the door closed behind them.

"Y'all just get married or something?" he asked.

The couple set to giggling again. Whispering.

"You might say that," the man said, turning his head to address them and then looking back at the road.

"I was supposed to marry Henry Brookshire," the woman said, twisting her body around and hanging her arms over the seatback. William realized she wasn't much older than him.

"But then I met Warren and it was, well, it was true love is what it was. And truth be told, I never did like Henry all that much. But his daddy and my daddy was always good friends and it ain't like there was a whole bunch to choose from in Etoile to start with."

The woman let her chin sink down onto the seatback and left it there for a moment and then straightened back up.

"Then here comes Warren," she said. "Pulled up to the crossroads where I was selling fruit. Pulled up in this very car right here and swept me off my feet."

"I asked her about her melons," the man said.

The girl laughed as if she might never stop, then slapped the man's shoulder and told him to stop and then laughed some more.

"Ain't he a hoot?" she asked them, and they nodded quietly. "Been the best twenty-four hours of my whole entire life."

"Y'all only known each other one day?" Ollie asked, and Lena elbowed him.

"We got to know each other pretty good last night," the man said.

The woman blushed but kept smiling.

"Sometimes it takes a while to get a fire started," she said, her hands animating her every word. "You gotta pile the kindling up and light it and blow on it and everything else. Other times, all it takes is a bolt of lightning. That's what Warren here is. A lightning strike."

She rested her head on the man's shoulder.

"And I guess you feel the same way, huh, Warren?" Ollie asked, leaning forward.

"Of course I do," the man said. "She's a great gal."

"I imagine old Henry thought so too."

William gave Ollie a stern look and the boy leaned back.

"Henry won't mind," the woman said. "He ain't much for anger. Or any kind of passion really. He just wants to live and die in Etoile, Texas. But not Warren here. He's been all over when he was playing for the New York Yankees."

The three of them looked at one another and the man glanced at them in the rearview.

"He could have been as good as Babe Ruth but one day a talent scout from Hollywood was at a ball game and he saw Warren and said—What did he say, Warren?"

"Oh, c'mon now, honey," the man protested. "They don't want to hear about that."

"Sure we do, Warren," Ollie said.

"Fine, I'll tell it," she said, giddy. "He said, put down that bat and come with me. You're too handsome to have someone throwing a ball at you all day long. So he's been in the film business ever since. That's where we're going next. The ocean, then Los Angeles."

The woman adjusted her dress.

"Warren says I could be the next Joan Crawford," she told them. "She's from Texas too, you know."

"You're much prettier than Joan, honey," the man said, again cutting his eyes to the mirror. "You'll give Mary Pickford a run for her money."

The woman settled into a pleased smile and looked out the window at the passing trees.

"And to think," she said. "My whole life might've been different."

They came into Colmesneil around noon and Warren said he knew of a pharmacy with as good a burger as they would ever eat.

"Scope it out during your pinstripe days, did you, Warren?" Ollie asked.

"What's that mean?" the girl asked.

"Nothing, honey," Warren said. "We just used to wear pinstriped uniforms."

"On the Yankees," Ollie added.

"That's right," Warren said. "On the Yankees."

Warren parked the car and the five of them climbed out and into the heat and looked down to avoid the sun but it was coming bright off the concrete as well. They staggered into the pharmacy and sat at the counter. There were only four stools and Lena insisted the others sit and she went to a small table near the window and sat alone.

Ollie leaned close to William and peered over his shoulder at Lena.

"What are you doing?" he hissed.

"Fixing to get the best burger in all the world."

"First off, you know goddamn good and well that Warren ain't to be believed—on burgers or baseball or anything else. Second, I'm talking about the girl. Lena."

"What about her?"

"Why are you so set on her coming with us?"

"Why are you so against it?"

"Because she'll rob us the first chance she gets. Or second chance, seeing as how she already tried it once."

"I don't believe she will," William said.

"Oh," Ollie slapped both palms on the table. "Well. In that case, don't let our firsthand experience get in the way of what you believe."

"She needs help, Ollie. She's out here alone, just like us. She's going southeast, just like us. Why not let her tag along?"

"Wherever she may be headed, she's running from something, bud. You gotta see that."

"Maybe. But there's strength in numbers out here."

"Strength in—" Ollie was dumbfounded. He looked up and down the counter as if there was someone else who might have heard and could join in his disbelief.

Then something else occurred to him and he slumped back some on his stool and looked at his friend.

"You're sweet on her," he said. "That's what it is."

William didn't react.

"I knew it," Ollie said. "I knew it when she got a man killed over her stealing his pistol. You didn't say a damn word. You would've scolded me to high heaven but you didn't so much as sigh at her."

"You lied for her," William said. "About the pistol. Might be that you had a hand in that man dying too."

Ollie shook his head. He was frustrated nearly to tears.

"You're gonna ruin this whole thing over a girl," he said, and it wasn't a question. "I ain't believing this."

"Don't believe it then," William said. "And keep your voice down."

Ollie just shook his head and looked down at the counter and when their burgers came he ate about half of his and sat staring.

Warren kept moaning every time he bit into his burger and the girl beside him was ever at her giggling. She'd ordered a grilled cheese sandwich with tomato soup and William saw her pick it up a few times but never saw her eat any of it. After a while she got up and went and sat with Lena by the window.

Warren finished and pushed his plate away and lit a cigarette and Ollie stood and walked down the counter to him and asked if he could bum one.

"Bum a ride. Bum a smoke," Warren said. "Somebody asking for handouts ought not bite the hand that feeds him."

Ollie nodded and Warren lit the boy's cigarette.

"Fair enough," Ollie said, inhaling. "You get a few medals for bravery in the war too?"

"I might have," Warren said, blowing smoke in Ollie's face.

17

They were rattling into Doucette in the afternoon and the sun was hot and it was hot in the car. The woman in the front seat had slipped off her brazier and she and Warren were back at their whispering. William squinted for the light as the community came into view and wondered in which of these little houses his father had betrayed their family.

Doucette was a small, haggard settlement playing at being a town. It was failing along with the country and in the years to come it would disappear altogether. The ruins of buildings would stand for decades like a half-constructed necropolis to some other time and then they would be torn down and there would be nothing left to prove the place ever existed except words on paper.

"This ain't much, even for a half-ass place," Ollie said. "And I know all about half-ass places."

"They sure ain't throwing a parade anytime soon," Lena added, and Ollie laughed despite himself.

There was a gaunt row of clapboard houses, little more than hovels and lean-tos and catslide roofs. There were gardens of dead plants and those that lived looked woeful and twisted and menacing. A thin layer of pollen covered the structures and the rotting porches where sat the dwellers of this misery.

"You can drop us here," William said.

There was a four-way, but the dirt road running east to west went dead into the woods on either side. There might have been seven buildings in all to constitute the downtown corridor.

The man slowed the car and raised his eyebrows at them.

"Y'all sure you wouldn't rather go as far as Woodville?" he asked. "At least they got a picture show."

"We're alright, Warren," Ollie said. "We're fixing to meet up with John Barrymore and Charlie Chaplin."

The man looked away angry and the woman looked lost and William thanked them both for the ride.

They climbed out and stretched their legs and looked around for the jakes and found a set of four lined up around the side of a pool hall.

William and Lena came out first and stood in the sun and waited for Ollie.

"Y'all ain't just standing out there waiting are you?" Ollie called from within.

"No," William said.

"Then why'd you answer?"

When Ollie was finished, William gave him some money and sent him with Lena to the mercantile across the street.

"Get us a sleeve of Fig Newtons and three Cokes," he told them, looking at his father's envelope and then looking down the street. "The address is right down yonder. I'm gonna go on my own."

They nodded and split off and William walked up the street looking at mailbox numbers. He had long been unsure what he would say to his father, but the added complication of a mistress tore at the calmness he'd hoped to project. With each step his hammering heart beat faster still until he was in front of an old building with a matching address. He pulled out the letter again and looked at it one more time and then stood looking up at the silhouette of the steeple against the bright sky.

The construction of the church was well known to him. It was not unlike the many country churches that dotted the counties and townships of East Texas. Its pier-and-beam foundation, weatherboard siding, and arched pine doors had been a staple of William's young life. Before her illness his mother rarely allowed him to miss a Sunday.

He could see her there in the nave of the chapel, in her plain tan dress and heavy ankle-high brogans. Hair pulled back and hands together, head bowed in prayer, and what had she ever asked for? What request had been so audacious that the Lord had seen fit to burden her so?

And still she remained loyal. Grateful even.

"I'm not afraid of dying," she'd told him after one of the doc's many visits. "In my father's house are many mansions and he goes forth before me to prepare my table. Death is already defeated."

The wind kicked up, ever so slightly. The rustling of pines. He closed his eyes.

He was on the two-seat sofa in the living room and she was there beside him and he couldn't have been five years old and he was crying. His hands covered the scrape on his knee and he wouldn't let her see it. She touched the side of his head and shushed him. Gentle. *It's alright, sweet boy. It's alright now.* She pulled his hands away. There was blood enough but she didn't react. Just kept stroking his head, talking to him. *We'll make it all better.*

That was, he contended, his single earliest memory. He didn't even remember how he'd gotten hurt. It was like the wound was born to him and the first thing he would ever know is her grace.

William stood on the church steps and the wind had died and he wiped his eyes.

"Yes," he said. "We'll make it better. We'll make it better right now."

He knocked on the doors and no one answered and in time he pushed one of them open and stepped inside and waited for his eyes to adjust. Even though he was out of the sun it was still hot. A thicker, more stifling type of heat. The church was long and slender and smelled like burnt pine and perfume. There was no one about. William walked down the aisle, wooden pews on either side, until he came to the pulpit and on that far wall the giant replica cross hung where all could see.

He was a long time standing, staring up at it. There were watermarks a few feet from the bottom of the cross where in years past the church had survived a great flood. Now came a drought. Do prayers change with the weather? the boy wondered.

He left out the back door and back into the light and even the brim of his hat did little good against the wrath of the sun.

Just across the courtyard from the chapel was the lych-gate and the cemetery beyond, where stood elaborately fashioned headstones in fine rows like Gothic soldiers awaiting some command. And further still there was the potter's field, where only simple crosses or crude stone pilings marked out the resting places of unnamed souls. The grass was thicker there, in the shade of a pecan tree, and the sacred cairns scattered below like mutant fruit.

William walked among the dead, imagining lions and lambs and streets of gold.

"Can I help you, friend?"

William looked up and a preacher was striding across the graveyard with an out-of-place smile on his face.

"Hello, son," he said, nodding toward his outstretched hand that the boy should take it.

William did so.

"Hello."

"Can I help you with anything or are you just visiting family?"

"Family?" William asked.

The preacher motioned at the graves.

"Oh," William said. "Nossir."

The preacher held a large glass jar of water.

"You caught me working on this week's sermon," the preacher said as he unscrewed the cap on the jar and offered it to William. "It's about forgiveness."

"Forgiveness," the boy repeated, waving away the offering.

"The foundation of all Christianity," the preacher said proudly.

William had heard it said in one such sermon that there were shades of Christ in every man and woman, and he thought now of his father and took silent measure of his own capacity for forgiveness and found it wanting.

"Well. I don't believe I'm cut out to be a Christian," he said.

The preacher laughed.

"None are, son," he said. "And that's the truth. But we are redeemed by Him. Our unworthiness is what He loves most. It's His grace what calls us home."

William shifted uncomfortably.

"I got a letter from this address," he said, ignoring the man. "You know my daddy, I believe. Thomas Carter."

The preacher frowned.

"Yes, I know Thomas."

"I'm here to bring him home to Shawnee Prairie."

"You must be William."

"Yessir."

"Well, I wish I could help you, William. But Lieutenant Carter left this place six days ago—maybe a week."

"Headed where?"

The preacher shook his head.

"I don't know. Rebecca Turner might, though I doubt it."

"Who's Rebecca Turner?" William asked and realized the answer before the preacher could speak again.

"Have the two of you not met?"

William stared at the man.

"Why in the hell would I have met the woman my father is sleeping with?"

The preacher struggled to not spit out his water. He was unsure how to respond.

"I believe your father and her husband were dear friends," he said. "There's little chance Rebecca and Lieutenant Carter were engaging in any sort of romantic relationship. She wouldn't even let him in the house, from what I saw."

"Why wouldn't she let him in?" the boy asked. "If her husband was supposed to be his best friend or something."

"Well, yes, but after what happened, Rebecca had"—the preacher hesitated—"difficulties with Thomas being here. I allowed him to stay in the chapel for a time."

"Who's her husband then and where can I find him?"

"Roger Turner," the preacher said, pointing to a grave that looked to be fresher than the rest. "God rest his soul."

The boy frowned.

"So he come here to see a dead man's wife?"

"Thomas had hoped, at least it is my belief, to find some sort of atonement here. Some sort of peace, perhaps. He and I shared many a fierce debate as to the ways of our Lord. A fascinating man, your father."

"Fascinating." William tasted the word on his tongue as if he'd never before tried it.

"He talked a good deal about you."

The preacher smiled at the boy but William only scowled.

"Did my letter make it to him?" he asked.

The man put his head down.

"I'm sorry to say it did not. I received it the very afternoon he left."

"That's about my luck," William said.

"There is no such thing as luck," the preacher said. "The lot is cast into the lap. But its every decision is from the Lord."

"You're not making quite the case you think you are," William told him. "I guess I'd better go talk to this woman."

"She lives right past that little brown cabin there." He pointed toward the small cluster of buildings. "Yellow house on the end. That's hers.

"Be patient with her," the preacher added. "She's suffered tremendously."

"So has my mother," William said and turned and then turned back. "Did he find it? The peace he was looking for?"

"I wish I could say. But the book of John tells us the only thing we are assured in this world is tribulation."

William nodded and went on through the graveyard and out to the road.

The house was painted yellow and the paint was peeling. All along the lap siding there were chips and stains and the backfill had pulled away from the foundation by more than a foot. There was a low porch, its roof steadied by short pillars with brick bases.

The skeleton of a Christmas wreath hung on the door and the holly leaves with their muricate edges had long turned brown and shriveled and much of the arrangement had been scavenged for bird nests or simply come loose to the wind.

He came up onto the porch and stood there and for a long while was just looking at the door when suddenly it came open. The woman was there in the entryway and she had been crying. She gasped when she saw him and her hands shot up to her face and wiped at the tears.

"I thought it was raccoons again," she said.

She was tall and thin with long blond hair that hung halfway to her waist. Her eyes were red and wet and looked sunken in, heavy and haggard. She guided her hair behind her shoulders with the back of her hands.

"I'm sorry," she said.

They stood there, the two of them.

"I'm William Carter," the boy said at last. "I'm looking for my father, Thomas Carter."

She had been staring at him with a tired sort of sadness that now all but disappeared. Her eyes widened and she uncrossed her arms.

"Oh that's low," she growled, and she hunched some at the shoulders like she might be readying an attack. "Even for Thomas Carter, that's good and low. Sending his kid to soften me up."

"He didn't send me—" William started, but the woman wasn't finished.

"If he thinks I'm just some delicate flower that will wilt at the sight of a child, he's got another thing coming. I'll tell you that much. I am not the least bit close to wilting. Do you understand?"

"Yes ma'am."

"And another thing," she said, and she was out onto the porch now and the boy had taken a few good steps back. "I never did like the sonofabitch. There. I've done and said it. I hope that self-righteous shit across the street heard me too. Reverend Greene. Always preaching at me. Forgiveness, he says. Grace, he says. Where in the hell does he think those things grow? Not out of this goddamn garden. It's anger that's got me out of bed every morning since the bastard shot hisself. Anger. Not forgiveness. I'm gonna live out of spite. I'm gonna suffer my own destruction slowly, just so the sonofabitch's ghost can watch the fire he set when he left."

The boy had stopped trying to interrupt and he was quiet so that when she stopped yelling there was no other sound but a few flies that zipped past the two of them and into the house.

"I believe we're in agreement there," William said at last.

She looked him up and down again and shook her head.

"Well come in," she said, throwing her arms up. "Coffee's on."

She turned away from him and went inside and left the door open behind her.

The boy's confusion had only grown but he followed her into the house and once inside he could smell himself and he smelled of sweat and soil and the cologne in Warren's car.

She led him through a small kitchen with dishes piled high in a wash bin and more flies abuzz above them. There were pale, faded rectangles on the wall where framed photographs had once been. The only thing left hanging was a round mirror and William glanced in it as they passed. He looked as ragged as he felt. Dry, cracked lips. Dirt pressed into creases in his neck. His clothes were thorn-tattered and stained with wet. If the woman was shocked by his appearance, she did not let it show.

"Please sit," she told him as they came into the parlor and William looked around and chose a place on the outermost edge of the couch. The couch was a dark green with a damask pattern of silver leaves and rolled cushions at either end. William did not feel comfortable sitting on it.

The room was dim and cluttered. There was a writing desk against the back wall that was piled high with stacks of newspapers, their lignin giving the room a muted vanilla odor. Next to the couch was what might have once served as a small dining table but it was covered in full by an ornate Christmas village made up of porcelain figurines and ceramic buildings that included such town staples as a hotel, café, and even a firehouse.

There was mistletoe hung along an exposed beam that ran the length of the room. In the corner was an old grandfather clock carved from what looked to be walnut. It was not ticking.

The woman noticed his staring and she forced a smile.

She sat across from him in a plain wooden chair that belonged to the writing desk behind her.

"Apparently there are biblical scholars who believe Christ was born in September," she said. "That's what my husband came to believe. This is all his doing."

She raised her hand and motioned at nothing in particular. At everything.

"He became convinced that the Bible had been misinterpreted. He and your father—well, they spoke quite frequently of it. That is, before Thomas put a gun in Roger's hand and told him to shoot himself just below the temple."

The boy was uncertain of how to respond.

"He did that?" William asked.

The woman paused and drank her coffee.

"He might as well have," she said. "Roger would've done anything Thomas asked, you know. Even things he didn't ask. Just look at where we live. I begged Roger after the war. Begged. Take me back to Chicago. Take me back to a living, breathing city. But I'll give you one guess who thought that wasn't a good idea. 'Thomas says he's staying in Shawnee Prairie,' he tells me. 'Thomas says the pastoral life is one to be proud of.' Thomas says don't ever listen to your wife or try to make her happy."

"He said that?" the boy asked.

The woman scoffed and drank again from her cup.

"And yes, he helped. Of course he helped. Roger wasn't right after the war. None of them were. How could they be? I mean, Christ on a cracker, what do people expect? But Thomas helped him. Until he didn't. Until he started in with all this 'nothing means anything' business. You plant a seed and the seed is planted," she said. "You're responsible for what grows. Thomas is responsible. You understand?"

"No ma'am, I can honestly say I don't."

"And then he shows up like you. Right there on the porch. I've just buried my husband and I'm stuck in Doucette, Texas, and who knows what will become of me? And he has the audacity to stand there and tell me he's sorry. To tell me he loved—"

Her words caught in her throat and she turned quickly away from the boy and composed herself and when she looked back at him her eyes were wet.

"To tell me he loved my husband," she said, and she leaned forward over the glass table and stubbed out the cigarette and blew away a last stream of smoke and then sat back and crossed her arms and stared at him.

"I loved my husband," she said. "Me."

"Ma'am," he started cautiously, speaking soft. "I'm sure sorry about your husband and whatever role my daddy played in it. But he didn't send me here. I'm looking for him is all. My momma's sick, back in

Shawnee Prairie, and I need him to come home. Do you have any idea where he was headed?"

"He wanted to stay here, if you can believe that," she said. "I told him no, of course. Spent his days lurking around the church like some lost dog. I would've liked to hear the 'discussions' he had with Reverend Greene."

She shook her head.

"Ma'am," William tried again. "Do you know where he went when he left Doucette?"

The woman was quiet.

"I'm sure she misses him, dearly," she said at last. "A wife always misses her husband. Worries about him. Hopes he is safe. I wish that for Roger, even now. Even after I watched them put him in the ground. I still hope."

"She misses him something fierce," William confirmed.

"Roger was so afraid," the woman continued as if William wasn't there. "Afraid of himself. His sins. He turned to other means of quieting the voices in his head. He fell into drink and gambling, perhaps other things as well, though he spared me any knowledge. He owed a significant amount of money. So I've been told. He was counting on his war bond being released. When it didn't happen, well—"

She looked back at the boy.

"I don't think he ever told Thomas. I think he was too ashamed. Maybe I was too. Maybe that's why when Roger—I wanted to blame someone else. I could've told Thomas about the debt, about the demons my husband was battling outside of his faith. But I didn't. I wanted him—wanted anyone—to feel the pain I felt."

"What did my father say to your husband that was so bad?" William asked, and he knew he shouldn't have but neither could he stop himself from asking.

"Your father is in Spurger," she said. "He and Roger have another comrade there."

"Homer Renfro," the boy said.

"You know him?"

William nodded.

The woman stood.

"Here," she said and she crossed the room and opened a drawer and took out a leatherbound journal and looked at it with a great intensity and then shook her head. She handed it to William.

"Take this," she said. "Thomas left it for me. He said it might help me understand the things he and Roger talked about."

"Did it?"

"I never opened it," she said. "Some questions are better left unanswered. Better still, if they're never asked at all."

William took the journal and she followed him to the door and shut it after him.

He stood for a minute in the street and flipped through the pages of the journal and found little form to the entries. They were not dated. Some read like a diary, others like poems. There were drawings. He stopped on one and turned the notebook sideways and studied it. It was a sketch of their cabin. Their home.

He looked back at the yellow house and he could see the woman watching through the front window and he nodded and she was gone.

Lena and Ollie were sitting in the shade of a sycamore with empty bottles by their side.

"We saved you a Fig Newton or two," Ollie said, "but your Coke was getting warm, so I had to drink it."

"Had to, huh?"

"Just couldn't see no other way around it."

"I sure do appreciate your sacrifice."

"Well, they ain't measured me for a halo just yet, but I do my best," Ollie said. "I'm guessing from the looks of things you didn't find your old man."

William relayed what he could from his encounter and Ollie and Lena listened without speaking and when he was finished Ollie laughed and shook his head.

"Homer Renfro," he said. "I should've known any sort of misadventure would spit us out at that crazy bastard's door."

"Spurger," William said. "That's another twenty miles."

"What do you think, bud?" Ollie asked him.

"We go home now, nothing changes. She won't go to Houston. The farm goes to the bank. Then what?"

"Then you're right back here, hunting your old man," Ollie said.

William nodded.

"I guess there's our answer," he said and turned to Lena. "We'll go south as far as Hillister if you wanna stick with us. But then we're headed east."

The girl nodded.

"You gotta be shitting me," Ollie said, and William thought he was complaining about Lena but the girl, too, was looking slack-jawed up the street. He followed their gazes.

Moving north to south through the tiny town of Doucette was Doctor Downtain's Mount Zaphon Medicine Show and its dozen wagons and horses and pack mules.

"You remember when Carl Platt ate them mushrooms and said it made him see things that weren't there?" Ollie said.

"Yeah."

"Well. I don't remember eating any mushrooms."

William shook his head.

"You know there's plenty of reasons for them to end up in the same place as us," William said. "They could be headed south. There ain't but four directions to start with."

"Yeah, and they could just be sharpening a cleaver to cut off one of my hands."

"He's right," Lena told William. "We shouldn't stick around to find out why they're here."

"Say that again, would you?" Ollie asked as they hustled southbound, past the edge of town. "The part where I'm right."

18

Lt. Thomas Didymus Carter

We are camped in the Anacostia Flats. What was just last week a dearth of swamp and bog is now home to hundreds of lean-tos and tumble-downs. Makeshift shelters and canvas tents line the grounds in long rows, and already there have been camp meetings to decide on leaders and officers and to set up activities for the children who have made the journey. Many people have come from all across the country. I hope their sacrifices have not been made in vain.

There is music and games, and the people here seem happy. There is a baseball diamond where the children play all day in long marathon games that have neither teams nor innings. There is a never-ending line of boys awaiting their turn at the bat.

This afternoon, I stood awhile in the heat of the day and watched them toss the ball and field their grounders and muddy their pants stretching singles into doubles. The vitality of youth and the joy that lies therein. It should have been a blessed moment, but the longer I stood, the more I saw William on the field. Chasing down a fly ball. Rounding third base. Smiling in the sun.

I have thought to write Laurie and tell her of the camp, but stamps have become more valuable than cigarettes. I also do not wish to upset her, as she begged that she and William might accompany me. I insisted they remain in Texas. I did not know the manner of welcome we would receive, and the last thing I wanted to do was put my family in harm's way. I pray she understands.

I know I have been too often gone. Perhaps after this, once the money is paid, I might rest my mind at home. It seems a wishful thing, but it is a wishful spirit that infects this place, and I am, for the first time in many years, not immune.

The House has passed a measure that would give us the money we are owed. The mood in the camp is hopeful as we await the Senate vote. And my own mood is no doubt lifted by Roger's arrival as well. He made camp this morning, and by the afternoon, he was laboring with the men building sanitation facilities. It is good to see his smiling face. It gives me strength now as it did all those years ago.

19

They were a few miles south of Doucette when the forest on either side of the road came to an abrupt halt. The country spilled out into low meadows and the shadows that had accompanied them through the trees were fled away all except their own and they continued along highway forty.

There were fields of cotton and fields of corn and there were hay fields dotted with cattle. Sheep and goats by the dozen, only a few of which raised their heads as the three of them passed by.

"You ever eat any goat?" Ollie asked.

"I've drunk the milk," William said.

"I don't think I'd eat any. There's something unsettling about a goat."

"You would if you was hungry enough," Lena said.

"Then I don't think I'd be hungry enough."

They came three-wide down the highway. Sunburnt and covered to the knees in the fine red dust that permeated the squalid world in which they wandered. Poor, broken world.

They fanned out across the road. Prospectors of a better nature.

The occasional car honked as it passed, but the cars were few and far between and none offered them a ride. Once a sedan slowed ahead of them and they thought the driver might be about to pull over, but he didn't.

The weeds and wildflowers alone stood at the selfsame height of the travelers who passed them by. Unruly stalks of fleabane ran riotous along the roadcut. Tall, unkempt bunches with their white flowers waving in even the slightest wind. And further along, with no regard for the sun's oppressive onslaught, giant thistle plants grew six feet tall. Grew leaning out into the road as if they would look to see what might be coming.

"They ought to figure a way to make clothes out of thistleweed instead of cotton," William said. "Be a damn sight easier to grow."

"They probably have," Lena said.

Ollie walked in front and at some point started to hum and a few minutes later he was singing.

"Momma bought a chicken, thought it was a duck, served it on the table with its—" He stopped singing and turned back to them. "How old were you when you quit believing in Santy Clause?"

They both looked at him.

"William said there was Christmas stuff everywhere in that woman's house," Ollie said, by way of explanation, and the two of them nodded.

"I must have been six or seven," Lena told him.

"What done it?" Ollie asked.

"We took a trip from Evadale to Houston. My mother had an aunt who was dying. I think she hoped there might be something for her—some secret fortune maybe," the girl said. "There wasn't. But it took all day to get there, and I just figured Houston must be on the other side of the world. When I looked at a map and saw how close it was, I knew there wasn't no Santa."

"You didn't figure his magic reindeer could fly that fast, huh?"

"Not on top of all the other work to be done—chimneys and presents and eating all them cookies."

"I must have been eight," Ollie said. "I come out from the bedroom hunting a glass of water and seen my folks getting everything ready. That was all she wrote. I think maybe I already had my doubts. What about you, bud? When did you figure it out?"

"I didn't," William said.

"Still think there's a jolly fat fella freezing his ass off up at the North Pole, do you?"

"My mother had to tell me. I guess she thought I was old enough to where I'd embarrass myself talking about it or something."

He shook his head.

"It just always made sense to me. Not the North Pole or the reindeer or any of that, but the thought that there was somebody up there keeping track of good deeds and bad ones, and then come December there'd be a reckoning."

"It didn't never bother you that everybody was getting toys instead of coal?"

"I guess I thought the world was full of good people."

"What do you think now?" the girl asked.

William looked at her and there was no malice in her face. In her eyes. There was no pity. Only understanding. Acknowledgment.

"I think if we don't stop soon the two of y'all are fixing to have to carry me."

They left the road and found a shade tree on the other side of the bar ditch and sat under it with their feet straight out before them and from above they looked a broken compass with no true north.

William checked the satchel. "We only got one can of ham left. We don't get to Spurger soon, we may have to start cutting new holes in our belts."

"We ain't the only ones," Lena said, and the boys looked up and followed her eyes to the road, where passed before them a slow-moving collective of migrants that numbered near one hundred. They trudged barefoot or in weathered shoes, the dirt clinging to their tattered clothing and coating their faces in dark shades whereby their eyes seemed to glow white. They rode in the backs of wagons or on the backs of skinny animals and they rode with a distant look about them.

There were old women and young children and there were proud, angry men and men who had already been broken. Men who walked by habit alone. Windup dolls of men who kept moving, kept breathing, but had been hollowed out long ago by a world that wouldn't stop taking.

A boy, teenaged, broke off from the group and walked toward the roadcut.

Ollie and William went out to meet him.

He stood staring at them.

"Y'all wouldn't happen to have any grub, would ye?"

William shook his head.

The boy wiped his dirty arm across his forehead. He looked as if he might spit, but his lips were too dry and cracked.

"Naw, I didn't figure ye did."

"Where you all from?" Ollie asked. "Where you headed?"

The boy looked at Ollie and at William and then past them at Lena.

"Headed to Houston," he said. "Come down from Stillwater."

"What's in Houston?"

"Hell if I know. Old man says the depression ain't down there," the boy told them, and this time he did spit and what little moisture he could muster never made it past his chin. "Course he also said we wouldn't have to leave Oklahoma. You bunch from around here?"

"Me and him are from Shawnee Prairie—a little place up around Manning," Ollie said. "Y'all might've passed close by."

"Might have," the boy said and wiped under his mouth. "What about that gal yonder?"

"We come across her in the woods a while back."

"Come across her, did you?"

Ollie nodded.

"Shit," the boy said, almost wistful. "I sure wish I'd come across something."

"Hot enough, ain't it?" Ollie asked, but the boy was still staring at Lena.

William stepped in his line of sight.

"How come y'all ain't over on 75?" William asked.

"Started out for Shreveport first," the boy told them. "Then we heard there weren't no work there neither. Heard the camps could get pretty bad. Violent like. Anyhow. We turned south. Had this one old boy with us. I didn't know him. He plumb and keeled over just before we got to the Sabine River. Speaking of the heat, I mean."

"Sorry to hear that," Ollie said.

"Like I said, I didn't know him," the boy said, and then he turned and went on with the rest of them in whatever sad march.

By the time the long procession had passed, the dust stood in the road six feet high and William and the others watched as it dissipated, settling slow over the country.

20

A last fire of sunset burning somewhere on the distant sky and then gray. And then gone. The night settled around them and they were alone.

They passed through Woodville and the main street was lit by a series of electric lamp posts whereunder thousands of insects swarmed and died and fell like some awful plague levied upon the town.

The caravan of migrants had held up in an alleyway and a night watchman and sheriff's deputy were reciting to them the local loitering laws and threatening arrest and the men stood with blank faces and crossed arms and the women were already gathering up their things.

They went on along the thoroughfare, the sounds of the unnatural night seeping from the buildings as they passed. Piano music from the hotel restaurant drifted by like a soft soundtrack from another world. Conversation, loud and undignified, carried heavy from the pool hall. A quick line from the picture show escaped as someone opened the theater door.

I have no soul. I'm beyond the pale. I'm one of the living dead.

And finally, the steam engine house, where within they could hear the hissing and thrumming of the two large dynamos powering this lively stretch of nocturnal happenings.

"Y'all got electricity in Shawnee Prairie?" the girl asked.

"They got some in Manning. You got it in Evadale?"

"Not yet. They say it's coming. Been saying."

"Why don't we get us a room?" Ollie asked, then looked at Lena. "Or two."

"I got five dollars left," William said. "I ain't spending it on a hotel room."

"Bath might be nice too," Ollie said.

"You don't want to sleep out on the range, cowboy?"

"Poison ivy and thornbush ain't no kind of range," Ollie said. "And whatever they're fixing in that hotel restaurant sure smelled good."

"Look there." The girl stopped and pointed, and up ahead was the car that had taken them to Doucette. It was parked a little ways down from the hotel in front of a café.

"You reckon they stopped for a little nightcap?" Ollie asked.

"They should've been a lot further than this by now," William said.

As they passed the window glass, they saw the man leaning hard over a table and whispering in a woman's ear.

"Y'all seeing this?" Ollie asked.

"That don't look like Mary Pickford," William said.

"Warren, you lying bastard," Ollie said, laughing. "Where do you reckon the girl's at?"

"Probably put her on a train back to Etoile," William said.

"Hard lesson," Lena said.

"Shit," Ollie scoffed. "She deserved every bit of what she got."

"I don't know, bud," William told him. "Tough to judge them that just want something better out of it."

"Out of what?"

"Out of anything. Out of breathing."

"Well. She could've been a little smarter about it. All I'm saying."

"I can't imagine they call you 'Ollie the Wise' back in Shawnee Prairie," Lena said.

"They just might have," he countered, "before I come on this little trip."

They went on in the dark for another mile south of Woodville.

"We can follow the road to Hillister," William said, "then cut east for Spurger."

"How far do you make Hillister?" Ollie asked. His pace was slowing.

"Nine or ten miles."

"Let's just stop and rest a minute. Might be that somebody'll come along."

William looked both ways in the darkness. He heard the drip of the cave.

"We might as well bed down," he said. "We start early enough and we'll still make it to Spurger tomorrow."

They camped not fifty yards off the road. They were exhausted, the three of them, and sleep came quick and deep and William dreamed of his mother. She was dressed in a white gown and her red hair fell down in front of her shoulders and she had walked barefoot into their camp. She didn't say anything. Just stood there over him and him looking up at her and her looking out toward the road.

"Momma," he said, and then he woke up.

The caravan was going by out on the highway. William could see the lights from their lanterns passing along in the dark like souls adrift. Silhouettes through the trees, passing one after the other, and often their dark shapes coalescing into some hybrid form of man. Many heads. Many legs. Someone quickens or slows the pace and the black mass separates like running ink. One hundred souls and no one spoke a word. The rattle of harnesses and long-turning wagon wheels with squealing axles and all else passed in silence. Even the children. Even the little children.

And when they were gone the night grew somehow quieter still.

There was no wind. William stared up at the firmament—windowed by the tops of the trees, but no less glorious. No less a source of constant awe.

He lay there for a long while and waited for a cool breeze that never came. No passing clouds in the night. No swaying limbs. Nothing changed. All was as it had been. As it ever was.

His stomach growled. In a way he'd become accustomed to hunger. And in a way that didn't much help at all.

Alright, Momma, he whispered to himself and stood up from his pine-needle pallet. He went quietly to the knapsack and took out the can of ham and put it in his pocket.

"Where you going, bud," Ollie asked, hushed.

"Nowhere," William said. "Go back to sleep."

He used the blue twilight to find the road in the dark. He snapped off a few dried branches from the nearest tree and laid them on the roadside in a patterned arrow.

He figured the migrants had the same idea he did—get a mile or two clear of the town and then make camp. He'd only walked ten minutes when he came to the first of their night fires. They were spread out in the ditches on both sides of the road. Some already asleep, others still awake. A few men were playing cards by lantern light and they looked at him as he passed.

The boy was sitting, his back propped against the wheel of the wagon he'd been trailing. His eyes were closed, but William didn't take him for sleeping.

"You awake?" William asked.

The boy didn't move at all, but his eyes came open. Staring.

"Here," William said and tossed him the can.

The boy caught it and turned it over in his hands.

"Guilty conscience?" he asked.

"That's our last can of food," William said.

The boy kept rotating it in his hands.

"You want some sort of prize?" he asked. "What? Were all three of y'all gonna take one bite each?"

"You can sure enough give it back," William told him. "If it ain't up to your high standards."

The boy clicked his tongue and gave a curt laugh.

"I'll keep it," he said. "Might come in handy if one of the dogs starts to starve."

"You ain't exactly the grateful type, are you."

"Look around, cousin," the boy said. "And try opening your eyes when you do."

21

He walked back in the dark. The road still warm from the day's heat. An owl hollered out. Something moved in the woods and there were glowing eyes and then they were gone.

A car went by and he held up his arms to block the harshness of the headlamps. Then it was gone and all returned to the blue black of night.

If he's with Homer, the boy thought, *maybe he'll be there a while. Maybe Homer will talk some sense into him.* That thought made the boy smile and shake his head.

Another car and again the bright lights cutting through the dark but this time it slowed and stopped and William blinked and squinted and tried to see who was driving.

"You out here by yourself, kid?"

"I don't need a ride," William said.

"Where's your pals?"

"I ain't got no pals."

He heard the hammer on a pistol click.

"Why don't you get in the car."

"You got the wrong person."

"No I don't. Get in the car."

"I don't know what you're talking about, mister."

"Yes you do. C'mon, boy."

"Let's just grab him," another man said. The driver turned to look as the passenger door opened and when he did the boy bolted into the woods.

One of the men fired a wild shot and William heard the bullet zip past twenty feet to his right.

"Don't shoot, goddamnit. I'm going after him," the other man called as he crossed the ditch and plunged ahead into the forest.

The boy went quick and quiet through the trees. Blackberry briers tore at his pants and the skin on his arms.

"I think I heard him over yonder," the man hollered. "Give me some light."

The driver turned the car perpendicular in the road and the headlamps threw into the woods like spotlights and William dropped down onto his belly and stayed still.

"Shit," the man called. "I don't see him."

He was a dozen yards to William's right and the light was in between them. The boy tried not to breathe. The man stepped into the light and stomped his way toward William.

"Come out, boy!" he hollered.

Another step.

William could hear the man panting.

"Can you turn it more to the left?" he called back toward the road.

"My left or your left?" the driver's voice came, small and distant.

"I don't— *Your* left. Wait. My left *is* your left."

"My left?"

"Just turn the fucking thing!"

"It ain't my fault you forgot a flashlight."

Another step.

William slowly moved his hand down into his pocket and felt for his pocketknife and found it. He wrapped his fingers around it. His hand was shaking. He closed his eyes and took his hand off the knife.

You can outrun him, he told himself. *You can outrun him.*

His muscles tensed and he placed both hands palm-down on the ground and readied himself.

"To hell with it," the man yelled. "I'm coming back. Keep them lights on so I can see where I'm going."

"He's gonna be madder'n hell when we tell him," the driver warned. "I've never seen him so upset about losing one. Must be pretty special."

"Then maybe we just don't tell him. He was right about them heading south. I bet we'll get another crack at it."

William stayed on the ground for another five minutes after the car had turned and gone back north and when he retook the road he did so at a full sprint and didn't let up until he saw his marker of sticks.

He went quiet into the camp and went to Ollie's side and squatted and put his hand on his shoulder and shook him awake.

"Kathy?" the boy said, groaning.

"Wake up," William told him. "Where's that bottle you stole?"

Ollie sat up and looked around and remembered where he was and then took the vial from the front pocket of his overalls and gave it to William.

William held it close to his face in the dark and studied it best he could. His hands shook from the adrenaline still coursing through his body.

"What is it?" Ollie asked.

"Two old boys from that medicine show just tried to jump me on the road," William said without taking his eyes off the bottle.

"What was you doing on the road?"

"Do you think there's a chance—" William looked out into the dark and then back at the bottle.

The idea that he was holding an actual miracle cure seemed preposterous, and yet the blood on his arms was still fresh from where he'd run through the woods to escape.

"What's going on, bud?" Ollie asked.

"Hush a minute," William said, and his mind was racing and his heart pounding and he untwisted the small cap and sniffed at the bottle.

He jerked his head back.

"Jesus Christ."

"What?" Ollie asked. "What is it?"

"Smells awful."

"That's because it's fox piss," Lena said, and the boys turned to her and she was brushing the dirt from her arms.

"What?" they asked in unison.

"Downtain's never been to India or anywhere else. The bottle is filled with fox piss. And those men aren't looking for y'all. They're looking for me."

The boys stood in stunned silence.

"I lied," the girl said.

"Seems like it," Ollie managed.

"The man my momma sold me to didn't live in Corsicana."

"It was him," William said. "It was Downtain."

She nodded.

William rubbed the back of his neck.

"Well," he said. "We'd better hear the story."

She told them.

She said her mother had sold her to Downtain when the medicine show passed through Evadale. He'd seen her and her sister in town and sent a man to follow them home. The next morning, Downtain was in the kitchen with her mother and the girl was gone with him before she could eat breakfast.

"And then what?" William asked.

"And then I worked for him. Belonged to him," she said.

"Why'd you run off?" Ollie asked. "Did he beat on you?"

"Would he have to? Is that the only way you'd justify my leaving?" She shook her head. "No, he didn't beat on me. But it was rough in its own way. All them people he has working for him—most of them are fresh out of the penitentiary. I didn't like the way they looked at me.

Mostly I just needed to get home—to get my sister out of that house before my momma could ruin her."

She wiped tears from under her eyes.

"If she was willing to sell me off, what do you think she'll do when Susannah gets old enough to catch a man's eye?"

William watched her. The moonlight on her wet face. He thought she looked beautiful and he felt guilty for thinking it.

"No," Ollie said, his arms crossed. "Something ain't right here."

William frowned.

"Why would that old boy go through all this trouble trying to track you down?" Ollie asked. "You stole something, didn't you? What was it? Money?"

"I didn't steal anything," she said.

"You by god stole a pistol. Tried robbing us."

"I meant from Downtain," she said.

"How much money did you take?" Ollie pressed her.

"She doesn't have any money, Ollie," William said, grabbing his friend's arm.

He leaned over close to Ollie's ear.

"You remember what them fellas were saying about Downtain back in Nancy?" he asked, his voice an urgent whisper. "About what he was doing with young girls in Missouri?"

Ollie twisted away from him.

"Yeah," he relented. "I remember. And I still think we ought to get as far away from her as possible."

"That would suit me just fine," she fired back. "You hadn't been nothing but ugly to me the whole time anyhow."

"Both of you, stop," William said. "There's a rail line that runs through the woods from Hillister to Spurger. We'll cut through the trees until we find it. We'll follow it east. Homer Renfro has a car. We'll explain things to him. He can drive you to Evadale while Ollie and me go back home with my father. We been going dead south this whole time. Downtain won't have any reason to think we turned east, and he won't have any way to track us. But we need to get further into these woods. We're too close to the road."

Ollie shook his head and sighed and made obvious his dissent but still they gathered their things and set out from one dark to another.

"We should've just cut her loose," Ollie hissed at William.

"Surely you know I can hear you," the girl said.

"Surely I do. And we should've just cut you loose."

"Hush," William told them. "Nobody's happy about the way this is all playing out. But tomorrow we'll get to Homer's and get everything sorted. Just hold off on killing each other for one more day."

Ollie mumbled his agreement.

The girl walked closer to William and he felt her take his hand in the dark. Neither of them said anything.

22

Lt. Thomas Didymus Carter

The Senate voted down the measure. It was not close: 62–18. I met with Rep. Wright Patman, who told me the news. Wright is a good man from Cass County. He served in France. Perhaps if they'd all been there, he told me, their votes would've changed.

In the press, we've been wrongfully linked to the Communist Party. There are communists among us, yes; and though I don't decry their position, I know that their presence will not help our cause. When an ideal is just and cannot be overruled with logic, the opposing party will attack the character of those who espouse it. Soon the papers will say communists are occupying Washington, DC.

Nothing is right. Nothing is fair. I sound like a child. So be it. My anger is growing in a way I have felt before, and I am tired of trying to quell it. So very tired.

Tired, and yet I fear sleep. Sometimes I begin to sweat at the very thought of it. Giving my mind over to itself is a proposition that terrifies me. I have awoken cold and shivering from fear of the memories that haunt me. The thundering tanks through smoke-darkened fields and screaming, legless horses. The smell of urine and the smell of phosgene and mustard gas. Bodies added to the wall of the trench, building it higher—dead men not yet released from their obligation to the cause. I no longer sleep with a knife within my reach for fear I cannot discern dream from reality. Would that I no longer sleep at all.

I often wander the camps at night. They have done well to make this place feel safe for the families. There are watchmen, the same as old Tidrick in Manning. They stop those men they don't recognize and ask to see their membership card. They no longer stop me.

Roger is the only comfort left to me in this place. I care for all of the men here, for their plight. But only Roger was by my side in France. When I see him, I am reminded of the true terrors we endured, and despite the disappointments that have confronted us here, they have come at the hands of democracy—voting, not violence.

Roger convinced me to join him in one of the church tents this evening to hear the word. The preacher spoke of suffering and spoke the words of Peter and Paul and James and their teachings that our present suffering does not compare to the glory that is to be revealed.

The preacher spoke of faith and steadfastness, and as he did, I looked at the eyes of those men and women and even the children who crowded the tent—the hot tent, damp with heat and damp with sweat—and in their eyes I saw no trace of mutiny. I saw that they would be—will be—loyal to the end. They have suffered and they suffer still, and yet they will not be moved from their faith. These are men not unlike myself. Soldiers. Men who have lost. Men who have taken. Men who have seen the dark heart that beats at the center of the world and, so too, in their own chests. And yet they remain unshaken.

Do I resent them? Do I aspire to them? I cannot say.

23

They went slowly in the dark for an hour or more and they were groaning at their own weight on their feet, and the railroad tracks they hoped to find had eluded them and they all agreed they had to stop and rest.

They found a sliver of flat ground among the trees and William unfurled the blanket.

"We'll take shifts," he said. "Two of us will sleep while the other takes a watch. I'll go first."

The others settled in and were soon asleep. Rhythmic breathing. Lost to the waking world. William thought of his mother's breathing. Her eyes closed, mouth muttering something soft and unintelligible. He thought of the string of days that led him here and he wondered where it had begun. Her illness. His father's absence. Something too long ago to trace. A desk in the back of a hay wagon.

William's eyes began to close and he jerked them open and they slowly closed again.

He'd memorized his mother's face and he thought of it now. He wondered if what he saw in his mind was true, or if it had been filtered with each recalling. Slight adjustments. Small inaccuracies. A lessening of the jaw here, a narrowing of the nose there. And with each recollection her face might have become someone else's entirely and him none the wiser, believing his own mind and the distortions therein. If enough time passed, might he see her on the street and walk right on by?

He slept.

The trembling of the ground shook him awake. Juddering vibrations come up seemingly from the earth's belly, like a vengeful god ill content with his own handiwork. Ready to clear the board and start anew.

Ollie and Lena scrambled up from the dirt, wide-eyed.

"Well," Ollie said. "I guess yonder goes your tracks."

The train came thunderous from the east, mining the dark for a path already laid. The headlamp, like an ersatz sun, shone off the steel rails and the nails in the crossties, and the crossties were revealed and swallowed up one by one as the train tunneled on into the night.

There were a dozen yards of trees between themselves and the tracks, and the trees were backlit by the train, blackened and shadowed, and the three young people narrowed their eyes as the light set upon them and then it was gone, the rest of the cars clattering past in the dark.

They stood still and watched. Silent witnesses to an industrious progression—a future made of transportation and technology. Raw material and rage.

William ventured out toward the tracks and eventually the trees gave out and he stood on the rocks with the train passing just above him on the lifted path. The cars trundled along and a few had doors slid open and even in the dark he could see the shapes of men sitting on the ledges with their legs hanging down. Hobos the world called them. Tramps. He watched them pass like appellants to the night. Ghosts in transit.

When he returned to the camp, Lena and Ollie were ready to go.

"Not long until first light," the girl said. "We ought to keep moving."

William nodded.

"You never woke us for our shift, bud," Ollie said.

"I didn't make it through mine," William admitted.

"Well. We survived one more night anyway, didn't we?" Ollie said. "Now let's see if we can survive Homer Renfro."

24

They started eastbound along the tracks, moving toward the rising sun like brave warriors sent to slay a fiery serpent. The sun did not cower. It rose up above them and in time passed them by with no concern or regard, such is the world in which they wandered.

A fox and her kits crossed over the tracks. There were little trailheads spotted here and there and then disappearing into the undergrowth of the forest.

"Who is this fella we're going to see?" Lena asked as they passed along the rail ties.

"He's the craziest bastard you've ever met," Ollie said.

"I've never met him."

"You meeting him or not don't have nothing to do with how crazy he is, and I'm telling you right now he's as loony as they come."

"How are we gonna find his place?" Lena asked.

"We'll find it," William said.

"I guarantee somebody will know it," Ollie said. "The townsfolk may have it roped off with warning signs."

In the afternoon, they heard voices rising from a shallow gully a few dozen yards ahead.

Singing. Slow and deep.

"*They nailed him to a tree,*" the voices called out in rhythm, "*and he never said a mumblin' word. Yes, they nailed him to a tree, and he never said a mumblin' word.*"

The tracks made a steep pitch and then flattened back out and there was a secondary set of tracks that split off and followed a little ridgeline down into the wood.

The three of them walked to the lip of the ridge and looked down and there were several colored men guiding and hand-skidding cut logs along a dry creek bed. They pulled together and lifted together and sang together.

"*Not a word, not a word, not a word.*"

To their left, there was a pair of flathead sawyers, each holding an end of a giant Simonds saw. The men were working the blade, crosscut and swayback, against virgin pines and they stopped only when their supervisor came running through the woods, waving his arms.

"Hold on," the man shouted. "Hold on, goddamnit."

The two men stopped, each looking at the other and then back to the out-of-breath supervisor.

"We ain't supposed to cut them virgin yellows," he said, wincing and holding his side. "Them turpentine boys and they mule skinners are gonna come through here after us. Just mark 'em and leave it."

The men shrugged and picked up their saw and moved on to the next tree.

William watched them cut the tree and watched it fall.

"*The blood came tricklin' down, and he never said a mumblin' word.*"

Two men leaned on opposite sides of the steam loader and a third hung his head and upper body overside the locomotive car.

William nudged Ollie and pointed and the three of them went over and waited to talk to the man driving the shay.

"Just get on up here," one of the men called as the skidders brought the logs closer. "Bring 'em on up. That's the way. Skid 'em on up."

The man in the shay climbed down and was cussing the train and the mill and the heat.

"You standing in a damn good spot to get squashed," he told William, "one of these logs comes off of here."

"Do these tracks go through Spurger?"

"Don't know."

"You don't know?"

"These tracks go yonder to the mill in Hillister." The man pointed west down the line.

"What about east?"

"Hadn't never been no further east than right here, right now. We make it a hundred yards or so, every day. If you want to wait here a few weeks, I'll tell you where the tracks go."

The other two men unspooled a two-prong cable yoke, and each affixed a giant hook to either end of the log. When they gave the all clear, the cable hoisted the log up and onto the steam loader.

They stood back and watched until the little train was full up with timber and a few of the men hopped onto it and the man who'd spoken to William climbed into the shay and pushed it forward with small bevel gears, the engine straining under the heavy load as it went churning up the steep grade. Soon the train's cabbagehead smokestack was billowing clouds of exhaust and on it went one way and them the other.

The tracks ran through the middle of Spurger and the three of them stopped into a little deli attached to a gas station and asked the proprietor if she knew where Homer Renfro lived.

"Renfro?" The old woman came around from behind the counter and untied her apron and threw it down on the floor. She crossed her arms. "He's banned."

"But do you know where he lives?" William asked.

"I don't know where he lives. I don't know *if* he lives. And I don't know what the good Lord was thinking when he wasted a beating heart on that no-good sumbitch."

Ollie looked at Lena with an I-told-you-so stare.

“He’s in an old L-frame headed out toward the river,” a younger man said. “Take that first road by the post office.”

The old woman bent and scooped up her apron and stalked over to where the young man sat.

“And how is it you know where Homer Renfro lives?” She glared down at him.

“I don’t, Momma,” the man quickly backtracked. “Not for a fact. I just—I just heard is all.”

She started to whack him with the apron and flour was coming off it like a light snow and the man held both arms up in defense and continued to insist his innocence.

Homer Renfro had served under the boy’s father. The two had been familiar with one another for some time, with Homer having a cousin in Manning and his family spending time both there and in Shawnee Prairie. While Thomas Carter had distinguished himself as a capable leader during the war, Homer had earned the reputation of a wild man—a fearless soldier who gladly accepted what his comrades called suicide missions, and somehow managed to always return. He also earned the love and admiration of William’s father.

Both of Homer’s parents had died from the Spanish Lady before he was back from the war and he had to come stay with William and his family for a short time thereafter.

The arrangement ended poorly, with Homer leaving a few weeks later after an incident with another man’s wife. That the woman’s husband was the pastor of the local church did not factor into Homer’s decision to leave, though it probably hastened the speed in which he departed. William’s mother, who seemed to harbor an everlasting capacity for grace, always seemed angered by Homer—a fact that fascinated William and somehow made Homer all the more compelling to the boy.

The last time he’d seen the man was Christmas Day of 1930. Homer had arrived in the dead of night in a brand new Model AA Ford pickup and brought presents for William and for his mother and father. The truck was bright red and he called it his sleigh and was clearly drunk and had been for some time.

The boy's mother had opened the door, with the wind blowing cold and the world all but black outside the little farmhouse, and Homer stood there with his arms out, grinning like a tippler. She turned and went back inside but left the door open and when her husband asked who it was, she told him, "The first of three ghosts," and went back to bed.

William had come down the hallway excited to see Homer and to open his present, which turned out to be a stack of Tijuana bibles.

"Laurie sees those and she's liable to shoot you where you stand," the boy's father told Homer.

"Gotta learn sometime, don't he?" Homer grinned.

"I know about girls," William said.

Homer belly laughed.

"You don't know shit about girls," he said. "And the fact you think you do, shows just how much you don't."

William was sent back to bed and though he tried to stay awake and listen to the two men talking he was soon dreaming of the things he had yet to learn. Hours to come he woke and the house was still dark and all was quiet save the sound of crying coming from the hall closet. He crept out of bed and into the hallway and opened the closet door and Homer was there on the floor, curled up with an empty bottle and weeping so hard he didn't even look up at the boy.

William woke his father and his father again sent him to his bedroom.

In the morning, Homer was gone and Thomas sat drinking coffee and smoking a pipe and William asked what he'd said to him.

"I told him to get a dog," his father said.

The boy nodded as if he understood.

"Are the magazines still here?" William asked.

"No."

25

The river was further east and they were just beyond sight of the town when a house with a long front porch with columns came into view. It had massive exterior chimneys standing at either end of the front wing. The house had been built at the edge of the woods and the woods now seemed to be seeking more territory. Branches from oaks and willows grew out over the structure and rested their weight on the dormers and on the roof itself. It looked like it had stood for two hundred years. It looked like it might not stand for two more hours.

"This the place?" Lena asked.

"I guess so."

"Well."

William knocked.

No one answered.

"You reckon he's off at work somewheres?"

"Homer Renfro working?" Ollie asked. "Sounds like a bit of a stretch to me, cousin."

They were about to come off the porch when the door opened a few feet and the woman who peered around it was wearing a nightgown such as they had not known existed, let alone seen. It was satin and lace and there was little to it.

"Y'uns looking for Homer?" she asked, and her voice was broken and smokey and William meant to say yes but didn't. Ollie stood blinking.

"Yes," Lena spoke for them. "This place belong to him?"

"Homer thinks everything belongs to him."

"You his wife?" Ollie asked.

The woman laughed.

"Darling there ain't enough money in the whole wide world to get me to marry Homer. I don't care how much sugar comes pouring out of his lying mouth."

She laughed at the thought of it or at something else.

"He's up at the four-way selling rotted vegetables for half price."

They looked around but didn't see a garden.

"He don't grow veggies," she said, answering their eyes. "He goes up to Schmidt's and gets the ones so bad they're fixing to throw 'em out. Entrepreneur, he calls himself."

"Sounds about right," Ollie said. "Last time he was in Manning he come by the funeral home trying to sell us on a new type of golden oak that made stronger caskets than anything else."

"What's golden oak?" Lena asked.

"It's oak that's been gone over with gold paint."

The woman shook her head and tried to shift her gown to a more modest position but failed.

"What do you want with him?" she asked. "He ain't one of y'all's daddy, is he? 'Cause he told me he didn't have no kids that he knew of."

"He's supposed to know where my father is. Thomas Carter."

"The soldier?"

"Yes ma'am."

"He just left here a couple nights back."

William closed his eyes.

"I don't guess you know where he was headed?"

"You'll have to ask Homer."

William was tired and he stood there in his tiredness and fought the urge to sit—to sit down on Homer Renfro's porch and let his problems and fears and the whole of the world go on without him. The woman was looking at him, impatient, and Ollie and Lena were quiet, as if they would wait for his final word on the matter.

"Alright," he said. "Let's go."

"Sure nice to meet you, ma'am," Ollie said, smoothing his hair down in the front.

The woman smirked and closed the door.

For a short time the wind blew heavy. Strong, merciful wind that pressed against the heat and sent invisible waves rolling through the grassy meadows. Oh, how the world danced, so suddenly animate and unchained. Pines swayed in an off-kilter rhythm like drunken sailors. Shimmering oaks and wildflower stalks that bent and righted and bent again. Long-dead leaves scooped up and tossed fluttering in the air. Then, just as abruptly, the breeze died down and the forest brought to heel once more. All was still, save the occasional darting of a bird from one shaded branch to another. The roar of cicadas and katydids filled the stale humid air. Small game sought purchase in hollow logs and shaded thickets, while larger creatures stayed near water. All were at the mercy of the sun once again. And the sun as merciless as the one who'd sent it.

"This is getting good and goddamn ridiculous," Ollie said as they labored along the road with yet another destination in mind.

"Feel free to head back to the Prairie whenever you're ready," William snapped.

"I didn't mean it like that, bud," Ollie said. "I ain't fixing to quit on you."

"It's hot," Lena said. "We're tired. That's all."

At long last they came to the crossroads.

Homer Renfro was sitting kicked back in a lawn chair with a western-looking cowboy hat pulled down over his face. He was barefoot. He wore no shirt and his shorts cut just across his thigh. Despite his Anglo heritage, his skin was a deep tanned brown save for his feet and ankles, which were pale from wearing socks and loafers.

"He don't look crazy," Lena said, and William didn't like the tone with which she said it.

Beside him was a mangy brindle dog with different-colored eyes and the dog spotted them and lifted its head and gave a halfhearted grunt.

Homer raised his hat slightly.

William stuck up his hand.

"Willie boy," Homer called out, sitting upright in the chair. "Are you shitting me?"

"What say, Mr. Renfro?" William hollered.

Homer stood and quickly dropped his shorts and bent over with his bare bottom exposed, six shades whiter than the rest of him.

"Well kiss my hairy ass," he said.

"What's he look like now?" Ollie asked Lena.

"My first customers!" Homer said clapping to himself as they reached his modest market.

There were a half dozen boxes of sad-looking garden vegetables at his side.

"How you been, Mr. Renfro?" William asked.

"Quit it with that shit. 'Mr. Renfro,'" Homer said. "I'm good. Hell, I'm great. If I was any better, I'd be twins. And look at you, all growed up. My god."

"You remember Ollie," William said.

"Why sure I do," Homer boasted. "The painter."

"I ain't a painter."

"Oil on canvas. Makeup on corpses. Different mediums of the same craft, son."

Ollie shook his head.

"This is our—" William looked at the girl. "This is Lena."

Homer frowned.

"Oh," he said. "Sorry about the hairy ass and all that."

"I don't mind," she said, and again William felt himself tense up.

"So y'all just out for a stroll in this lovely weather?" Homer asked. "You know I seen the devil himself stopping under a sycamore not ten minutes ago. Said he had to cool off in the shade."

"I imagine you know why we're here," William said, and Homer stopped smiling. "Do you know where he was headed next?"

"Where *who* was headed?" Homer asked.

"We done been by your house and talked to the half-naked woman," Ollie said.

Homer sighed.

"Well, in that case, and with my deepest and most sincere apology for y'all having come all this way, I ain't gonna tell you."

"What?" William said.

"Your daddy's business is his own."

"You chickenshit!" the boy hollered.

Homer took a step forward. He was a half foot taller than any of them.

"I'll give you that one," he said. "I'll let you have it, free of charge, because I love your daddy. But I won't take no more lip off you than that. And I damn sure won't be called a chickenshit. You get me, boy?"

The dog stood up and growled and Homer snapped at it without turning around and the dog laid back down.

They were still and quiet and then Homer took off his hat and slicked his hair back and laughed.

"Whoa," he said and sounded as if we were talking to himself. "Things got hot real quick-like. Gotta cool it down. A drink."

"A drink?" he said again, this time as a question to the three of them.

"I've done swore off the hooch," Ollie said, and Homer howled with laughter.

"What are you, twelve years old?"

"I'm sixteen."

"Sixteen and joined the temperance movement, have you? Well good on you, undertaker."

"Will you at least tell me what he was doing here?" William asked.

"Why he left Doucette? Hell, why he didn't come home in the first place."

Homer went over to his truck and opened the door and came back with an unmarked bottle of amber liquid and he drank straight from it and sat back down in his chair, his limbs folding over it like some giant spider.

"You ever take them Dr. Miles pills if your head is hurting?" he asked after a while.

"Every now and then."

"Well, Thomas is trying to stop his head from hurting too. He just ain't found the right medicine yet."

"Is that what he wanted from you?" William motioned toward the bottle. "Medicine?"

"He wanted to talk is all." Homer took another pull and offered the bottle to them and they each declined in turn and he went to screw the cap on but stopped and took another drink and then capped it and set it on the ground next to the chair. "He goes all around all the time checking on everybody from the old squad. But I'm the only one that ever came to see about him."

"So what did you talk about?"

"Our favorite colors."

"C'mon, Homer."

"I don't know what you want me to tell you. He was here. Now he ain't. Go on home to Miss Laurie and see about your cotton. It ought to be the harvest coming up."

"Momma's sick," William said, and at this Homer softened.

"What kind of sick?" he asked.

"The dying kind."

"Shit," he said and picked up the bottle and turned it over in his hands and then set it back down. "Thomas don't have no idea."

"Would it matter if he did?" William asked.

Homer's face tightened.

"What the hell sort of question is that? Of course it would matter. Your daddy loves Laurie."

"Yeah? Then how come he spends more time gone than he does at home? How come he ain't home with her right now?"

"How come *you* ain't?" Homer challenged.

"Because I'm out here in the goddamn heat looking for him," William all but screamed back.

"Right," Homer said, his voice lowering. "But you had a choice, didn't you—to come hunting him or stay with her? And you made the choice you thought was best. And so did Thomas."

Homer shook his head.

"There's not a soul on this earth that understands unless they were there," he said. "You just can't even imagine."

He sat with his eyes closed and his head in his hands as if he would replay it all there before them.

"And it was worse for your daddy than anybody else. Because when somebody died, it was on him. You understand? He was the one responsible. Or *felt* responsible, since he was in command. One of a hundred great things your old man did for me was beat me out during that election. I saw what it did to him. I could've never handled it. Shit, I can barely handle things as it is."

When he sat back up he reached and pulled a cigarette down from out of his hat band and asked if they had a light and William dug in the satchel for the matches and tossed the little box over to him.

Homer stood and walked to his truck and jacked one foot up against the running board and left it there and leaned forward.

"Imagine losing all them men, and then the ones you are able to bring home, well, they end up poor and depressed and destitute like. And you can't save them over here no more than you could over there."

Homer lit his cigarette and held onto the box of matches. He looked up at the sky.

"Now imagine you make a friend like Roger Turner. A man who sticks by your side. A man who loves you in every way you can love a person. And then that man kills himself and you think it's because of something you said."

"Homer," the boy said, pleading. "I don't know what he's feeling. I don't know what it's like. But what I do know is that my momma needs him. And if what you're saying is true—that he would want to be with her—then take us to him."

Homer took a drag and blew out a long stream of smoke and shook his head.

"That's the demon your daddy is wrestling right now."

"Fine," William said. "Now you imagine something. What's that weight gonna look like when his wife dies without him being there? And what's he gonna say if he finds out you knew and you didn't help us?"

Homer scratched his head with the thumb of his cigarette hand.

"C'mon, Homer," Ollie said. "It's the right thing. You know it is."

"He's in the Thicket," Homer said. "Or headed that way."

"Where?" William quickly followed up: "What for?"

Homer looked put out. He sat and smoked and looked at William curiously.

"There's a rumor," Homer said, "a while now, about an old woman lives somewhere deep in the baygall. Swamp-like. Supposedly—and I ain't saying I believe it—this woman is a healer. Strong medicine, they say. You and me might call her a woods witch. Anyhow, they say she can do things."

"What sort of things?" William asked.

"Miracle things. Take pain away. Fix a man's mind. Fix his heart."

"And you believe that?"

"What I believe don't matter."

"My father believes it," William said.

"He might," Homer nodded. "A fella that was staying with me for a few days got to talking about this old woman and the lieutenant seemed real interested. Or maybe he's just so desperate to get back to you and your momma that he'd try anything."

"He could come home anytime he wanted."

"It ain't that simple."

"It is," the boy insisted. "It is that simple. We needed him and he wasn't there."

"I'm sorry, William. And I sure wish I could explain it to you. Sometimes a man loves something so much, he knows he has to stay away. As much as he don't want to. For what it's worth, I tried to stop him. To talk him out of it. But he wouldn't hear it. Wouldn't hear anything. The most stubborn goddamn man I ever met, your father. And with Roger gone, well . . ."

"Take us down there, Homer. To wherever he's headed."

"I can't, son. Honest. I'm due up in Texarkana day after tomorrow to pick up two hundred pounds of yeast."

"What in the hell do you need two hundred pou— Oh," Ollie said, nodding. "Right."

"Let us borrow your truck," William said.

"I need the truck to tote the yeast," Homer said. "Listen, just come on back to the house with me and get a bite to eat. Beth can fry up catfish like you wouldn't believe. Cuts all the gray out of the meat and everything. What do you say?"

William thought about it. He looked to the others. Ollie shrugged.

"Do you have a phone," William asked.

"There's one at the barbershop in town. Old Nick won't charge you for it."

"Take us there first?"

"I can do that."

They walked to the truck and Homer opened the passenger door and clicked his tongue and the dog came running and hopped into the cab. Homer closed the door and looked at the three of them and pointed to the bed.

26

The barbershop was small with a low ceiling and there were three people waiting in the three chairs by the front windows and one boy younger than William was having his hair cut and they squeezed into the shop the four of them. The old man with the scissors looked up at Homer and started shaking his head.

"I told you not to come back in here, Renfro," the old man said.

"Aw, hell, Nick, that was months ago."

"It took the doc three hours to stitch that Jenkins boy up," the barber said, and William could see the back of his balding head in the mirror opposite the chair, and along the counter were pomades and razors and jars of shaving cream lined up just in front of the mirror to where they touched their reflections in the glass.

"But he *was* able to stitch him up," Homer said. "And I bet Wes Jenkins don't ever disrespect Little Dog again."

"I ain't getting into this with you, Renfro. You ruined my favorite thinning shears."

"We're just here to use the phone, Nick. Calm down 'fore you get to shaking and snip the top of that boy's ear off. Letting yourself get all worked up over nothing."

The kid in the chair grew wide-eyed.

The barber threw his rag down onto the hair-scattered floor.

"I'm not getting wo—" he started and then stopped and closed his eyes and raised two fingers up to his neck and felt himself breathing.

"Fine," he said, straining a smile. "You got three minutes."

The phone was at the back of the shop and the rest of them waited while William asked the operator to put him through to the Manning switchboard and he gave the number to the doctor's office and the line rang and rang and no one answered.

"Probably visiting with her right now," Ollie said, encouraging.

William hung the receiver back on the wall and turned and looked up at Homer.

"Come back to the house," Homer said. "I'll draw you a map."

The woman was already frying the fish when they came into the house. She had put on a sundress and was smoking a cigarette and standing with her hands on her hips and one hip kicked out to the side. The catfish medallions were coated in a kind of cornmeal, and they were quivering and popping in an iron pan filled up halfway with grease.

"Y'all want hushpuppies?" she asked without taking the cigarette from her lips.

"Does the pope shit in the Vatican?" Homer said.

She rolled her eyes.

"How about that map, Homer?" William said.

"Here in a minute," the man said. "Just sit down and let Bethie fix you a plate."

"Beth," the woman said.

"Bethie," Homer said again, grinning. He squeezed the woman's bottom and she shooed him away with a rag.

He was drinking regularly from his bottle and William noticed his speech had gone a little lazy. Eyes taken for a bit of a swim.

"Sooner the better," William told him. "On that map."

There was a knock on the door.

Homer peered through the window.

"Shit," he said.

"What is it?" Beth asked.

"Nothing, honey, I just gotta talk to a few gentlemen about some business for a minute."

Homer opened the door and William could see three men over his shoulder and they looked at Homer and then at the rest of the house.

"How about we go into town to hash this all out?" Homer said. "I wouldn't want to bore my company."

"Homer," Beth said, but he shook his head at her.

"It's fine. I won't be gone long," he said, and then looked at William. "I'll draw you that map when I get back."

The brindle dog started for the door but Homer told him to stay and the dog did.

Beth sat at the kitchen table with the young people and smoked one cigarette after another and she looked at each of them in turn but never asked a question and so they just sat, the four of them, in a strange silence for nearly an hour until Ollie announced he was going to bed.

"There ain't but one bedroom," Beth said.

"That a problem for you?" Ollie asked, and the woman rolled her eyes.

"You can sleep in the barn," she said.

"Wouldn't be the first time," Ollie said, nodding at William. "Y'all coming?"

"I am," Lena said.

"I'm gonna wait for Homer," William told him.

He watched his friends leave the house and head across the backyard toward the barn. He leaned over in his chair and scratched the dog behind the ears while Beth scrubbed dishes.

"What was that about?" William asked.

"What was what about?" Beth said without turning around.

"Them boys didn't look too friendly. And Homer sure didn't seem happy to see them."

Beth shook her head.

"That would be Homer coming face-to-face with his worst enemy."

"Who?"

"Himself," she said. "He goes out on a drunk just about every other night and half the time he brings a stray home with him."

"Dogs?"

"Every now and then," she said. "Mostly people."

She flung her dishrag down and sighed.

"Last week it was some sort of priest or friar or some such. Let him stay here. Him and your daddy slept right yonder, on the floor in the den. Next morning the little bastard had stole two barrels of whiskey. The real problem being that them barrels was done and paid for. Promised like."

"To the men at the door?"

"To the men, or the men they work for," she said and lit another cigarette. "Everybody's on edge these days. What with the Volstead about to fall."

She shrugged and then tipped the ash of her cigarette onto one of the plates she'd just washed.

"You don't look much like your old man."

"I'm not like him," William told her.

She gave him a pitying smile.

"Every little boy is like his daddy," she said. "Especially when they try not to be."

The dog rose and went to the door and started to whine. Homer came in a minute later. The left side of his face was swollen and there were cuts on his left cheek and forehead.

Beth pursed her lips and nodded and tried not to tear up.

"I'm alright," he said, wincing as he pulled out a chair and sat. "Any catfish left?"

"I'll bring you some," she managed.

"Bring me a pen and paper too," Homer said, working his jaw to both sides. "I gotta draw Willie Boy a map."

The dog stood beside the chair and laid its head sideways in Homer's lap.

"I'll get it from you in the morning," William told him, and Homer nodded and patted the dog and smiled at the boy through bloody lips.

27

When William woke the following morning, Homer was already up and had fixed them all heavy plates of bacon and eggs. While they ate, Homer passed William a hand-drawn map.

"Here you go, as promised," Homer said.

William stopped chewing and stared at the lines of black ink.

"Half of this is just the river," the boy said.

"Yes, it is," Homer said, grinning. "Just you wait."

"You try wrestling a bear last night, Homer?" Ollie asked.

"Ben Lilly killed all the bears," Homer said. "I had myself what you might call a minor disagreement with some fellas."

"I'd hate to see a major one."

"It's all sorted now," Homer said. "Y'all hurry up and eat and let's go."

They loaded into the truck and he drove them to the Neches River and pulled off the road down a little dirt trail that turned quickly to rock and grass. They jostled around the truck bed until Homer brought the truck to an abrupt stop and they all lurched forward.

"Here she is," Homer said before they'd climbed down.

William came around from the back of the truck and looked to where Homer was pointing.

A sad, scraped-up flat-bottom was tied under a cypress and bobbing there in the shallow water.

"A boat?" the boy asked.

"My boat," Homer said. "And for today, your boat."

"Look at that motor," Ollie said, walking toward the water. "Is that an Evinrude?"

"Don't be ignorant, son," Homer scoffed. "That there's a Johnson Sea Horse."

"I don't know how to drive a boat, Homer," William told him.

Homer waved off the boy's concern.

"You'll get the hang of it. It's a helluva lot easier than learning to swim."

"I can drive it," the girl said. "I grew up near the river."

"Well, hell. There you go," Homer said. "Amelia Earhart of the Neches."

He smiled at her and William told himself her cheeks were red from the heat.

"What about Evadale?" he asked her.

"This'll get me closer faster," she said.

Homer put his hand on William's shoulder.

"Now look, you know how to gauge a mile?" he asked him.

"I can get pretty close."

"You're gonna go about twenty miles downriver. That'll take you to the Hardin County line. There's a big old sandbar on your right. Just pull the boat up onto that sandbar and leave it. I got a buddy down there who can bring it back. I'll let him know you're coming. Once you're on dry land, head west by southwest into the Thicket. You'll run into Black Creek. Follow it. They say she has a little cabin somewhere in the baygall."

Lena and Ollie pushed the boat into the water and climbed in and Homer kept his hand on William and wouldn't let him go.

"We all do things we ain't proud of," he told the boy, and William looked at him blankly. "Just keep that in mind, son."

William put one boot in the water and the other in the boat and the girl pulled the rope on the motor and it sputtered and started and Homer clapped his hands together from the shore as they awayed and then he turned from the water and asked forgiveness.

28

Lt. Thomas Didymus Carter

Our legislative defeat is weeks past, but the camp remains. It is, in my estimation, foolish. And yet, if the men are here, I must stay with them. The papers have taken to calling us the Bonus Army. I'm unsure if this is meant to be a mockery. I suppose time will tell.

Men make promises in the moment, to get what they want: "Just let me, just this once, and I will marry you. I will love you forever." "Just give me your vote, and I will put your interests above all others." "Go and fight this war for me, and I will give you the money you deserve—the money you are owed." And now the maiden has been blooded, and she has come to demand her prize. But our own government rejects us. They will not pay what was promised. "Patriotism . . . bought and paid for, is not patriotism." I hear Coolidge's words even now, eight years hence. And Hoover has proven himself to be no different. Another Republican. Another disappointment. Without our money, we have been thoroughly bedded and cannot even call ourselves whores.

29

The river was low and the girl kept the boat near the middle and navigated with expert precision around submerged logs and protruding islets and they were with the current and making good time.

The boys sat in the middle of the boat and William turned and looked at her and the false wind blew in her hair and she narrowed her eyes against it. Stern face. Steely and determined. She caught his stare and he looked away and Ollie said something to him but he didn't hear for the motor and the water and the wind.

William leaned over the edge of the boat and watched the river unzip before them. The bow of the boat peeled away the water and the miles and they passed in solitude for a long while and then there were fishermen on the banks and then other boats. Men running trotlines. Men in long waders going forth to pull up nets and traps. Hard-faced women washing baskets of clothes in the roiling water.

The winter had been wet enough to bloat the bottomlands and even as the river waned in the summer, life sprang up around it. All along the muddy banks grew woolly rose mallows and rose pogonias. Pale pitcher plants and great orchid varietals—lady's slipper, three birds, crested coral-root. Alligators, half-submerged, marbled Jurassic eyes peering out from amid floating heart lilies and swollen bladderwort. Strange, slender shorebirds stilted about the sedge and rush of this riverine country.

The locals gave them long, concerned looks as they passed. No one waved or nodded or regarded them as anything other than interlopers.

The river narrowed and there were six naked children perched belly deep in the brown water and their mother standing watch on the bank folded her arms and eyed the boat as it passed. Lena slowed the flat-bottom so as to not create a wake and the woman stared with unblinking eyes and further up the bank a man squatted and drank from a jug held in the crook of his elbow.

"Some friendly folks down this way," Ollie said. "You think they got any idea there's a depression on?"

"Who would know to tell them?" William asked.

"We're natural goddamn pirates, ain't we?" Ollie hollered, and William gave him a nod.

Hours to come, they reached a long sandbar and Lena pointed and the boys nodded and she guided the boat toward it. It was just before sunset when she ran the nose ashore and raised the motor out of the water and locked it. The three of them pulled the boat onto the bank and looked around but saw no trail leading away from the river.

Ollie conferred with the map.

"You think we pulled off too soon?" he asked.

"Might have," William said. "But this is a big-ass sandbar on the west bank. The miles seemed right."

Lena was crouched near the boat, running her hand along the siding.

"What is it?" William asked her.

"Did this boat seem heavy to y'all," she asked. "I thought we were sitting low out on the water, and just now when we pulled it up on the bank . . ."

"I don't know how heavy a boat's supposed to be," William said. "Do you think we've been twenty miles?"

"I'd say we have. But we might could put it back in the water and run a little further downriver," Lena said. "There ain't a lot of daylight left though."

"What's the gas situation on this thing?" Ollie asked.

"I didn't even think to look," William told him. "I guess let's poke around some and see if we can't find the trail Homer marked. Could be a little growed up since last time he was down here."

They each went a different way and each fought through greenbrier branches and wild-growing alder and twice William found himself in poison ivy. The sun had not yet set in its entirety but there was little light in thick woods and soon they called to one another from their various positions that they should return to the boat. William tried to take a different route back to the river but it was no less difficult and when he pushed through the river cane and stumbled out onto the short beach, Ollie and Lena were already there. So was a second boat.

There were two men with shotguns facing Ollie and Lena and a third man who was rolling up his sack of tobacco having just inserted a wad into his cheek.

"This'un with you?" the man asked.

"He is now," Ollie said.

"C'mon, you," the man said and motioned to William.

He was tan and covered in dirt and sweat and his shirt once had buttons but they were gone and the sleeves torn away so that he wore it like an open vest. The lower legs of his denim trousers had also been cut away and he was barefoot even in such terrain.

William joined the others.

"Homer Renfro's boat," the man said and raised his eyebrows as if it were a question. His eyes were sapphire against his tan face and he looked directly at William and waited for a response.

"Yessir, it's Homer's," the boy said. "He let us borrow it."

"Bar it?" the man asked, doubtful. "Bar for what? Lil' ole joy ride?"

The man giggled at his own words and flashed a near toothless grin at his companions and they laughed much in the same manner.

"We're looking for my father," William said. "Thomas Carter. There's supposed to be an old woman who lives off in the woods down here somewhere. Homer said soldiers went there sometimes and she—this woman—helps them. Said maybe my father was there."

The three men looked at one another and laughed again.

"Soldier?" the tobacco man asked. "Ain't no soldiers down here. Ain't no woman. Watchyou see?"

He spit.

"This *our* river, here," the man said, nodding toward the water as if it were evidence of his claim. "Homer done been told don't to come down here. Him and John Jay both. But here you are."

"Yeah, but Homer's not with us."

"Don't matter. You work for him."

"We don't work for nobody," Ollie interjected.

"Hush now, boy, 'fore Les puts one in you. Watch him, Les."

"I'm watching."

"Listen here. You work for Homer. That's Homer's boat."

The man walked over to the boat and made a full circle around it. He stepped over the side and stood in the middle of the boat, inspecting it. He spit tobacco juice in the hull.

"Watch here," he said, and the man bent down and with great force jerked up on the middle seat and it came completely off from the boat and there was a hollow space beneath it.

The man grinned and reached down and came up with two milk-crates full of corked whiskey bottles.

"Goddamnit, Homer," William said.

"You say you ain't work for him," the man said, "but you running his whiskey. How come that is?"

"We didn't know," William said.

"Ain't know?" the man squawked and turned to his partners and they were already laughing.

Ollie was cursing Homer under his breath and William looked past him to where Lena stood and her right hand was halfway behind her back moving slowly under her shirt toward the notched handle of her stolen pistol.

In his head he screamed no but she was already wrapping her fingers around it to draw.

A motor revved and all turned to the water, where an old canoe that had been outfitted with an Evinrude was now speeding toward the sandbar with its nose lifted five feet out of the water.

The canoe hit the bank and went airborne. It landed with a sharp crack in between the two parties and flung water and sand and broken wood into the air as it came skidding to a stop.

There was no time to process the event. The two men inside the canoe raised Thompson submachines and in a few short bursts of sound the other men were dead in the sand.

"Stay put," one of the gunmen said to the kids without ever looking at them.

They did as they were told. Or perhaps they were too stunned to move. It all happened so quickly and there was a strange anticlimactic nature to the way the two men dragged their fallen foes into the river and let the bodies go.

"John Jay," one of the men said, walking back up the bank and holding his bloody hand out.

"William," William said but didn't shake the man's hand.

"Thanks for the help, William. I been wanting to shoot Leroy Cryer for a year and a half. But he hides, you know. All them Cryer boys hide. Slipping around in the Thicket, thinking they have the only say in Hardin County. But you brung him out in the open. I'm indebted to you."

William looked at the crates of whiskey and the bloody sand.

"Did Homer know?" the boy asked. "Did he know this would happen?"

"Well sure," John Jay said. "If he'd tried to come down here hisself, they would have shot him before he ever got to the bank. Cowards like they are. But he figured they might not be so quick to kill a bunch of kids. He didn't tell y'all any of this?"

"No."

The boy's hands were clenched into fists.

"Jesus Christ," the man laughed. "Well. Homer does things his way, I guess."

William was near to shaking with anger.

"Canoe's a little busted up," John Jay told his companion. "Let's get that motor off from there and mount it up on Cryer's boat. I'll take Homer's. You take Cryer's."

"You don't think he'll mind?" the other man asked, and the two of them were laughing and John Jay moved to pick up a crate and William stepped in front of him.

John Jay scoffed.

"What are you doing, boy?"

"We almost died for this," William said. "For a crate of whiskey. I'd say that makes it ours."

"William," Lena said. "Don't be stupid."

"What are you gonna do with a shipment of Frog's Finest, boy?" John Jay asked him.

"What are *you* gonna do with it?" William said.

"Sell most. Drink some."

"What do you sell it for?"

"What?"

"How much money for a bottle?"

"Seven dollars."

"William, c'mon bud," Ollie said, "let's just go."

"There's what, twenty bottles?"

"Eighteen," John Jay said crossing his arms.

"And what do you pay Homer?"

"Seventy-five if he brings it down here. Fifty if I have to go up north to get it."

William did the math in his head.

"You'll make fifty dollars," he said. "If you sell every bottle."

"Fifty-one," John Jay told him. "And considering how much Homer owes my boss, he's lucky that's all we take."

William looked at the man. Looked for regret or pain or even uncertainty but there was none. The boy saw nothing. And it was the nothingness that defeated him. His shoulders fell.

He moved out from in front of the crate and walked across the sand and sat and watched them wrestle with switching out the motors. For fifty dollars, three men were dead and the river had not stopped running.

Ollie came and sat next to him.

"You alright?"

William's eyes watered and stung and he wiped at them with dirty hands.

"He don't care anything about me," William said, and Ollie wasn't sure if he meant John Jay or Homer or someone else entirely.

"You think Homer was lying about everything?" Lena asked. "Black Creek, the woman. All that."

The blood caked the sand together where the men had fallen.

"Homer's a gold-plated son of a bitch," Ollie said. "I wouldn't put nothing past him. Could be that William's daddy is anywhere in the country right now. Could be that he's headed back to Shawnee Prairie as we speak."

Ollie looked at the other boy.

"For what it's worth," he said. "I think that's what we ought to do. Go back home."

William knew what truth was waiting there. Home. But he wasn't sure if he could yet face it.

"There's a Black Creek," John Jay called, looking back as he pushed the boat into the water. "It's southwest of here. Not far. Can't speak to any old woman."

William stood. He grabbed the map from Ollie and looked at it.

"How did you know to be here?" he asked, walking down the short beach toward John Jay.

"My cousin come and told me early this morning," John Jay said. "Homer had phoned him down at the sheriff's office."

"Your cousin's the sheriff?" Ollie said.

"Deputy sheriff."

"Did Homer, or your cousin—did anybody say anything about Thomas Carter," William asked, "or about what we're doing out here?"

"Said you were hunting your old man," John Jay told him. "Didn't say anything more than that."

John Jay stood erect and then put his palms on his lower back and leaned back from the waist.

"But if he's out there," he said, motioning to the vast expanse of dense forest, "you ain't gonna find him. Not if he don't want to be found. Y'all ought to just come on with us. We'll drop you in Buna."

"That's east of here," William said.

"Yeah. Well. East is where we're headed."

William looked at Ollie and he could see the boy was waiting on an answer.

"I'll find him," William said, defiant. "If he's out there, I'll find him."

Ollie's eyes dropped and John Jay shook his head.

"I guess some people don't want to see the truth, even when it's right in front of them."

"Maybe it wouldn't be the worst thing to go with them," Ollie said.

"Yeah?" William asked. "Why don't you go right ahead. I'll find him myself."

William was shaking and he couldn't tell if it was the gunplay or his anger and he grabbed his satchel and walked past Lena and Ollie and into the dense forest.

The other two looked once more to John Jay and the other man and then followed William away from the river.

They went a while without speaking and in the distance they heard the boat motors start up and then fade away and William stopped in front of a dogwood tree and stood there before it like some woeful petitioner.

It grew in the shade of larger trees. Gray-black bark like ash. Heavy wood and close-grained, with the shallowest of fissures spidering through.

He tried to see a larger map in his mind. Judge how far he was from home—how far he was from anything. But the answers, like the darkening forest floor, were hidden from him—from the light.

He could feel the frustration rising through him like a thing alive and growing and malignant. Like something he would have to purge if he were to survive. Like the rotten bolls of cotton. The men on stage and the helpless ape. Like the wars past and present and every war yet to come. Like all violence, born from hurt and anger and sadness. Men born shapeless into the dark of the world and no father to guide them. Long is the night. Lonely is the child.

He took out his knife and flipped it open and the others just watched him.

He grunted and stabbed the bark. The blade stuck and he wrenched it free and gritted his teeth and stabbed again and there were tears in his eyes and he hated Homer and he hated his father and he thought of his mother dying and in that moment he hated her too.

Ollie moved toward him but Lena pulled the boy back.

Thirty-nine times William Carter drove the blade into the tree and when he yanked it free after the final blow he slumped down onto the ground and stayed there weeping until the other two pulled him up by his underarms. In time he apologized and they waved him off as if his actions were normal and the boy wiped his eyes and blew his nose and looked around.

"I don't know," he said, though neither of them had asked any question.

"Lena," Ollie said, not unkind, "if you're looking to get downriver toward Evadale, you ought to see if that canoe back at the sandbar will float."

"You still trying to get rid of me?" she asked, but he could hear in her voice she didn't mean it.

"I just got a feeling things are fixing to get real uncomfortable."

Lena laughed, and it occurred to both boys they had never heard her laugh before.

"As opposed to the lap of luxury we've been living in," she said.

"He's right," William said, slowly coming back to himself. "It's about to get worse."

"Either way, let's sleep here tonight," the girl said. "See what worse looks like in the morning. It's fixing to get dark before it gets anything else."

She was right. The swift abdication of the sun, and in its wake the pink and purple hues of the eventide. The trees black against the falling light. They made a haphazard camp beneath a rock overhang, using broken branches to whack at the shrubs and tall grass in hopes of ridding the place of snakes.

They made no fire.

They slept.

30

Lt. Thomas Didymus Carter

It came to violence, as now I must believe all things do. There have been spats here throughout the week. Yelling and pushing. Fisticuffs. Yesterday there was gunfire. The police shot two men. Both died. Before we could even hold their memorial, General McArthur himself rode us down with cavalry and tanks. Many of the men here brought their families. Women and children running scared. Their tents, and all the possessions left behind, were burned by the very government sworn to serve them. It was not unlike the visages of France. Towns afire. Hopes dashed.

My own thoughts were hauntingly familiar. I helped rally these men to be here. I am responsible for them. And again I have let them down. Their danger is my failing. The loss of life adds yet another link to my chains.

I stayed longer yet on a hill just beyond the swamp and saw there the rising flames and pillars of black smoke, and beyond the fire stood our nation's capital. I could see the flag through the smoke.

The war is over. The war has just begun.

III

THE THICKET

31

They slept past the sunrise, exhausted as they were. The birds were in full song by the time Ollie shook William awake. They gathered their things and wandered a little ways in the woods before coming to the creek. It was mostly dried out and there were drifts of black sand gathered up in the bed.

"I guess this is it," William said, and then no one spoke for a while and William thought about the hanging man on the old woman's card. About the look on his face.

"We'll do both," he said, and they looked at him. "We'll go home and we'll try to see about this miracle worker on the way."

He drew two circles in the dirt.

"This is us. This is Silsbee. The creek runs southwest through the Thicket. Silsbee's southwest too, and it's liable to be the closest train station anywhere out here. So that's where we'll go. And if what we're looking for falls into our lap before we get there, all the better. Lena, you're welcome to come with us and take the Silsbee line to Evadale. But I wouldn't blame you for sticking to the river."

"I believe I've had enough adventure on the high seas. I'll go with you as far as Silsbee."

"Well," William said. "Alright then."

The Thicket was a poor place to pass through, no matter the reason. The air itself was different. Dense, like the trees and underbrush that surrounded them. Thousands of acres of unchecked growth, cut off from the world without.

There were hunters and trappers in the arid sandylands and those who worked the river for fish and game. In the bottoms there were whiskey makers and rice farmers, societyless drunks and backwoods prostitutes who would barter for their trade.

There were those who were born, lived, and died, without ever leaving the Thicket. Without the knowledge of wars, depression, or who'd been elected president. A clannish people. Families that had warred with one another from the time of the last Indian. No common enemy, but still slaves to their own violent nature.

A pregnant daughter, a lying son from across the creek. A feud that might last three generations. Might last longer. Stolen squirrel meat or a drunken insult, and bodies begin to turn up downriver. Some sheriff in Jefferson County looking north and wondering what ceaseless battles must be raging.

There were those who were darker still. Self-described healers who turned to the black brackish water to mix their potions and spells. Gypsies who carried cards that could tell of a man's life. Of his death. Shadowed figures who haunted the Thicket, just out of sight. A man standing amid the stalks of trees, watching, and when you look back, he's gone.

In such a place the light was little and less. The world turned gray and wasted.

They felt near to starving by early afternoon, having not eaten the day prior. The boys were contemplating which berries were poisonous and which could be consumed when Lena shot a rabbit with her pistol.

They were walking along the slope of a hammock just beyond the river and William felt her beside him and then felt her stop and before he could turn to see what happened she fired the gun and William flinched and Ollie dropped to the ground.

Neither one of them said anything. They watched her walk a dozen yards into the brush and when she returned she was carrying a dead swamp rabbit by its hind legs. She asked William for his pocketknife and he obliged and she took it and knelt and the body slid onto the ground like liquid, gray and brown fur clinging to limp muscle, and she started to gut it and the boys stared at her, open mouthed.

"Y'all just gonna stand there or can you get a fire going?" she asked.

"My goodness, that's a canecutter if I ever saw one," Ollie said. "I knew bringing you along was a good idea. I've never contended otherwise."

They gathered wood and tried the matches but they would not light.

"These matches are wetter than an otter's pocket," Ollie complained.

Lena went into the brush and came back with a palmetto chord and piece of wood and threw both down by the rabbit.

"Go get me some dead grass."

"Do what?"

"Go run your hands through some bluestem or whatever you see first. Just spread your fingers like you're coming your hair. That'll bring up all the dead stalks."

"Is she fixing to try hand-drilling this thing?" Ollie asked.

"Just do what she says," William told him.

The two of them went out in search of dead grass and other kindling and when they returned Lena had carved a hole in the wood and inserted the palmetto chord and she took their offerings and laid the dried grass near the friction point and began to spin the chord between the palms of her hand.

"Son," Ollie said. "We've done gone and teamed up with a genuine frontiersman."

"Frontierswoman."

"Sure enough."

"Y'all quit gawking and get a bed ready."

They sprung into action, assembling more grass and dried leaves and a few small sticks nearby. Lena soon had a spark and an ember and the kindling was smoking then burning and then producing a few small flames.

"Careful now," she said as they transferred the fire to the bed.

She blew softly on the flame and it quivered and diminished and then came back stronger and soon there was a proper fire and William looked at Ollie and Ollie shook his head.

Lena stood and wiped her hands on her trousers.

"Let's cook this coney," she said.

William was impressed by her skills and the humility with which she deployed them but there was a wildness about her that infatuated the boy. There was a resolve in the way she went about things that signaled to the world that it would not soon break her. William himself felt near to a breaking point almost every day. And yet here she was with circumstances no kinder than his own but she had taken agency over the outcome. She had acted rather than merely reacted. He admired her. Selfishly, he liked having her with them, as if perhaps he might siphon off some of her courage and keep it for his own.

He knew it was also possible he only wanted to appear courageous in front of the girl—that perhaps his newfound valor was merely some version of testosterone-fueled strutting.

Either way, the boy thought, real or imagined, she makes me brave.

They ate the rabbit and Ollie talked about a radio preacher who said it was the end times.

"I ain't one for doom and gloom, but the fella was pretty dang compelling."

"Compelling?" Lena said.

"It means he made a good argument for it," Ollie said.

"I know what it means. I'm just surprised *you* do."

"William don't believe in hell," Ollie announced.

"So?" the girl questioned.

"So nothing, I don't guess."

"Then why waste time talking about it?"

"What do you believe?" William asked her, but the girl just shook her head and kicked dirt on the fire to put it out.

"Let's go if we're going," she told them.

32

Minutes in the Thicket felt like hours. Hours like lifetimes.

They passed along thin uplifts, telluric causeways that wound through dry floodplains and low-lying marshlands where roosted flocks of mallards with oil slick feathers and heads wet with green. Bluebirds from the east, early in their migrating, and already contending with the native horned larks and crowned sparrows over resources.

The creek bed was deep, near ten feet in some places, but the water itself was scarce. They followed along beside it as best they could, cutting further into the woods when the way became too thick or otherwise unpassable. They followed it southwest and William and Lena shared a handful of glances at one another as Ollie presented his thoughts and theories on the world at large.

"The thing about Kathy is that she acts like she don't like me but then she gives me that little smile," he told them. "Y'all know what I'm talking about. That little ole smile that might as well be a wink. Might as well be her saying, 'Oliver Leek, me and you are fixing to talk business.'"

"Talk business?" Lena asked.

"What do you call it?"

"I don't call it that," she said. "What about you, William? You got a Kathy waiting on you?"

The boy shook his head.

"Nope."

"He ain't that type," Ollie said.

"What type?"

"The talking-to-girls type."

"I talk to girls," William said. "Just this past week I talked to—"

Ollie raised his hand.

Just through the brush was a cookfire where huddled two men and their dogs and the dogs rose up and growled and the men were skinning out an ocelot and they stopped their work and watched the young people but didn't speak.

"Keep moving," William said, and they did but it was different now. More unsettled. As if the men had broken some spell. They were more aware of themselves, the sound of their voices and the sound of their passing.

For hours they saw no one else, until in the near evening they passed two sad cabins built one beside the other and not but a few feet between the two.

On the porch of one of the cabins was a gaggle of children ranging from what looked to be one to fourteen and they all stood or sat shoeless and held similar blank stares on their faces. There was a shared strangeness about them that made William uneasy.

"What is this, an orphanage?" Ollie asked, and the oldest of the children, a boy, spit off the porch.

"These your brothers and sisters?" Lena asked, and the boy looked at her and then looked quickly away as he answered.

"Yes'm," he said.

A second boy pushed forward and crossed his arms. William thought him no more than ten years.

"You with the Census?" the boy asked.

"No," William said. "We're just with ourselves."

"Y'all better get on 'fore Daddy Farris wakes up."

Some of the other children looked toward the adjacent cabin as if perhaps the mere mention of the man might bring him forth.

"He don't like folks walking by?" Ollie asked.

"He don't like nothing," the first boy told them.

"Let's go," William said.

"Y'all wanna take Jonah?" the second boy asked.

"C'mon," William said again.

"Which one is Jonah?" Ollie asked.

"The baby," the boy said and pointed to a blond child who sat naked and expressionless with his back against the cabin door.

"We ain't in the market for a baby right this minute," Ollie said. "And I don't imagine your momma would appreciate it none either."

"My momma ain't got nothing to do with this."

The oldest of the girls looked away from them and walked to the other end of the porch.

"Y'all got any whiskey?" the boy asked, his arms still crossed.

"How old are you, kid?" Lena said.

"Daddy Farris says we ought to always ask. About whiskey and about Jonah."

"Daddy Farris sounds like a surefire bastard," Lena said, gripping her pistol. "Why don't you go get him for us."

A few of the children gasped.

"Let's go," William said and this time pulled Lena away from the porch.

"They're better off without him," Lena said through gritted teeth.

"No," William told her. "They're not. Ollie, c'mon."

But Ollie had gone around the side of the porch and was standing below the girl. She was crying quietly as he watched her.

"Darlin'," he said, soft. "Do you need help?"

She sniffled and shook her head and turned from him and looked at the baby who had begun to grunt and babble with his arms up in the air.

Ollie reached up and took the girl's hand and she looked down, startled, but didn't pull away.

"Is that—" he started, but there was a loud groan from the other cabin and the children cowered and the girl jerked away her hand.

"Take me," the girl said, not much more than a whisper.

"What?" Ollie asked.

"Take me with you."

"The baby?" Ollie motioned.

"I don't care nothing about it," she said. "Just take me with you."

"Ollie," William said again.

"Please." And now the girl was pleading. "Take me with you."

She was on her knees.

"Don't leave me," she said. "You're Ollie? Please don't leave me, Ollie. I'll do anything you want. I'll do anything for you, Ollie. Don't leave me here."

The baby had begun to cry and Ollie looked past the begging girl to where the baby sat in his own piss.

"Don't worry about it," the girl shook her head, desperate. "It's not even mine. I don't even know anything about it."

She, too, began to cry.

Ollie was all but frozen. He looked from the girl to the baby and back again. He felt a hand on his shoulder and flinched.

"Leave it, bud," William said. "We gotta get."

Ollie frowned but followed the others and he kept looking back as they went. At some point the girl stopped crying and picked up the baby to comfort him and Ollie thought he heard the door to the second cabin finally open but he couldn't see and soon the trees had swallowed them up.

They trudged on through the dusk and for the rest of the evening Ollie did not say a word.

The dying sun left hanging in the trees like a fresh kill until at last it disappeared entirely and the sky thereafter went from pink to purple to dark of night.

A half mile into the pitch black, fighting briars and blackberries, they entangled themselves in a thick patch of Jackson vine. They cussed and grunted and tried to work free, the thorns ripping at their clothes and at their skin.

"We keep on like this, we're liable to get snakebit or worse," Lena said.

"Like a goddamn knife fight," Ollie mumbled, loosing his arm from the vine.

William felt their frustration and it nearly matched his own.

"Let's just stop," he said. "It's been a long day."

They worked out of the brush and found a space just wide enough for the three of them to lay side by side with their supplies at their feet.

They were close together and could hear one another's stomachs grumbling and could hear every breath, and late into the night when Ollie thought the others were asleep, they could hear him crying softly to himself.

33

Lt. Thomas Didymus Carter

I said things—a great many things—to Roger last night that I believe now I will never be able to remedy. I might have had such an opportunity as he stood to leave. He looked at me then, and I saw in his face that he wanted me to take it all back, but I did not. I denied him. I watched him leave, out from the tavern, and when I went to the station this morning, his train was already gone. He is headed back to Texas, and I linger here in my own disgust. My thoughts turning more and more toward melancholia. I am ashamed. The physical implications of my falling to drink last night are well worn this morning. Deservedly so.

In my overindulgence, I broke a promise to myself made long ago to not behave as mine own father. And as I scold myself, I feel his judgment from beyond the grave.

I believe boys would grow up mostly happy if not for their fathers.

Mine was raised in Walker County, working alongside my grandfather as a tenant farmer. The corn and cotton grew so close to their house there was little room for a footpath, let alone a garden. But the simple and pious life of a farmer did not suit him. Nor did the coldness with which my grandfather regarded him. My father's very existence was a reminder of my grandmother's death. My grandfather never said it plainly—that thing they both knew—but they knew it all the same, and it would always be between them.

I think the old man regretted it in the end. But by then it was too late. My father was already gone and chasing whatever it was he felt would make him whole.

He worked steamboats up and down the Mississippi and later the Sabine River. He was well into his twenties before he met and married my mother. She was the disgraced daughter of a disgraced politician—both of them were out to set the world afire. Having children did little to slow them down. I remember, growing up in Houston, not seeing my parents for days at a time. My brother became a surrogate father to my sister and me.

I learned later about the gambling. About how my parents had accumulated tremendous fortune and unimaginable debt, living for the most part by the turn of a card.

"Bad luck," my father would say when there was no money.

The worst of their luck, however, came not at the pharaoh table but in the San Jacinto River, where my brother drowned under circumstances never known to anyone beyond that he had indeed drowned—his body washing ashore a half mile downstream from where he'd been fishing.

"Bad luck," my father said, and then he never spoke of it again.

I vowed to never be like him—my father—and yet the first thing I did when I came of age was to rebel against him, just as he had done with his father.

I moved back to Walker County, where my grandfather still lived but was ailing. It was there I fell in love with the land. With the fairness of it. You get what you put in—or so I thought at the time. It was freeing to me to be unburdened from the traffic and the trappings of the urban world. And now I can't help but wonder whether, had I been raised on a farm, I would have yearned instead for the energy and vitality of the city. Is, perhaps, the most common trait among men simply our tendency to desire that which we do not already possess? Even my faith was likely a product of rebellion. My father's notion of luck, good or bad, was something I could not abide. I craved a certain stability. A guiding hand. And so it was that in those few short weeks with my grandfather before his passing, I came to know the power of belief. I filled myself with it, sealing every crack created in my youth. I made myself strong. Worthy.

But long had the pressure been mounting, and last night, with Roger, the dam finally broke.

34

The following morning William woke before the stars were down and he thought his mother was asleep beside him but it was the girl. Ollie was gone.

He sat up and grabbed his boots and turned them upside down, one and then the other, and shook them and then slipped them on and stood. He looked down at the girl where she slept and then went to look for Ollie.

He found him by the creek, sitting on a moss-topped log with one leg over the other.

"You thinking of crossing over?" William asked.

Ollie didn't look up.

"Ain't nothing to cross," he said.

"It'll rain," William told him. "It'll fill back up. This drought will end or it'll be the first one that never did."

"That baby belonged to that little girl," Ollie said.

"I know it."

"You think it was her daddy?"

"Who knows."

A red fox stood watching them on the far bank, head cocked, one paw raised off the ground. Its eyes glowed in the dark, as if there was some light within it that would not be extinguished. Could not be.

"Somebody," Ollie said. "Somebody knows."

"Yeah."

The fox went on and turned its head back once more and then was gone forever.

"What are we doing here?" Ollie asked, at last looking up at William. "Just what in the hell are we doing?"

"I'm sorry, Bud," William told him. "I shouldn't have made you come."

Ollie shook his head.

"No, not you and me. Not this. I mean all of us. I mean every beating heart from here to China. What are we doing that something like that can just happen?" he asked.

Ollie pitched a clump of dirt toward the creek. The boys heard a thud somewhere in the dark.

"I've seen all kinds of sorrow," Ollie said. "Lived with it my whole life. Hell, my family's turned a profit on it. And death, well, death is one thing. It's coming for all of us whether we're worried about it or not. There's an equality there, you know? But seeing that girl and seeing—and them out here in the wilderness like this, out here where the world really is—I don't know, it just did something, I think."

"Did what?" William asked, and he looked at the boy next to him with his small frame and his knees drawn up to his chest.

"I can't really say." Ollie shook his head again. "But I'll tell you one thing."

"What?"

"You didn't *make* me do anything."

There were tears in his eyes when he spoke and in his voice.

"You hear me?" he asked. "When we were little I called you my best friend and I damn well meant it. But I've give it some thought these past few days, and I don't figure there's many ways this can end with you staying in Shawnee Prairie. Whether it's Houston or somewhere else, I don't imagine things are gonna stay the same."

William opened his mouth to argue but Ollie kept going.

"I've done and made my peace with that," he said. "And I'll make it all over again when the time comes, but you ain't rid of me yet, you know?"

William nodded. He felt the flush on his face.

"Not today," Ollie said. "Not when you still need me to keep you from doing something dumber than you've already done. Now, do you know it?"

"I know it," William said, and he looked away, something like embarrassed.

They both took a breath.

"Shit," Ollie said, wiping at his eyes. "Lena up?"

"Not yet. I was fixin' to wake her."

"Well. Let's give her a little longer," Ollie said. "It's almost nice this morning, without the sun."

William knelt in front of Ollie and looked at him and his pale face there in the dark.

"You alright?" William asked.

"I'm alright."

"Yeah?"

"I'm alright," Ollie insisted. "I just gotta take a minute to feel sorry for everybody that's ever lived."

William left him there and backtracked to the blackberry vines and crouched and began to pick what few ripe berries he could find. He had never seen his friend in this light and it unnerved him. Like something that didn't belong. A house beneath a lake. He had so often relied on Ollie's optimism. Perhaps even taken it for granted, he thought. Something else occurred to him. *It's my fault.*

Ollie, and now too the girl, were here because of him. His life had somehow usurped their own, and yet he had been thinking only of himself. Another unnerving revelation.

He had worked the land his entire life and he understood the give-and-take of nature and the wildness of weather and the unpredictability of a spooked horse and the swiftness of a deer, and in all these things—and in everything, he believed—there was evidence of a certain magic. An ineffable perception, or perhaps awareness, that something tangible but altogether unexplained was taking place around him at any moment. At all moments. The unmistakable hum of the earth what came alive to him, purring there just beyond his sight—beyond some veil he could not decipher but nonetheless could feel. And in such a feeling he sensed it may be readying to open—to tear itself apart and expose the very secret of existence that the boy knew must be hiding within.

For had God not peeled back the sky so that the Malakim might send messages to men?

You spoke to others. Speak to me. Tell me what I'm supposed to do.

As he squatted and gathered the berries, the boy searched for such a happening. Such a feeling. It was not there. The forest was made of trees and the dirt made of dirt and he was alone.

35

The girl was awake when he returned and Ollie was there and they ate the berries and moved on. The going was slow. They hunched and contorted to get through the undergrowth crowding the forest floor. The girl moved athletic, almost creature-like through the woods. As she twisted and stretched, her cotton shirt rose up from her waist and exposed the softness of her stomach and lower back and William watched her and told himself not to.

He and Helen Harper had kissed one another on the lips in fourth grade and then never talked about it again. But he had, for several years, held that quick kiss as a testament to his not being behind in the ways of romance. Now he was less certain. Even with all the troubles that surrounded him, the boy still felt a nervousness when Lena looked at him. He wished he could ask Helen if she'd liked the kiss.

In time they came to a semi-actualized trail. Too wide to be a game path but too small and overgrown to have been cut in the past few years. The trail stuck close to the creek and they followed it southwest and they could feel the land beneath them softening.

As they ventured further the red clay lessened and much of the ground turned to white quartz sand and the underbrush sprang up with

Gulf Coast yucca and eastern prickly pear. The stinging hairs of bull nettle harassed them as the trail grew still more narrow and the brush thickened and the earth sloped toward the sea.

Here the creek held water and there were pools of water standing in depressions and near great cypress roots that grew in and out of the ground like a swarm of eels.

Even the birds seemed to transform. Great blue herons, their slender alien legs stalking about in pools of shallow water. Osprey gliding in the thermals and calling out to one another in short shrill bursts.

Unchanged was the heat. The sultry air. Their bones ached from days of walking. It was nearing noon when Ollie stopped and looked back the way they'd come and then up ahead in the direction they were headed. It was much the same.

"We hadn't seen the first footprint or piece of trash or any other sign of life out here," he said. "If I ever see Homer Renfro again I'm gonna coldcock the bastard right between his eyes."

The others were too hot and hungry to do anything but nod.

"Any more of them blackberries?" Ollie asked, and William shook his head.

They went on for a while without talking and the woods were still and quiet so that when they heard the gunshot it echoed from every direction.

William's first thought was of the two men who'd chased him through the forest and he felt the same cold discomfort run the length of his spine.

The seconds drew out and no one moved and then the screaming started.

Piercing. Shrill. Human.

"That's somebody hollering," Ollie said.

They stayed put.

"We gotta help, don't we?" Ollie asked, and William did not know the answer.

Finally Lena nodded and took off down the trail and the boys followed her.

There was a boy staggering about, just off the path, and he was screaming and stumbling into vines and holding his hands over his face.

"Who's that?" he said, turning his whole body but keeping his hands up like some sort of shield. "Is that somebody?"

"What happened?" Lena asked.

"I'm blind," the boy moaned. "Oh god, I'm blind."

"Is somebody after you?" Ollie asked.

William knelt on the ground near the trail. There was a silver canister laying on its side near a divot where it had been buried. He reached to pick it up.

"Don't touch it," Lena hollered and yanked him backward by the collar. "It's a coyote-getter."

The wounded boy had slumped down with his back against a tree and was crying.

"Stupid bastard," he said, and they weren't sure if he was talking to himself or them or someone else altogether.

"It's a trap for coyotes and bobcats and the like," Lena said. "You smell that?"

"Smells like almonds," Ollie said.

"It's cyanide," she told him. "That's what they fill it with."

"Camden Raines," the boy was mumbling. "Kill that sumbitch."

"Can you breathe alright?" the girl asked.

"Kill his whole goddamn family."

"Hey," Lena tried again. "Can you breathe?"

"Yes, I'm breathing," the boy snapped. "The bastard shot me in the face, not the lungs."

"Shot you?" William asked.

Lena frowned.

"I'm gonna move your hands," she told him, gentle.

She reached out and the boy flinched but she took his arms and guided them away from his face.

His right eye and a good deal of his face was swollen and already bruising. There was some blood as well.

She studied him. Touched him. He recoiled.

She walked over and looked at the ground where the trap had been.

"I've seen this," she said. "They use a .38 cartridge to hold the cyanide and then prime the whole thing like a gun. He must have stepped on it and it went off."

"Shot me in the goddamn face."

"Quit worrying about your face," Lena told him. "You ain't blind. It hit your cheek, not your eye. But you need to get somewhere quick and get washed. If that poison ain't bothering you now, it's sure fixing to."

They led the boy stomping and staggering to the creek and helped him kneel there before the water like a supplicant come to beg forgiveness.

"Wash your face as best you can," Lena instructed, and the boy leaned and splashed water onto his injured face and winced and cussed and tried to stand but Lena put her hands on his shoulders and forced him back down.

"More," she said. "That was enough poison to kill a coyote. You gotta make sure it ain't on you. Get your arms and your neck too."

"Get your own neck," the boy complained, but he did as he was told and then stood and ran his wet hair through his hands and looked at the three of them and frowned.

"Who the hell are y'all?"

"William Carter," William said. "Ollie Leek. Lena . . ."

"Forester," the girl said.

"Lena Forester," William repeated, more for his own benefit than that of the boy.

"Paul Fuller."

"You gonna make it, Paul?"

"I'm alright," he said, embarrassed. "My cousin's dog tripped one of them getters when they were out looking for whitetail last hunting season. Said it made him shit everywhere but that was about it."

"The dog?"

"What? No. My cousin. The dog died."

"Oh."

"Anyhow. I've done and told Camden Raines if he puts one more of them bastards on this side of the creek, I'd kill him."

"So what are you gonna do now?" Ollie asked.

Paul looked at him confused.

"I'm gonna kill him. Like I said," Paul told him. "I always know'd I'd have to one day, on account of him murdering my brother."

"My god. He murdered your brother?"

"Well, my brother Matthew had shot his daddy. But his daddy had shot at Matthew thinking it was my other brother, Pete. Pete had run off with Mr. Raines's daughter about a week before. So Matthew shot back and killed Mr. Raines and then Pete brought the girl back for her daddy's funeral and Camden Raines shot and killed Pete thinking it was Matthew. They was twins."

"We figured," Lena said.

"Matthew lit out after that, not wanting to get anymore caught up in the mess than he already was. I don't know what happened to the girl. Rumor was that she was swollen up with Pete's baby and Camden put her out before he'd have anything to do with a Fuller under his roof. But now it's just me and Camden and his brother James Jr. down here and they keep setting traps on my side of the creek. Trying to provock me."

"Provoke," Lena said.

"Huh?"

"He's trying to provoke you."

"Yeah," the boy nodded confidently, "I believe he is. And once I purge whatever of this cyanide is in me, I'm gonna go oblige him."

"If you kill Camden, won't James Jr. try to kill *you*?" Ollie asked.

"He can damn well try," Paul said. "Now y'all come on to my house and let me repay the kindness so I can get it off my conscience."

The boy told them he lived nearby two other families a mile or so to the south and from his cabin it was only a day's walk to get to Silsbee.

They walked a ways with the boy and he talked at great length about the blood feud between the Fullers and the Raines and they asked him if he knew about the depression and he asked them if he looked like an invalid. He said of course he knew about it, but it just didn't matter much to him or anyone else he knew. He said his people were more concerned with prohibition rumored to be on its last leg.

"Y'all are for it?" Ollie asked.

"Gotta make money somehow. These woods is all but trapped out. Trees cut or fixing to be cut. There ain't a whole lot left to turn a dollar. This land is just about worthless after what they done to the pines."

"What'd they do?"

"Used to there was nothing but big ole longleaf pines all through here. All but blocked out the sun. Only thing would grow along the ground was broom sedge. Maybe some bluestem. Then the timber companies come in and took it all down. I heard somebody say they done something like seven hundred and fifty million board feet in a single year. But don't worry, they said, they'll replant everything they cut. And they did. Replanted with weaker trees. Goddamn loblolly."

The boy spit the word from his mouth.

"Why?" Lena asked.

"'Cause they grow faster. You can harvest 'em quicker. That's what the company men say—'harvest.' Harvest the trees. Anyhow. Loblolly's a shit tree. Shallow roots. Along comes a windstorm and down goes the trees. All of sudden the canopy starts to open and this undergrowth starts to happen—bloodroot, trillium, mayapples. You name it. Junk forest, you ask me. Good for ticks and timber mills. Wouldn't want anything to do with either one of them. Like I said, worthless."

"Tell that to the bank," William said.

The boy nodded.

"You got me there, cousin. My granddaddy come out here—him and Granny—and they built up our cabin in the deepest woods they could find. Creek for water. River close by for fishing. And there was all sorts of game at the time. I heard it said once that the deer couldn't hardly take a step without tripping over the rabbits and if the rabbits tried to hop they'd land on the back of a black bear."

Paul smiled and looked off as if he would remember such times himself.

"Folks told him he ought not come out here. Stay, they told him, be a part of this here new civilized society. But he growed up during the War Between the States and all that mess that came after. He said he'd done and seen what happens when too many people get together and he didn't think too much of it. He was alive the first ten years of my life and I never knowed him to take a dollar. Different breed, them old-timers."

When they reached the cabin, Paul looked at it and frowned as if he'd forgotten where they were headed. The structure was ruinous and crumbling. Fallen boards and broken windows. One end of the cabin was scorched black from a past fire. A bearskin hung over the door cut, and the whole of the building was at a sharp and obvious slant where the ground had shifted beneath it.

"Well, this is it," Paul said. "Y'all want to come in? I got some mayhaws put back. Deer jerky too."

"You live here alone?" William asked.

"Most of the time."

"What about your old man?" Ollie said.

"He's down in Beaumont, working oil. Comes home now and again and brings a few supplies. Sleeps like a grizzly for a week or two and then he's back at it."

"All the rest of the time you're on your own?"

"Lucky, ain't it?" the boy asked. "Y'all come on and stay a while. We got the right number to play Wa-hoo, if I can find all the marbles. I can go kill Camden Raines some other time."

"We gotta keep going," William said. "But we appreciate it."

Paul did not hide his disappointment.

"Well," he said. "If you gotta go, I guess you gotta go. Not a lot of visitors out here is all."

"My mother's sick," William told him. "We're trying to get back to her."

The boy nodded.

"I can understand that," he said. "I never knew my momma."

He didn't volunteer any more information and William didn't ask.

"Say, Paul," Ollie said, and Paul looked up, hopeful. "You know anything about an old woman lives in a cabin somewhere out in the swamp?"

"You mean the Haint Lady?"

"I don't know. Maybe," Ollie said. "We heard she was something like a witch."

Paul shrugged.

"Might be," he said. "She lives six or seven miles from here. You gotta keep south then cut west and do some swamp-wading after the trail peters out. But you'll see her bottle tree from a ways off."

"Can you take us to her?" William asked.

"Shit no," Paul said. "I heard whatever she tells you, it always comes true."

"So maybe she'll tell you something good," Ollie said.

The boy thought about it, then shook his head.

"I don't believe she can tell lies," he said.

They left him at his cabin but not before he gave them strips of venison jerky and filled their canteen with well water.

"Y'all see a gal named Martha in Silsbee, tell her Paul Fuller says he sure is sorry."

They said they would and they went on their way.

36

Lt. Thomas Didymus Carter

From the gallows pole are hanging men, no longer will they fight
They cannot tell the hot from cold, nor know the day from night
They cannot see the sun go down, nor see it up again
Nevermore shall they feel pain, these dead and lucky men.

For years, others have told me as I have told myself, the things I did, I did for the greater good. But if there is no greater good—no possibility of a higher power or higher calling—and the actions are taken on their own, are we not monsters? And if the changing of words can make us such, then are we not already? If there is no God, then we are not made in His image. What shape then do we take?

I have heard it said and seen it many times written that there are those who believe we are all connected. In some cases, all men; and in other cases, men and animals and even the shared grass beneath our feet. I've also heard men of certain faiths condemn these thoughts. But such writings and such beliefs are not so different than Romans chapter twelve, verse five, in which Paul writes that we are all members of one body.

If this is true, in either sense, in any faith, have we not looked into our own eyes, our own soul, countless times and pulled the trigger? Have we not already committed one thousand murders? Died one thousand deaths?

I do not know if I would disavow God's plan or simply deny His existence entirely. I feel a fracturing in my soul. Doubt grows in me like a noxious weed, and yet it is my own mind that tends it. Feeds and waters and watches it devour all other notions of good.

I do not wish to drag others down with me. I do not wish to be here myself.

37

They stuck south on the trail until it ended at no destination in particular and they turned west as the boy had instructed. Further into the Thicket and into the moisturized heat—the air so wet it boiled around them. The wind offered little reprieve. Aeolus asleep at his post. They stuck as best they could to the bowers and understories where shade might spell them from the onslaught of the sun but still they faltered, stopping two and three times each hour to rest and drink the smallest rations of water, for who knew when the next creek would appear and what condition they might find it in.

Their feet were tired and torn. The ground was an uneven mix of duff and loam, but on they went until the trees gave way to a long narrow field in which a windmill stood, its wooden sails turning ever so slowly.

"You don't think . . ." Ollie said and let the words fall away as if not wanting to curse the question.

"Maybe," William answered anyway, and when they reached the windmill Ollie's eyes widened.

"Looky here, looky here," he said, taking down a tin cup hung from a nail on the side of the structure.

There was a pipe coming up from the ground and a little spout that fed into a tin tub. The tub was nearly empty but for a thin, two-inch layer of murky water that sat in the bottom.

"There ain't no telling how many animals have drunk from this since the last time it had anything fresh in it," William said.

"I don't care if the Kaiser hisself has drunk out of it. I'm thirsty and that's well water. Besides, animals drink from creeks all the time and that don't stop you. Shit in there too."

William looked at Lena who shook her head. The boy shrugged.

"Whatever you say, bud," William told him. "I guess some lessons are better learned than taught."

Ollie scooped water into the cup and drank and twisted up his face and then, sensing they were watching him, scooped up another cupful.

A few hours later Ollie was off in the woods somewhere violently expelling the water and Lena and William sat under a mulberry tree and waited.

The girl took off her shoes and socks and rubbed her feet.

"What was it like?" William asked. "Being a part of that whole deal."

Lena shook the dirt and sticker burrs from her socks. She didn't look up.

"It was awful," she said.

She stretched the socks out longways and laid them across her lap.

"That's a lie," she said. "It wasn't all awful. Getting to see some of the places was alright."

"Like where?"

"Like everywhere," she said, and she told him about cow towns to the west and men who wore giant sombreros and men who spoke only German or only French. She told him about beignets and about the ocean and about how she'd never been on a mountain but once she'd seen the shape of them in the distance and it was like nothing she could even describe.

"That sounds like a lot more than I ever saw in Shawnee Prairie."

"You the type of person who wants to see more than where you grew up?" she asked.

"I don't know," he said. "Tell you the truth, I hadn't thought much about it one way or the other. I've always liked the songs though, about people heading out west. Me and Ollie used to talk about it some. But, hell, I've never been further than Groveton, far as that goes."

Her face turned somber.

"I've been to Groveton," she said. "That's where Downtain bought Kushim."

"The gorilla come from Groveton?"

"Downtain knew a man who was trying to put together some sort of traveling zoo. But he never could get it going. All he ended up with was Kushim and a crocodile. Lord knows where he got either one of them to begin with. But he was trying to sell them off, use the money for some other idea he had. You know people like that—no staying power. One thing gets hard for a minute so they go on to something else."

"What happened to the crocodile?" William asked.

"I heard tell nobody wanted it, so the old boy turned it loose in the Trinity River."

"I guess that probably hampered some fishing holes."

"Swimming holes, more like," Lena said, and they both laughed.

She ran her hand through her hair and looked out to where the light and the shadows played soft under the pines.

"When Kushim first came on, it wasn't a fighting bit," she said. "There was this fiddle player from out in West Texas somewhere that had joined up and he would play the fiddle and Kushim and I would dance."

"Dance?"

"Sure. He was a better dancer than I was. Charleston, foxtrot, Texas Tommy. He knew every step."

"Damn," the boy said.

"One time, a drunk cowboy in College Station threw something at us while we were on stage. Kushim raised up and was about to jump off into the crowd but I was able to stop him. Calm him down. But Downtain said he'd seen something that gave him an idea. He said when it looked like Kushim might go rip that fella's head off, the man was scared as hell, naturally—but he said the rest of the people there didn't look scared at all. They looked excited. Not long after that they started the fighting act. I went back to selling things in the tent every night. Washing laundry during the day. Trying to stay out his way."

"When he . . . bought you," William said, and the word came out awkward and strange, "nobody in the show said anything?"

"No. There were a few who would give me these looks, like they were sorry or something. They worship him though, like some kind of prophet. They may even think he is."

"Is what?" William asked. "A prophet?"

The girl shrugged.

"Why not? Think about how crazy it probably sounded when Jesus told everybody who he was."

She looked at him and shook her head.

"I don't want to talk about him anymore."

"Alright," William said. "Let's talk about something else."

"Like what?"

"How old are you?"

"Eighteen," she said.

"How old are you really?"

"Sixteen. What if your daddy won't go back with you?"

"You turned that table right quick didn't you?"

"I wanna know," she said. "If we do find him, but it don't go the way you hope—what happens then?"

William leaned his head back and looked up to where the sunlight cut through the fat green leaves and there were silkworms descending in slow sleepy spirals.

"I been asking myself that for the last four or five days," he said.

"Does yourself have any answers?"

"No, he's about as sharp as a box of marbles."

She rolled her eyes.

"You know, some people would praise the heavens if their daddies would go away and never come back."

"It ain't some people I'm worried about," he told her. "My mother is going to die. And I don't know that finding him will make a difference in that, but she needs him there with her. He owes her that much."

The boy nodded his head.

"That much he owes her."

The girl ran her finger along the bark of the tree.

"She doesn't want you there with her?" she asked.

"I didn't say that."

"But you aren't."

"What?"

"There with her."

They heard Ollie tromping through the brush and they looked up as he emerged and asked if they were ready and they nodded and the three of them packed up and moved on and William felt as if he might be sick as well.

38

Lt. Thomas Didymus Carter

There was a man in our unit descended from German lineage—Karsten, he was called. He was from some small town in Kendall County, out west in the Hill Country of Texas. The other men were distrustful of him on account of his heritage.

On the ship across the Atlantic, the anxieties of war and the realization of what it truly was we were embarking on began to manifest. A few of the boys cornered Karsten in the mess hall below deck.

"Why would you fight against your own countrymen?" they asked him.

"They are not my countrymen," he said. "I am an American."

"You don't pray," one said. "When Roger or Lieutenant Carter leads the prayers, you don't bow your head, don't close your eyes."

Karsten nodded. There were six or seven of them surrounding him, but he stood calm, holding his slop tray. Me and Roger stood up from our table and went to deescalate.

"I have no one to pray to," he said, and he looked at us as we walked up. His head was high and proud. "The world is an oyster without a pearl."

"Infidel," one of the men said and stepped forward, but Roger grabbed his arm and yanked him back.

"We are brothers in this unit," Roger said. "On this ship. In this army. Brothers. We do not judge our brothers by anything but their ability to protect us and protect themselves. Private Karsten is a better shot and better soldier than the lot of you. So leave him be and pray he is the one watching your back on the battlefield."

The men grumbled, but they dispersed.

"You're not going to try converting me now, are you?" Karsten asked.

Roger shook his head.

"No, friend. I try to do what's best for people because my God tells me to. And he doesn't tell me to help only when the man in need is a man of faith."

Karsten nodded and went on with his tray, and Roger and I returned to our table.

"You should be the one leading this outfit," I told him.

Roger smiled, but it did not mask his troubled mind.

"The things I say, and the things I feel, are often at odds, Thomas. Do you ever feel this way?"

"More often than not," I told him.

"What do you do in those moments—to reconcile the two?"

"I think of my son. My wife. I think of the peace my grandfather must have known as he pushed his single-blade plow through the East Texas dirt. Even if such peace is not mine own, it is something to aspire to before the sun is setting on us all."

Roger smiled, and this time I saw it was a true smile.

"What?" I asked. "What do you think of?"

"I think of you, Thomas. Of your certainty. Your leadership. And most of all, your friendship. You will bring us through whatever we are about to face. I have faith."

"Faith." I repeated the word, and Roger nodded. "Well, save a little faith for Karsten too. Like you said, he's a better shot than all of us."

Roger laughed, and his laughter brought me the peace of my

grandfather's plow, and before our meal was finished, the officers were calling all units to the top deck. We had arrived.

I long now for the rawness of his laugh. I hear it in the dark of night. A brief, imagined solace stolen by the wind. Carried away across the Acheron.

Word has come from Texas. Roger is dead. I am lost.

The shell has been ripped apart, and there is nothing inside.

39

That evening, they were attacked by a full battery of insects. Gnats and mosquitos by the tens of thousands. They swarmed the heads of the three travelers and the heads of deer come to drink from near-dry creeks and waning ponds. The insects guarded what little water there was. Guarded it for the survival of their species. For their bloodthirsty future.

They were no strangers to mosquitos but never had any of them seen swarms so dense they became nearly impenetrable.

"Lord help us, this is like something out of the Bible," Ollie said, and when he did several bugs ended up in his mouth and he spit and swatted and started running.

They all ran. They ran through the swarming hordes with their hands and arms covering their faces and they sought higher ground and when they finally found it they set about making a fire. Lena at the wood and the boys at the brush and they blew all together and altogether desperate.

Finally the flames rose up and the wood was smoking and the majority of the bugs retreated to a less choked environment.

"I'm one tore up sonofabitch," Ollie lamented, walloping his elbow where he thought a mosquito might be, then scratching at a spot on his forearm. "One more missed breakfast and I imagine they'll be able to just carry me off."

"You think complaining keeps the bugs away?" Lena asked. She was breaking thin branches off a witch hazel tree.

"It can't hurt. Maybe it'll turn my blood bitter and give some pause to these little bastards. And if not, at least it makes me feel better."

He was itching at every inch of exposed skin.

"And I'll tell you something else. The fella that comes up with some sort of poison for these things is gonna find himself with more money than Johnny Rockefeller."

"Shut up, Ollie," Lena told him. "And take your shirt off."

The boy's eyes widened.

"What?" he asked.

"Both of you," Lena said.

They looked over at her. She'd pulled the early yellow blooms from a pile of hazel branches and was crushing the flowers in the palms of her hands.

William brought his soiled shirt over his head and held it and walked to where she was sitting and knelt down. She dabbed at her palm with one finger and then used the finger to paint William's bites. Along his arms, the back of his neck, down toward his chest. Her mouth hung slightly open and she tilted her head back some as she doctored each red welp.

"Here, get me too," Ollie said, stripping off his shirt and joining them.

When she was finished, Lena told William to hold out his hand. She crushed what was left of the witch hazel into his palm and then turned her back to him and pulled off her shirt.

William and Ollie looked at each other like stunned mice.

"Go on, bud," Ollie whispered.

William touched his fingertip to the yellow powder and reached out and pressed it against a red bite at the base of Lena's neck. The skin on her neck turned to gooseflesh and he felt her shiver.

"Sorry," he said.

"I'm alright. Keep going."

He did.

"Well, I believe I'll go . . . get more wood for the fire," Ollie said too loud.

Before William could stop him he'd stalked off into the woods.

"Sorry," William said again. "He's not used to seeing girls out of their shirts."

"But you are?" she asked, turning her head back, chin down.

"No, I—"

"I'm teasing you," she assured him. "And that's not why he left."

William knew as well as she did why Ollie had suddenly and awkwardly departed. He felt his heart raging against his chest. He reached out again with his finger and this time she turned and faced him and they were only inches from one another and when he realized he was staring he quickly jerked his head up.

She smiled. Patient.

"Are you gonna kiss me?" she asked.

"I had a mind to," he said.

"And?"

"I got distracted."

"By what?" She took his arms and guided them around her waist.

"By thinking of what might happen."

"If I didn't kiss you back?"

"If you did," he said, their foreheads now touching.

"Well. You wanna find out?"

He kissed her.

40

Across the valley the full moon had yet to rise but the horizon was aglow with its coming and the whitetail moved quiet through the scrub oak and yellow pines and one by one they stopped and raised their heads toward that eastern light. The sun reincarnate spoke unto them in the gentle gloom. *I am here to stay the darkness. I am here to hold it back.*

They'd kept the fire burning but were laying a good distance away to try keeping halfway cool for the night. Ollie slept on one side of William, and Lena on the other. He could still smell her on his skin. Sleep was hard to come by.

He watched the stars rise and fall above him. Listened to the screech owls and the frog songs and the occasional sigh of soft wind through the trees. He thought of his father and tried to see his face but couldn't.

The fire was fading and William went to it and crouched and cupped his hands and blew. The ashes delivered up a glowing ember and the boy blew again. Soon was the flame and William laying pine needles and twigs all about it. He tipped over a larger, half-charred log. He watched it smoke and catch and begin to burn.

He slipped his father's journal from his bag and in the low light of the small fire he continued reading.

He heard something moving through the dark, the dried thatch and burnt grass crunching. An armadillo, he imagined, but then a twig broke nearby and the boy closed the journal and shot up and there, at the edge of the camp, a man stood smiling. William could see the white of his teeth in the moonlight.

He was carrying a brown leather bag slung over his shoulder and he came now, stepping around Ollie and passed the girl, and squatted down near William.

"Howdy," he said, his voice quiet but somehow menacing, even at a whisper.

"Howdy," William said back.

His mouth felt suddenly dry.

"Y'all having a little campout?" the man asked, loosing the bag onto the ground next to him.

"Nossir. Just passing through."

The man looked at William as if he would judge the answer on the boy's face, and the boy looked back at him, and the two of them were quiet and still as they studied one another in the dim, pallid light. The man's hair was parted just left of center. He wore slacks and a long sleeve shirt rolled up to his elbows. Black dress shoes, nearly flat and barely a scuff on them.

"Where you headed?" he asked at last.

William found he'd been holding his breath and took in a quick suck of air before answering.

"Silsbee," he said, not wanting to explain anything else.

"Silsbee. That's a fair stretch."

"Yessir."

The man smiled. He eased himself onto the ground beside the bag.

"Be a good deal easier to take a train," he told William. "Hitch a ride, maybe. But here you are in the Thicket."

"Yessir," William said again.

"So. Who is it that you're running from?"

"We ain't running."

"No?" The man seemed amused.

"Nossir."

"Sure you are. Everybody is."

"I know who you are," the boy said. "I've seen pictures in the paper."

"Alright then," the man said, and if he was concerned with being recognized, he did not show it.

"Are you gonna rob us?" William asked.

The man shook his head. He had unzipped the bag and was fishing around inside it.

"No. I don't believe there'd be a whole helluva lot to take, would there?" he asked, and then offered up from the bag a half-eaten sack of peanuts.

"Nossir."

"I didn't think so."

"What are you gonna do?" William asked.

The man shrugged.

"I plan on just eating these peanuts," he said. "I'm waiting on somebody. Thought I might have a friendly chat in the meantime. Don't get to do that so much these days."

"I guess not," William said.

"Yeah? What else do you guess?"

"I didn't mean—"

"What does your pa say about me?"

"What?"

"You said you know who I am, yeah?"

"Yessir."

"So what does your pa say about me?"

"I don't know. I hadn't seen him in a while."

"Why is that?"

"I don't know that either," William said. "Why is anything the way it is?"

The man smiled.

"You ask that like there's not an answer," he said.

"Is there one?"

"Sure there is. Everything—anything—is the way it is because of a thing that happened before it. And that thing happened because of something else before *it*. You see? . . . Shit. You think I started off like this? I was about your age, they sent me to jail for stealing a turkey. Now, well, here I am."

"Maybe you ought not have stole it," William said, and immediately he regretted saying it. "I mean, if it's been all this trouble."

The man laughed softly.

"What tells you that? The Law? The Bible?" he asked. "Ain't neither one of 'em worth nothing. You ever been starving, son? So hungry you can't hardly get up out of the dirt?"

"Nossir. I been pretty hungry, but probably not like that."

"Well imagine it. Now imagine your little sister's that bad off. Worse even. And you having to just set there and watch her suffer."

"You could have asked."

"What?"

"You could have asked whoever's turkey it was if they'd let you have it."

"You're right. I could have."

The man leaned back over the leather bag and without much consideration came up with a Colt .45 and looked at it carefully as if he'd make sure it was the right one and then he pointed it at the sleeping girl and thumbed back the hammer.

"And you could ask me not to shoot."

The boy didn't speak, breath heavy in his nostrils.

"No?" the man said. "Well here, take my .32 then."

He went back into the bag with his empty hand and emerged with a smaller pistol and pitched it sideways at the boy's feet.

"Pick it up," he commanded, and the boy did so.

"Now, I'm gonna shoot this girl here on the count of three."

"No." William shook his head.

"Too late for no. You want to stop me, you have the power right there in your hand. One."

It's not real, William thought. *You're dreaming. It's a nightmare. Wake up.*

"Two," the man said, and William lifted the pistol and the man said "three" and the boy did not shoot.

"Pow," the man said, puffing his cheeks out. "Now she's dead."

William flipped open the chamber of the pistol and saw that it was empty.

"What?" the man asked, looking pleased with himself. "I wasn't gonna shoot her, so I couldn't have you shooting *me*. Can you imagine? You would've been the most famous man in Texas come daylight. But that ain't how I'm gonna go. I done been shown."

"By who?" William asked, but the man stood and shouldered the bag and looked toward the darkness.

There was a whistle, quick and shrill.

"That's my lady," he said. "Keep the gun. Tell whoever you want. Nobody'll believe you."

The man reached the edge of camp and stopped and turned back. He flipped a bullet toward William and it hit on the ground near the boy and then he was gone.

William did not sleep. He sat next to the dying fire until morning. He turned the bullet over in his hand and wondered at his cowardice to not pull the trigger.

When the others woke, he told them Clyde Barrow had given him a gun. They laughed and asked where he'd found it.

He shrugged.

Nobody will believe you.

"Just sitting there on the ground," he said, and then handed it to Lena. "Here. There's only one bullet and you're the better shot."

The girl tucked the pistol into the waist of her pants, opposite the other gun, and she looked like some outlaw from the cover of a dime novel and the boy thought she looked beautiful.

41

Lt. Thomas Didymus Carter

I hereby confess to murder, though no law will ever charge me, nor will a court convict me. But if there is a God, perhaps He will hear my confession. Perhaps He will hold me accountable. I hope that He does. In fact, I challenge Him to. Do something just, you miserable bastard.

Our argument plays out in full. Over and over and over. I cannot be rid of it. Perhaps I do not wish to be. Perhaps I would rather keep the blood on my hands than attempt to wash it away.

The manifesto I laid out for Roger on the last night of our meeting was one of seething hatred. Bitterness and blasphemy.

It was Roger who advocated strongest for my election as lieutenant. Homer Renfro had nominated himself against me, but even back then, Homer wore his instability right there in his eyes. The men might have chosen me anyway, but Roger's speech in my favor was rousing. Though we had only just met, sharing a bunk during basics, he called me a true leader. A man they could follow.

Of the fifty-seven men who elected me, twenty-two returned home. Well under half. I remember their names. The names of their children.

Roger was an assured man. Certain of things. Quiet, but certain.

His was a stoic steadiness that is much welcome in battle or any other hardship. We leaned on him greatly for his strength. I leaned on him.

He struggled after the war, as did so many. He hid his guilt beneath his cloak of faith. He often wrote letters to me detailing some new interpretation of the Bible that he believed proved one of his theories. He used his faith as a shield against his demons, and the shield held them at bay.

After the police had shot and killed two men, the camp was overrun. Roger and I met in a tavern across the Virginia line. We both drank heavily. I more than he.

"We will regroup," he told me. "We will try again."

I would not hear it. I did not.

Fool, I called him. "You goddamn, pathetic fool."

And when I looked at him, I did not see my loyal friend and faithful comrade. I saw only the things I had come now to despise. Naivety. Hope. Faith.

Forgiveness, Roger says, is the cure. As if my indignation were an affliction.

There is a great fury in my heart. Fury at the ugliness of the world and those who inhabit it. Fury at all those things we are made to suffer and made to watch others suffer. We are made to wilt and die. Made to struggle and watch others struggle. Evil men who lie about what can be clearly seen. Clearly felt. And worse, we lie to ourselves. So, where then is my forgiveness warranted? What has the world done to deserve it?

"But the beauty," Roger says. "What of the beauty of this place?"

The beauty, I tell him, is the most egregious of all cruelties. The beauty of this life—the beautiful things that wield hope like daggers and espouse the possibilities as if there are possibilities. As if the truth is a malleable, makeable thing. It is not. And no beautiful thing can make it so.

"What of William?" he says. "What of your son, your wife—the things you think of when the world grows too dark around you?"

Roger and Rebecca so desperately wanted a child that I will admit there was a small pang of guilt each time I spoke to him of William.

But Roger, in his grace, never denied me my moments of fatherly pride. He listened to my stories, to my boasting, and he smiled all the while.

"The Lord's will," Roger had said.

Of all that I said to him that night, I regret most of all the mentioning of children.

Children are made to suffer unimaginable horrors at the hands of evildoers or the hands of their own families. "And yet it is God's will that you be denied a child," I tell him, "when so many undeserving fools are made parents? How can you not be enraged?"

He is quiet.

"What of my son?" I say, voice raised. "I hope he is a simpleton, for any true thought given to a man's life will surely expose the horror he has been born into without consent. The weight of knowledge would hang about him like chains."

"You are not yourself, Thomas."

"*Lieutenant*," I say, reprimanding him, denying him even our friendship.

"And I am only myself," I tell him. "All else is a lie. Your life, your god, your faith. There is not but desolation in this life. There is not but sorrow. We are alone and godless, and if by chance there is a God, then the truth of the world is made all the worse, for he lacks either the pity or the power to cease the cruelty which he created."

"God will forgive you," he says. "As will I."

"I don't need your forgiveness, *friend*," I tell him, my words now venomous at every syllable. "I know what you are—coward. You wanted me to have command because you knew what it would do to me. To any man. You knew you couldn't bear the responsibility and the anguish and the dead men in your dreams, so you made sure you wouldn't have to. *You* are the source of my pain."

In this moment, he is quiet. His face betrays nothing. He stands. Looks down at me. What does his face say? Then he leaves and is gone. And is gone forever.

IV

THE CABIN

42

Progress was slow. Near day's end they came into a copse of locust trees and navigated gingerly among thorns as big as their hands. They clambered carefully down through the sloped forest then crossed through the palmetto flat and into the baygall. The land here was dead and depressed and poorly drained. A few inches of water covered the ground for acres at a time.

Great cypress trees shaded their smaller brethren. Magnolias and hollies and wetland pines. Ferns and fetterbush filled in the gaps between the broadleaf trees, and late-blooming azaleas shone white against the backdrop of brown, roiling water.

All about them the country was dark and acidic. Ochre-stained from the tannins of rotting plants. Choked off from oxygen. Impenetrable swaths of earth where sunlight had not ventured in millennia. Longer.

"I've had bad dreams that didn't turn out as disagreeable as this mess," Ollie said.

They moved forward in slow, sloshing steps, stopping half a dozen times to let snakes pass. Sleek black bodies winding overtop the shallow water with raised heads and flickering tongues.

"There ain't no way somebody lives out here in this shit," Ollie said. "Woods witch or not."

"I guess that just growed up on its own then," William said, pointing ahead as bits of a small ramshackle cabin appeared beyond the thick curtains of vegetation.

"I'll be go to hell," Ollie said.

"We might be right here on the doorstep."

They stood panting.

Their legs were heavy from the hard slog through the swamp and though they were in perpetual shade each of them poured with sweat, beset on all sides by the unrelenting humidity of this bleak riparian purgatory.

They moved closer, forearms and elbows tore at by saw briers and honey locusts alike, until at last they emerged from the Thicket and into a small clearing, where sat the cabin, raised one foot off the ground by squat wooden stilts at each corner and through the midsection. Vines grew unchecked up the walls, along the porch boards, and even through the door that stood half-open.

"You think anybody lives here?" Ollie asked.

"If they do, they ain't real big on upkeep."

In the yard, such as it was, was a single laurel oak that stood stately on a small mound of soil, as if it might address the rest of the bog trees, reprimanding them for their unsightly condition. From the limbs and branches of the big oak were hung a hundred glass bottles of every color, shape, and size.

"What'n the hell is that?" Ollie asked.

"They're meant to catch spirits at night," Lena said. "Haints and the like. They pass through one side of the bottle, but they can't pass back out. So they're trapped there, until daylight."

"If it was me," Ollie said, "I believe I'd just go around the damn tree and be done with it."

"Spirits ain't like that," the girl warned. "They get affixed on something bright colored like that, something shining in the moonlight, they can't help but float towards it. Can't help but see what treasure's waiting inside there."

Ollie looked at the bottles. They hung, turning slowly one way and then back the other. They touched, softly in the breeze. Subtle breeze. Bottles clinking as glass met glass and then, caught by the sun, a spectrum of brilliant light thrown forward. Fragmented light through the trees and reflected there in the twisting bottles and suddenly the great oak alive and shimmering and the wind stronger now and beginning to howl and the chiming glass and Ollie could hear them, the trapped spirits, and they were calling to him from somewhere behind the light and he strained to hear and to see and then something grabbed his arms and he screamed.

Lena let go, laughing. The wind calmed.

William looked at Ollie.

"It ain't funny," Ollie said.

"I didn't say a word."

"Y'all come on," Lena called back to them. She was climbing the porch, pressing her weight onto the warped wood and feeling it give a little.

Half of the sloped roof sagged lower than the other, overhung as it was by limb and leaf and moss that grew there along the north side.

Once they were all on the porch, William knocked at the tattered door and then saw it had no knob so he pushed it open. He helloed the cabin and there was no response and the three of them went inside and stood in the shadows and took in the must of the place and looked around. It was dark and the air within somehow thicker than the humidity without. Dust motes hung and floated in rogue stripes of sunlight. The walls smelled of soil and smoke from long-ago fires.

On the kitchen counter and the shelves above it there were glass jars full up with pickled vegetables and jams and a few substances William could not name. The jars looked to be untouched—coated with dust and all aligned there on the shelves like relics or specimens from some other world. He picked one up and turned it in his hand and there was a perfect brown circle where it had been and he put it back just so.

Deer skins were strewn about the wood floor and hung on the walls and draped over windows like Gothic curtains.

On a table in the middle of the room and in various corners of the cabin, hardened wax collected at the base of candles that had not been lit in years. And if there was a chair in the place, William did not see it.

"You think this is the place?" Lena asked.

"Either it is or it ain't," Ollie said.

"What's that mean?"

"I don't know. I just say things sometimes."

"When you're scared?"

"I ain't scared."

There was a loud thump and Ollie flinched as if he might leap onto the table.

Another thump.

Shuffling from the backroom

"Who's in my house?" the woman called, and the sound echoed throughout the cabin.

They looked at one another, surprised not so much that they weren't alone but that anybody might call such a place home.

"You come back to rob me?" the woman said, and when she appeared in the room, William took a step back.

She was not four and a half feet tall and she carried a knotted stick that stood higher than any of them and she leaned on it with both arms, frail and poorly balanced.

Her hair was long and white and unkempt. The skin on her cheeks reached down to her jaw and the skin of her brows hung heavy over her eyes, so that she had to open them wide to see. And her wide eyes scanned the room with a sharp urgency. Feral madhouse eyes.

"We're not here to rob you, ma'am," William said loudly, sensing the need.

"I don't know what you think we'd take," Ollie said, and Lena elbowed him.

"Three of you," the woman said, scrunching her nose up as if she would smell their number. "And young too. You oughten have need to be here."

"We're looking for someone," Lena said. "A man."

The three of them huddled together near a collapsed beam, wary of the woman and whatever power she may possess.

"Man just left out of here," the old woman said. She went forward on her cane into the kitchen area and stood and looked at her jars and mumbled to herself.

"Thomas Carter?" William asked.

"Who?" she asked sharply.

"The man. Was his name Thomas?"

"I don't know nobody's name. He wore a soldier's boots. Like yours, only brown."

William nodded at the others.

"When did he leave?"

"Sometime before now. Yesterday maybe. Or last year. Time is a memory and memories are funny little shits."

"Did he say where he was going?"

"Sure he did. The train station in Silsbee. In a hurry too. Got family he had to get back to in New Orleans."

As quickly as the boy's heart had lifted, it came crashing down.

"What about Shawnee Prairie?" he asked. "A soldier from Shawnee Prairie?"

There was panic in his voice.

The woman was unbothered.

"I get plenty of soldiers," she said, moving purposeful about the kitchen. A cabinet had come loose from the wall on one end and fallen tilted onto the table below it and the woman opened it and the dishes were all at one end and she took a bowl from the leaning stack and shut the door.

"Crestfallen preachers, and men who killed their brothers, and men who sought to kill themselves."

"And women?" Lena asked.

"Women. Sure. But women don't despair so easy," the old woman said. "Even had a monk in here, if you can believe that."

"Do you work miracles?" Ollie asked. "Like they say?"

"Miracles," the woman said, "are for jackasses."

Lena stifled a laugh.

William had walked back to the doorway of the cabin and stood looking out.

"Not the ending you'd hoped for?" the old woman called. "Well. Here's one: There were shepherds in a hut, feasting themselves on mutton. Passing by was the wolf. He says to them, 'You would kill me for such a thing.'"

"What does that mean?" William asked without turning around.

"What do you want it to mean? Something valuable? Something funny?" She turned to Ollie. "Something miraculous?"

No one answered.

"The lost souls what cross o'er my threshold come for all sorts of reasons and all them reasons are the same."

She held Ollie in her gaze.

"I seen a white moth this morning," she said. "That mean anything to you?"

"I've heard things said. Omens from old grandad times."

"Only one time," she told him.

"What do you say to them—all these people who come here?" William asked, returning from the doorway, his arms crossed.

"Come sit," she said, and she tapped the floorboards with her cane and they came forward cautiously and sat crossed-legged on the cabin floor.

"Do you know the Atakapan creation story?" she asked, circling behind them.

They shook their heads.

"The ocean," she said, "threw a great oyster onto the land, and inside it were the first people."

They waited for more but the woman was quiet.

"Ain't much of a story," Ollie said.

"Well, it's their story. And the Caddo people believe the first men crawled out of a cave called the crying place," she said. "And some tribes believe we came from inside the earth, and others believe we came from the sky. And whatever your tribe believes is the truth."

"It can't all be the truth," William said.

The woman smiled.

"Why?" she asked.

"Somebody has to be right. Or maybe they're all wrong."

"If everyone can be wrong in a different way, why can't they all be right?"

"I don't know," he said. "It just don't work like that."

"On the other side of the world, a boy lives nearby an elephant and he believes the elephant to be the largest creature in the world. A boy in Montana believes there is nothing bigger than a buffalo. Who is right?"

"The elephant boy," Ollie said.

"Neither of them," Lena said. "There's whales bigger than elephants and buffalo."

The woman smiled again.

"But these boys don't live anywhere near the water. They don't know anything about whales."

"They're still wrong," William said.

"I agree," the woman said, pounding her cane twice into the floor.

She walked back to the kitchen and took down a jar and smelled of it and then pinched off some of the leaves therein and ground them between her finger and thumb over the bowl. She did the same with the contents of another jar.

William stood.

"Is that it?" he asked.

The woman looked up as if she were surprised to see him.

"Not the ending you'd hoped for?" she said again. "I see that lesson's gonna take more learning."

"Is that what you tell them?" William said. "A story about a boy and a buffalo?"

"Yes."

"Then what?"

"Then they leave," she said. "Sometimes we have sex before they go."

Ollie nearly fell backward.

The woman opened yet another jar, this one containing so foul-smelling a liquid that their eyes burned from across the room. She poured a small amount into the bowl and quickly screwed the lid back into place.

She stirred the mixture and leaned forward over it like some storybook witch.

"If I told you that nothing has anything to do with you," she asked, "would you see it as a condemnation or a freedom?"

"Can you tell me when I'll die?" Ollie asked.

"No," the woman said, still stirring.

"Then what can you do?"

"I can tell you to look at my face and count to ten."

Ollie frowned.

"Let's go," William said. "I'm tired of these riddles. I'm tired of everything. Can you tell us how to get to that train station? I'm going home."

"Good for you," the woman said, and William couldn't tell if she was mocking him or not. "It's past time you stopped running."

"I'm not running."

"In any case," she said. "Keep near the creek. Three miles to a clearing called Ackerman's Field. Another mile and a half to the highway. Station is just before you come into town from the north."

When they left, William did not look back at the cabin where, inside, the old woman moved hurriedly about, preparing for their return.

43

They camped a mile west of the cabin. They were quiet, the three of them, in the evening gray.

"I'll fetch some water," Ollie said and took the canteen and went off into the dusk toward the creek.

The air smelled richly of pine and the evening had brought with it an altostratus of half-gray clouds and a slight breeze out of the north. The girl lifted her hair from her neck so that it might cool in the wind and William watched her and she caught him staring and she quickly put her chin down and cast her eyes up at him as if she were embarrassed by her own loveliness.

William looked away.

"We'll be home," she said, "by this time tomorrow."

The boys would take the train north. A day's travel to Huntington, where they would wait for the SH&G that ran between there and Manning and then William would go on foot back to the Prairie. The girl would make the much shorter trip from Silsbee to Evadale.

"I'm never going to find him," he said. "Am I?"

"It shouldn't have never been your burden to begin with," she told him. "You know that, don't you? All of this is his doing, not yours."

"Maybe. Or maybe he really is just doing what he thinks is best. And maybe I am running."

"Running from what?"

"I don't know. The truth?"

She shook her head.

"No," she said. "I don't believe that. Look at all you've done. How far you came to try to find him. If you wanted to up and leave you could have just hopped a train for anywhere else. Instead you chose to hack and hike through the woods, through the swamp, in the dadgum heat. That's not running."

"No," he agreed, "it might be worse. Convincing yourself you're doing the right thing when really you know you're too chickenshit to do anything else. At least hopping a train wouldn't have been a lie."

"There's only one lie, William, and it don't have a thing to do with some choice you made or didn't make."

He stared at her. Unbridled anger made lovely as autumn. Pulsing. Burning. Eyes searching for a thing not seen. Eyes afire with passion. Eyes engulfed by the same fury the boy held in his own heart.

"Why are you looking at me like that?" she asked.

"I don't know. Because I love you."

He leaned in to kiss her. She pulled away and touched his face.

"What?"

"You don't love me," she said.

"Sure I do."

"No. You just think you do because I'm the first. But it don't mean what you want it to."

"What does it mean?"

"Something. But not that."

He scowled. Looked away.

"You gonna sull up on me now?" she asked.

"Well. Do you regret it?"

"Regret what?"

"You know what," he said. "Are you sorry it happened?"

"No," she told him. "I don't regret it. If it was something I was going to regret, I would've never let it happen. You understand? Nobody owns me, William. I get to choose."

"And you don't choose me."

"I don't choose anybody but myself," she said. "That's it. Doing whatever it takes to make sure I'm safe."

He frowned.

"And my sister too," she added quickly.

He nodded and she laid her head on his shoulder.

"But I am sorry," she told him. "Truly, I am."

"It's alright," he said, looking off at the fading colors of day. The dark stone-washed sky pulling down to meet the edge of the earth. The shapes of birds rising soundless into the air. Beautiful things.

44

The dawn tarried. The woods were gray and black and birdless. Small trees and tangles of vines took on the muted shapes of unknown beasts what stalked the night. William watched the stars vanish from the bleak gray sky. Baleful sky.

Lena stirred to his left. She yawned and pulled herself to sitting and he followed suit.

"You been awake long?" she asked.

"No," he lied.

They looked at one another and William couldn't tell what the sadness was that so clearly painted her face. Would she miss him after all? Or was it some deeper despair? Something without words to it—a long, mournful melody.

William started to ask but a woodpecker broke the silence, hammering away at a distant pine. Its work emanated throughout the bottomlands and the morning birds began to emerge and soon there was sunlight filtered clean from the east and Ollie was up and looking with menacing intention to see where the pounding echo might be originating.

"I guess that needle-beaked bastard's got stronger coffee than the rest of us," Ollie said, wiping angrily at his eyes.

A single doe had wandered out from the palmettos and stood with twitching ears and looked at them and then moved on. Squirrels barked as she went.

Ollie yawned and stretched and then nodded to himself as if he'd come to some satisfying decision.

"I believe I'll piss," he announced. "Then, let's get the hell on home. Once more unto the breach."

He laughed to himself and walked off toward the creek.

William had avoided the obvious but he could turn away no longer. By the end of the day, he would be face-to-face with it. His mother was alive. His mother was dead. Only one of those things could be true. He felt a cold creep along the back of his neck. His arms weakened, then his legs. For a moment he thought he couldn't breathe and then he thought perhaps he'd forgotten how. It felt as if he were back in the medicine show tent. The whole of the past week some strange dream. He had the urge to cry.

The woodpecker halted its proceedings and Lena touched William's arm.

"I'm sorry about last night," she said. "There's something I need to tell you. Something about Downtain."

Ollie howled in the distance. A strange, terrifying sound.

"Son of a no-good goddamn bitch," he hollered. "It got me, bud. Oh, goddamn it, it got me."

William stood unsteady and started toward the trees and Ollie met him coming the other direction and holding one hand with the other. His face was drained of blood. Pale as the corpses of his craft.

"What is it?" Lena asked.

"Cottonmouth son of a bitch," Ollie whimpered. His tears were less from the pain and more from the fear of what would happen next.

"I'm gonna die, ain't I?" he asked, voice quivering.

"Let me see it," Lena said, and took his hand away and studied the bite and then gave a worried look to William.

"Oh god, I am," Ollie wailed. "I am gonna die. Jesus Christ, I'm sorry Kathy."

"Shut up, bud," William said as he struggled to find his own breath. "You ain't dying."

"Do me a favor," Ollie pleaded. "Marry her for me, would you?"

"Shut up."

"If it can't be me, it ought to be you. Fair is fair."

"I wish the snake had bit your tongue," Lena said. "We gotta wrap this up. Tie it off like a tourniquet."

"Then what?"

"Then—" Both of the boys looked to Lena but she shook her head. "Then I don't know."

"The cabin," Ollie said. "Take me back to the old woman."

"We're not going ba—" William started, but Ollie yelled over him.

"Take me back, goddamnit," he cried, and William nodded and Lena was already gathering their gear.

"Carry him," she said.

"What?"

"We need to move quick, but the faster his heart beats, the faster that venom will spread. You have to carry him."

William nodded and scooped his friend up into his arms and started back toward the swamp.

45

They came crashing through the trees and their adrenaline was such that they didn't notice their bleeding arms or blistered feet. When they reached the cabin, the door was open and they called out for help and the old woman stood patiently by the table with the bowl in her hands.

"He's been snakebit," they repeated multiple times upon entering.

"Get him up on the table," she told them.

They laid Ollie on the table and the woman unwrapped the cloth tourniquet and looked at the boy's arm and then wrapped it up again.

"You're gonna save me, right?" Ollie asked over and over until it sounded something like a mantra. "You're gonna save me."

The old woman looked at him.

"Drink this," she said and offered him the bowl.

"Is this antivenom?" Ollie asked. "Did you know? Am I dying?"

"Drink this, then look at my face and count to ten."

Ollie drank and within seconds he was unconscious.

"What'd you do to him?" William demanded.

"He'll be out for at least an hour," the woman said. "But it won't take me that long."

"To what?"

"I'm going to cut off his hand."

"Like hell you are," William said.

"Ah, well, if you'd rather let him die . . ." She shrugged.

William took an angry step toward the woman but he knew she was right.

"You do it," he said, "and he'll live? You promise?"

"What do you think a promise like that is worth?" she asked. "It would only be said to pacify you."

"Then pacify me, goddamnit," William said, and he began to cry and in his heart he cursed everyone and everything and so too he cursed himself. And he looked then at Ollie and put his head in his hands and knew there was no path forward in which he would ever forgive himself.

"Do it," he told her through gritted teeth and tears. "Just please save him. Please save my friend."

William waited on the porch. He chewed at his dirty fingernails and tasted the soil beneath them and tasted the salt of his own tears. Black clouds rolled overhead like a curtain being drawn shut and the wind played at the bottles in the tree like chimes and the boy thought surely this time there would be rain but there was not. The clouds moved on and the sky lightened and William could hear the old woman inside giving instructions to Lena about what to hold and what to hand.

He began to mumble first one prayer and then another. The same powers he had denied he now appealed to, such was his desperation. Such was his confusion.

"Please," he said, and he repeated it over and again, and he closed his eyes and saw Ollie and saw his mother and saw even his father and there was no way he could know his sister's face but he saw it too. "Please. Please."

His prayers were answered by the baying of hounds. He stood and looked out at the swamp and didn't see any movement. The hounds called out again and this time he spotted them splashing through the low water and now coming up the hill.

The first dog skidded past the bottle tree and pulled up hard, growling and baying and pacing at a distance. He was a Hudspeth with orange and white coloring that looked nearly blue in the shadowed light what filtered through the trees. A wolfhound came barreling in alongside him with her ears laid back, listening.

They circled the tree and looked up at the bottles and whimpered and growled and whimpered again.

William looked past them but the swamp was still and empty. Then, as quickly as they'd come, they were gone. Back into the Thicket and out of sight and all was quiet again.

46

William sat against the wall in the back bedroom while Ollie lay sleeping in the old woman's bed. The room was nary as big as a closet. The boy could hear Ollie's every breath. It reminded him, all of it, of his mother. Five days and no closer to an answer and now he sat at the bedside of yet another person he loved.

There was a small window above his head and it was opened and a breeze came through and stirred the thick buckskin curtains. William looked up at them. When he looked back down Ollie was staring at him.

"She asked me if I wanted to keep it," Ollie said.

"Keep what?"

"The hand she took."

"Why would you want to keep it?" William asked.

"That's what I asked," Ollie told him. "She said some folks are sentimental that way."

They both looked down at the bandaging where Ollie's hand had been.

"I been working on this line in my head," Ollie said. "As long as I got one hand to hold you, I'll be just fine."

"Huh?"

"That's the line I'm gonna say to Kathy."

William nodded.

"Well, you know you're talking about my wife, don't you?" he asked.

"You wouldn't have done it," Ollie said, scoffing. "You're too far gone with that one in the front room."

"Sure," William said. "She says it don't mean nothing, our being together, but if I can talk her out of saving her sister and have her come back to the Prairie with me, I'll ask her if she wants to go for a walk through my foreclosed house where my momma's laid up dying. That ought to bring her right around."

"You sure paint a pretty picture."

"Why are we talking about me?" William said. "How are you feeling, bud? When can I take you out of here and get you to a real doctor?"

"She says I ought not go anywhere until tomorrow. Says we can stay the night."

"You trust her?" William asked.

"I don't believe she saved my life in the day so she could kill us come midnight," Ollie said. "If that's what you're asking."

Ollie glanced over at the door.

"But I will say," he told William. "Whatever she give me—to put me out like that—there was things attached to it."

"Things?"

"Dark things," Ollie said. "Things I don't think we're supposed to see. But I saw."

"What did you see?"

"People I've seen before. Them that's been dead and in my hands at the mortuary. But they were alive, or standing up at least. Standing out yonder in the woods. In the dark."

The curtains moved again.

"What were they doing?"

"Calling to me. Singing like. *Ollie*, they said. *Ollie*."

Both boys were quiet.

"Hey," the old woman said loud from the door, and they both flinched. "It's time to re-dress that wound."

She shuffled forward with a bowl of white liquid.

"What is it?" William asked.

"Dakin's," she said. "Now get out of the way. You're taking up my doctoring space."

William squeezed by the woman and went into the hall. Lena was waiting there.

"C'mon," she said and took his hand. "Come lay down with me."

He asked no questions. He followed her into the den. He suspected he would follow her anywhere.

Ollie awoke sometime in the devil's hour. He felt at first confused and then quickly overwhelmed by a great sadness. The old woman was on the floor, asleep and snoring. He looked at his freshly changed bandage and stood, groggy and unbalanced, and went slowly from the room. He made his way down the hall and stood in the den and looked to where William and Lena lay entangled in one another and then he went on. He reached for the front door with a hand that wasn't there. He used the one that was.

He went out onto the porch and then down into the yard and stood before the bottle tree and closed his eyes and listened.

Footsteps in the dark.

Whispered voices. "Hello, boy."

47

William woke to gunfire.

Lena came awake beside him and they both sat up and it was still night out and the old woman was standing just to the side of the open window and holding a smoking rifle.

"Anymore gunplay will be answered, madam," came a voice from outside, and William and Lena looked at one another in disbelief. Both scrambled to the window and looked out.

Downtain stood beneath the bottle tree with four men and two of them with a tight hold on Ollie. The two hounds trotted back and forth in front of them.

"Let that boy go," the woman called.

"Gladly," Downtain said. "Just send out my daughter."

"You can't have her," the old woman said and leveled the rifle to prove her sincerity.

William staggered back. He looked at Lena and her face held the truth and there was no denying it.

"We could do this the hard way," Downtain said.

"They'll be especially hard for you, devil," the old woman said. "'Cause I ain't aiming at nobody else."

Downtain smiled.

"Boy," he called. "I know you're listening. Did she lie to you like she did the others? This isn't the first time she's run off. But a man has a right to his daughter. Isn't that so? Shouldn't a child be with their parent?"

William looked at the girl and she wouldn't meet his eyes and it felt as if his very heart beat with anger and anger alone.

He moved to the window and stood opposite the old woman.

"She don't want to go with you," he said, and the girl looked up, surprised.

"Very well," Downtain said. "We are camped in a field three miles west of here. Not far off the county road to Silsbee. We leave in the morning. Bring her to me, or I cannot speak to the length or quality of your friend's life."

"I'm sorry, bud," Ollie said, and one of the men hit him the back of his head and he fell to his knees beneath the tree.

"Don't you touch him, goddamnit," William cried, but there was nothing he could do and the men slunk back into the darkness, their lanterns swinging like pale sabers slicing away layers of the dark only to have the dark return again, filling a void where the light had been but could not hold.

48

The old woman kept watch by the window and the two of them sat alone on the floor of the kitchen.

"Tell me again, because I'm trying hard to understand," he said to the girl.

"He has women," Lena said. "In all these little towns. He makes promises to some, to others he doesn't bother. Just forces it. He don't much care one way or the other. He told my mother he'd love her forever. Take her to see the world. She believed him. It's easy. It's so easy to believe something like that when it gives you a purpose. Tells you you're special. You mean something. He would come back, every few years, when the show passed through. More promises. 'Soon,' he'd say. 'Soon.' All that time he'd be gone, she would just talk about how great he was. How great our lives were gonna be. Then one day he showed up and said he was taking me but not her. I don't even know what he said to her. More lies. And she just let it happen. Let him take me away, like I wasn't nothing to her. Not compared to him and all his false signs and lying wonders."

She looked up at him.

"I hate her. If I ever see her again, I'll tell her that and then I won't say another word to her for the rest of her miserable life. I'll be gone forever."

"What about your sister?" he asked, and she looked away.

"Another lie," he said.

The girl nodded.

He sat paralyzed. He kept opening his mouth to say something but there were too many things to say, and yet nothing at all.

"Why?" he finally asked. "Why would you even want to go back to Evadale if you don't have a sister and you hate your mother?"

She was quiet and then she asked if he really wanted to know the truth.

"If that's something you're even capable of," he told her.

"There's a boy down there waiting on me. We've been gonna get married since we were kids. He managed to get a letter to me, through some kin of his, that he had a job lined up in New Orleans working for his uncle at a sugar factory. Letter said he was leaving in two weeks. So I run off.

"I'm sorry," she said, and William didn't respond.

He started collecting his things and putting them in his pack and she reached out and grabbed his elbow.

"Say something," she said, and he straightened up and looked her in the eyes.

"You ain't no better than any of the rest of them," he said. "Not even a little."

She scoffed.

"I could've got back in that boat and gone straight down the river and been in Evadale two days ago but I didn't."

"And I'm supposed to thank you for that? Because of you, my best friend is snakebit and now who knows what else."

"And here you are, the noble one," she said. "Only wanted me to come along so you could screw me."

He turned.

"Tell me it ain't true," she challenged. "You didn't have any idea who or what I was, but you sure started making me something in your own head, didn't you? I know boys like you. They think a girl is gonna come along and save them. Give some sort of purpose to their shitty lives. Well I'm not here for you, William. I have my own life, and I don't aim to spend it with that evil bastard. You think having your daddy around is always a good thing? You don't know. You don't know what men are capable of. And I'll tell you right now, you keep hunting your old man and something really bad is going to happen."

"What?"

"You're gonna find him. And then you won't have me to blame for everything that goes wrong."

There was nothing rational to his thoughts. Something in him had at long last come apart. Every betrayal undergone was here manifested in his hatred for her. The strength of his passion turned against him.

He grabbed the pistols from the table and pointed them at her.

She glared at him, unafraid.

"Go," he told her. "Get out."

"You need my help to get Ollie back," she said.

"I don't. I don't need you for anything."

"Son," the old woman said, and William swung one of the pistols her way.

"Stay out of it, witch," he said. "I appreciate you tended to Ollie but this don't concern you anymore."

The old woman didn't seem bothered.

"Just not the raspberry," she mumbled.

"You can't make me leave," Lena challenged, and William fired a shot just past her ear and a jar of jelly exploded dark red against the wall.

The old woman shook her head.

"You used us," William screamed. "You used me."

His face was red and his arms were tight and straining and the pistols began to shake and at last he lowered them and lowered his head.

"Please," he said. "Please just go. I don't want your help. I don't ever want to see you again."

Lena looked at the old woman and the old woman looked away.

"Fine," the girl said, and she went to the doorway and stopped and stood and then went on.

The girl had been gone for half an hour and William felt shame and guilt heavy in his stomach and looked out the window as if she might reappear there in the night.

"Regret it already, do you?" the old woman asked.

"I should have made her stay," William said. "I should have marched her into that camp and traded her."

The woman laughed.

"She doesn't seem like the marching kind."

"I would've made her. Or she would've got a bullet in the leg."

"You're not the shooting kind," she said. "Surely you know by now."

"You don't know anything about me."

"Alright then," the old woman said.

She looked out the window. The bottles shifted and clinked though there was no wind.

"Your father stood under that tree," she told him.

The boy tightened.

"What?"

She turned to him and the wildness in her eyes was gone and there was only pity. Only sorrow.

"Three days ago. He stood there and I gave him a choice and he chose to leave."

"I don't understand."

"He is full of anger, your father. Bitter and resentful."

"You didn't help him?"

"He didn't want my help."

"He came all this way."

"So did you. And you don't want my help either. You just needed a place to hide."

"Hide from what?" William asked, but the woman ignored him.

"He wanted someone to blame," she said. "Someone perhaps even to punish. If such a someone were to exist—well, then—might that he could no longer blame himself. You understand? When I told him I could not offer him such, he continued on his own path."

"What's his path?"

"Only he knows."

"You said you gave him a choice."

"I did. I asked that he choose between his rage and his pain. In pain there is growth, there are the seeds of empathy and kindness and grace. In rage there is nothing. It is a mindless endeavor. Weak and unaccountable. But he was not ready to part with it. It has consumed him, I'm afraid. Will you let it consume you as well?"

"I'm not anything like him."

The woman raised her eyebrows.

"No?"

"I don't abandon the people I love."

The old woman stared at him. She reached out and took his hand and pulled him toward her. Her gaze was intense and unsettling and the boy felt a rush of heat.

"What did he tell you?" she asked.

"Who?"

"The young doctor, when you asked him if there was a chance she might live. What did he say?"

His breath caught. He snatched his hand back and looked at her in some sort of awe and terror and curiosity.

He moved away. His heart hammering.

"The sun will be coming up soon," he said. "I've gotta be at that camp when it does."

"Denial," she said. "Running. What do you think you'll do in this camp?"

"I'll save Ollie. I don't know how. I'll figure it out when the time comes," he said and then hesitated. "Unless you want to tell me how it all plays out."

She moved away from the window and shook her head and trudged past him toward the bedroom.

"The same," she said. "Everything always plays out the same."

49

Lt. Thomas Didymus Carter

When I was a boy, not yet seven years of age, my brother drowned. He was older than my sister and me. Stronger. Smarter. With our mother and father so often absent, taken to drink and gamble and galivant with the dregs of society for long stretches of time, it was my brother who watched over us. He was, in a sense, denied his own life so that he might care for ours. And yet he never showed resentment or bitterness, at least not in front of us. He was exceedingly gentle. He would take us almost daily to the small park near our home in Houston and sit on the iron bench and watch as we played at whatever games our children minds might conjure. Once in the park, on a particularly hot day, there was a boy we had not seen before, and I don't remember his face, but he wore a red shirt. And the boy in the red shirt had grabbed hold of a large stick fallen from one of the oak trees, and he chased the other children, us included, and he hit us with the stick, and we all cried in turn, and finally, a woman came and took the stick away and scolded him, and then she hit him with the stick and asked, "How does that feel?"

The boy cried and sulked, but he did not bother us again, nor did he attempt to play with us. He sat alone, and I can only imagine now that his anger and embarrassment brewed within him some deeper, more formidable darkness.

Then a man on a bicycle came into the park with an ice cream cart, and we all lined up and paid our three cents and took our treats. The boy in the red shirt and the woman—who I thought at the time must be his mother, but I now suppose could have been his sister or caretaker—did not buy any ice cream. My brother saw this, and he went and spoke with the woman and then went and bought another treat and took it to the boy and watched as he licked it and then asked him, 'How does that taste?'

I was, at this time, still too young to question my brother, but our sister demanded to know why he had given ice cream to the boy who had chased everyone with a stick. "Irresponsible," she called it, and I will never forget her using this word because, for one, it was a word our parents hurled at one another when they fought—the irony all but lost on them—and also because my brother said it back to her. "If we are to be irresponsible," he told her, "then let us be irresponsibly kind. Let us show the grace of our creator to all those we encounter, including—and even especially—the awful little shits with sticks."

In less than a year my brother was dead. A few years later my sister fled our parents, and I could not blame her, though I often tried as I sat alone in our room. For a lifetime I have tried to live by my brother's words. No longer.

Would that I might speak to him in earnest and hear the truth from his own lips. When the rushing river overcame him, when he knew all hope was lost, did he feel cheated? Did he feel his time was too little? Or was that only left to the rest of us?

I sully his memory with such thoughts. The afflictions which I carry with me must not be allowed to harm my wife and son. They cannot be exposed to these maladies lest they see their own faith tested, lest they see it falter. If I can spare them, I must. I must.

50

In the early light of dawn he crouched at the edge of the field and watched the towery pines give birth to great shadows that reached out across a tideless sea of blooming bunchgrass, its purpletop tridens put to a balletic bending by the first wind of the coming fall.

The main wagon sat in the middle of the other carts and trolleys. The first thing William noted was that there was no one about. He couldn't smell coffee or bacon and he couldn't see any cookfires. The second was that Ollie was asleep in a locked cage and the cage was strapped to the front end of a Dearborn wagon. Next to him was the cage that held Kushim. The great ape sat with his back against the bars.

William crept through the field and into the camp and still he saw no one. He made it to the cages and the ape watched him with disinterest.

"Ollie," William hissed, and he tried to reach the boy's foot to jostle him awake.

"Ollie," he said again, slightly louder and looked around the camp to see who might have heard. The ape rose and crossed his cage to where it butted against Ollie's and he reached his arm through the bars and with a casual flick of his wrist he managed to roll the boy over.

Ollie, startled, scrambled to his feet and struck his head against the top of the cage and then sat crouched and unsure, holding the stump of his arm.

"What are you doing here?" he asked William. "Where's Lena?"

"I'm busting you out. Where are the keys?"

"Shit if I know," Ollie said. "Was that your plan? Ask me if I had a spare key?"

William looked around the camp.

"I didn't know you'd be locked up."

"You need to get out of here," Ollie said. "And don't let Lena get anywhere near this place. That Downtain is a twisted sonofabitch."

"Can't do it, bud," William said. "You just sit tight, and when the time comes, hold onto your ass."

"Wait," Ollie said, but William was already moving behind a row of wagons toward where the horses were staked.

There were a few men emerging from tents and William stayed low and moved quickly. The first horse he came to was a blue roan and she stirred some at his approach.

"Easy there," he said, holding out his hand. "How'd you like to pull a wagon this morning?"

The horse stamped a bit and then steadied and William scanned the area for tack and found a single harness with crupper and breeching rested against a tree. He drug the harness over to the roan and the horse gave little protest as the boy worked her into it, cinching up the girth and bellyband.

He led her at a slow walk behind the other wagons and toward the cages, the traces of the harness dragging the ground behind them.

"No, you're right," Ollie said as William returned with the horse. "Let's just hunt for a key."

"Get ready for a bumpy ride, bud," William told him, but the horse reared suddenly and the lead rope came out of the boy's hand.

He lunged for it but the horse had turned quickly and was at a full trot in the opposite direction.

William and Ollie watched her go.

"It's the ape," Downtain said, and both boys whipped their heads back around. "The horses get quite spooked around him."

Kushim rose and made a huffing noise and turned in a circle and sat again.

Downtain stepped forward.

"Well," he said. "So much for my little trap. It seems you've come empty-handed. And here I thought we had a deal."

"You're a serpent," the boy said. "There ain't no making deals with somebody like you."

Downtain laughed off the insult.

"There is nobody like me," he said.

William pulled the pistol from the back of his pants and leveled it at the man. Downtain did not react.

"Give me the key to the cage," the boy said. "Let me take my friend and leave, and I'll let you live."

A few of Downtain's men were making their way to the cages, guns drawn. Downtain held up his hand to them.

"It's alright, boys," he said. "He's not going to shoot."

William looked down the barrel of the gun and took a breath in. He moved his finger to the trigger. He felt its weight. Exhaled.

He lowered his arm.

Downtain pointed and three of the men grabbed the boy and he let himself be taken and the pistol too. He was on the verge of tears and he couldn't bring himself to look back at Ollie as the men dragged him to a tent and tossed him inside.

"Let's talk," Downtain said, following them in.

Downtain took off his hat and rested it carefully on the back of a chair and then bypassed the chair and sat instead on a three-legged stool. He ran his hands through his hair and then rested his elbows on his knees and William thought he looked, for a moment, tired.

"Well, that was our moment of excitement for the morning," Downtain said. "Where's the girl?"

"I don't know," William said.

"Yes, you do."

"I don't. I run her off last night. You were right. She lied to us the whole time. Takes after her father, I guess."

"Is that what you think I am, boy? A liar?"

"Does the fox piss smell any different in India?"

Downtain seemed to consider this.

"When people purchase my products—rather than steal them like your friend outside—what do they give me?"

The boy didn't answer.

"They give me paper," Downtain said.

"You mean money?"

"The dollar is paper, is it not? Paper made from trees. And who advocates for the trees?"

"The trees?" William asked, lost.

"Yes," Downtain said and motioned with his hands toward the walls of the tent as if he would imagine the forest that surrounded them both. "These here, the ones still standing. Those, out there, the ones already gone. Who shall be their keeper?"

"I don't know. Not me."

"No." Downtain laughed. "No, certainly not. Since the beginning of time the synchronicity of nature's survival system has mandated that all depend on the every. Bees and birds and squirrels carry pollen and seeds and nuts, and water comes from the sky, and the earth drinks it and gives it back, and even the dead help fertilize the living. And when disaster strikes there is no answer, for disaster itself is a tool of evolution—a tool of balance.

"But what can nature do against the power of man?" Downtain asked. "Man who can take something used by nature since the dawn of existence and give to it a new use and a new meaning."

"I don't know. And right this minute I don't much care."

"Nor are you obligated to. If in one hundred years the trees are gone, man will adapt. Will have adapted already. There is like to be someone right now—young boy or girl—sitting at a desk and sketching out a world devoid of trees. What it looks like. How it operates. Solutions to the problems we ourselves create.

"So you see, we no longer wait on evolution. We have long outpaced it. Whatever the natural is, we are its antithesis. We have found ways to survive that no other species has or will ever approach. We are the only living creature whose greatest enemy is itself. A wolf from one pack may kill a wolf from another, but she won't kill twenty thousand wolves in one day. I go forth in the world and walk up and down in it. All I see is the power of destruction. Greater even than the power of creation. And it is I who offers respite from it."

"But you're not saving anyone. You're just lying to them."

"Ah, and they need the lies."

"They need the lies," the boy repeated.

"Of course they do. We all do. There was a time when everything we did was to survive, now everything we do is to distract ourselves from the fact that we won't. The whole of humanity has turned to one distraction or another. What do I sell that the churches don't? The fortune tellers, even the doctors—peddlers of lies, and who are we to blame them? Do we not tell ourselves lies? You told yourself you would kill me if given the chance, did you not?

"See? We are all liars here," Downtain said. "And you are the worst among us. Because you are lying to yourself."

"Just let us go," William said. "Me and Ollie. We don't have nothing to do with any of this."

"Oh, now," Downtain said. "Don't sell yourself short. There may be uses for you yet. I have friends with all manner of tastes.

"Bring the other one," he told one of the men, and the man nodded and left the tent.

"Is that what they locked you up for in Missouri?" William asked. "Your tastes?"

"Something like that," Downtain said. He looked amused that his reputation was known to the boy. "Prison turned out to be a wonderful training ground. And a consistent pipeline of employees willing to turn a blind eye to some of my more peculiar enterprises. Even some who choose to partake. As I said, any respite from death should be celebrated, not judged."

Someone shouted from outside the tent and Downtain stopped talking and listened.

"Fire," the shouts came again. "She set it on fire."

When the ferrocerium blew, it all but incinerated the wagon that held it and everyone in the tent fell to the ground as those wooden fragments that weren't instantly burned came tearing through the fabric at violent speeds.

The sound of the big bang was so loud in William's ears that he wasn't even concerned with how or why he was facedown in the dirt. He pushed himself up and ran toward the tent flap but Downtain caught his arm. The other men were already outside and Downtain followed them, dragging William a step behind.

Other wagons had caught fire in the explosion. Horses were running through the camp as people tried to pick themselves up off the ground.

A flash to his right and William turned away just as Ollie launched himself shoulder-first into Downtain. The man let go of William and the two boys ran as Downtain lunged at them from the ground.

"Now, that's how you bust somebody out," Ollie said.

William didn't understand nor did he stop to ask. They fled toward the woods.

The camp had fallen to chaos. Some men were dragging their tents away from those that had already caught fire. Others were trying to corral the horses that had broken loose and were tramping about the field. The grass itself was burning. There were people screaming about the fire or the horses or where was Anthony, he was right here. No one seemed to pay the boys much mind.

William looked back for Downtain but did not see him. Much had disappeared in the smoke.

They were at the edge of the camp when he saw her there at the cages. She had a ring of keys and was trying to free the ape.

"Lena," he said, and he stopped.

"C'mon, bud," Ollie urged. "We gotta keep going."

"Go," he said to Ollie and pushed him toward the trees.

William headed for the cages and was still a dozen yards away when Downtain grabbed him from behind.

"Throw yourself down, boy," Downtain said, his voice wild.

He twisted the boy's arm behind his back and William cried out and went to one knee.

He looked to the cage but the girl was gone and so too the ape. His arm felt as if it would snap.

He slapped backward at the man with his free arm but Downtain only laughed and wrenched the other arm tighter. William felt his shoulder rip from its socket.

He screamed.

Downtain was laughing even harder now—manic-like—as if the mayhem only made him stronger. Horses ran smoking from the burning encampment. Men in their underwear chased after them, coughing and choking in the unnatural brume. A woman sat crying on the ground then praying, reaching out her arms to something unseen. Some specter among the flames.

A gunshot.

William felt the pressure release from his arm and he spun away from Downtain, who was looking curiously at the blood near his left shoulder.

Lena was ten yards in front of him. She fired again. The bullet tore through Downtain's left bicep. She was moving closer. She pulled the trigger again. The pistol clicked.

She stopped. Her eyes went wide. Downtain looked at her, grinning and snarling, and running forward, lunging at her.

No, William thought he yelled, but he didn't hear a sound and all he saw was a flash of darkness and now Lena was standing alone, still holding the empty pistol.

A dozen feet away, Downtain was on his back with Kushim roaring above him and there was a true and all-encompassing fear on the man's face.

The ape brought both fists down and William thought he heard the cracking of ribs and Downtain was screaming and the ape pummeled him again and again and the screams stopped but the ape did not. It howled and hammered until the remains beneath were unrecognizable as not just one man but any man at all.

At length Kushim stood and moved away and without turning back he crouched and galloped through the field toward the swamps, and deeper still into the thickest of country, where his story might not again intersect with these, his more barbarous relations.

Lena helped William to his feet.

"I told you I didn't want to see you again," he said, his arm dangling by his side.

She nodded.

"And?" she asked.

"I'm glad you didn't listen."

They ran into the forest as the fire spread and the other men and women had flushed from the camp like startled pheasants. Some stood naked or in undergarments or wrapped in blankets. Most of the blue paint had been washed from their faces. Their dotted patterns yet to be drawn on. They were skinny and tired and they watched the wagons burn with something like deferred amusement. Something like relief. One of the women covered her mouth with a cloth and went back into the smoke and stood over Downtain's body. She looked at it for a moment and then unceremoniously bent down and went through his coat pockets and took his watch and a few coins.

"Come on," Ollie called to the two of them from up ahead. "Let's find that county road and get the hell out of here."

The three of them once more awayed into the woods, each holding onto the others for support.

V

GOING HOME

51

They came out of the Thicket onto a dirt road and William was bleeding badly from a cut on his head and the girl looked worse for the wear, and then there was Ollie, with not but the soiled bandages of his bloody stump. The road led south into Silsbee and the first building they passed was a government sewing warehouse and there were three women taking a smoke break and all three of them dropped their cigarettes and came running.

The women worried over them and asked them more questions than they could have possibly answered and asked to take them to a hospital. William and Lena looked at Ollie.

"You want a hospital, bud?"

The boy looked to where his hand would have been and shook his head.

"Get me home," he said. "I just want to go home."

They were at the train station in Silsbee by midafternoon. Standing on the platform, they were like oddities from some other race of man. People stared. Men frowned. Women put their hands up to their mouths. No one dared get too close.

Trains came and went out in the railyard and the hiss of steam brakes and the smell of burning coal filled up the hours. The three of them stood quiet and exhausted. At some point an older woman handed them sandwiches without saying a word. She sighed, like it was an inconvenience or some great obligation she was duty-bound to fulfill, and then she boarded a train to Kansas City by way of Dallas and didn't look back at them.

They ate in silence. The white bread sticking to the roofs of their mouths.

There was a traveling apothecary on the platform and the doctor took a look at Ollie's wound and marveled at the story of how it came to be and gave the boy a handful of pills to help with the pain. He put William's arm in a sling and gave him a few more pills for good measure.

"What do we owe you?" William asked, and the man waived him off.

"That tale alone will cover it, son."

The man boarded a train to Houston.

The afternoon sun shone white on the steel rails and the people on the platform shuffled under awnings to follow the shade.

"I know y'all," a girl said, and they turned their heads, synchronized, and it was the young woman from Etoile and they did not see Warren, nor did they expect to.

"You bunch look like death warmed over."

"That's about right," Ollie said, though the pills had put a lax smile on his face.

"Well," she said. "I imagine you're wondering where Warren is."

They were not, but she held her head high and told them anyway.

"I'd gone to touch things up in the ladies' and when I come out he was chatting up a waitress right there in the middle of the restaurant. Had his hand on her rear end and everything, if you can believe that. I was so hopping mad I didn't know what to do."

"What did you do?" Lena asked.

"I called him a sonofabitch is what I did," she said. "Walked right on out of there."

"How'd you end up here?"

"I gotta grandma lives in Silsbee. I figured I was already halfway here, might as well come on and see her."

"Heading back to Etoile now, are you?" Ollie asked.

She laughed at him.

"Don't be ridiculous," she said. "I started out for Galveston and that's where I'm going. Warren or not. Something don't go my way, I ain't just gonna tuck tail and run home. Life's full of people with their feet stuck in the mud—I don't want mine to even touch the ground."

A whistle blew and the girl squealed.

"There's mine," she told them and walked forward on the platform and then turned back. "I don't mean to hurt no feelings, but y'all ought to think about a washhouse."

They watched her go.

"I'll say this for her," Ollie said. "She may not know Yankee pinstripes from prison stripes, but she sure wasn't gonna stand for that bastard two-timing her, was she."

"Almost sounds like you admire her," Lena said.

"She's sure enough got some sand to her."

52

The train to Huntington came in the late afternoon.

"You sure you don't want us to wait with you?" William asked Lena, whose train did not arrive for another three hours.

"No, y'all go on. I've caused you enough hardship."

"We've brought plenty of it on ourselves," William told her, and Ollie nodded.

"Thank you," Ollie told her. "For coming back like you did."

"I heard somewhere that friends are supposed to look out for each other."

"Are we friends?" Ollie asked.

"We are," she said, and he came forward and hugged her and almost knocked her over and she laughed.

When she turned to William, he was staring at her.

"William, I wanted to say that I really am—"

"You were right," he said. "You don't owe me anything and you don't belong to anyone. But there is somebody waiting on you. Don't make him wait any longer."

She kissed his cheek and said she didn't know how to thank him.

"You stuck your neck out for me plenty," he told her.

"I lied to you," she said.

He nodded. "Yeah, and I've lied to me too. I guess we'll both have to work on forgiving ourselves."

"Deal," she said, and they shook on it and then they embraced and when the boys boarded the train they looked out the window to where she stood watching them. In time the train lurched forward and began its journey and the girl passed out of the window with the other faces on the platform and then the platform was gone and the window filled up with sky and the boys put their heads down and didn't say anything for a long while.

They were on the train heading north and the passengers on the train stared at them but no one said anything and eventually there were other matters to attend to and the boys sat alone and unencumbered.

William stared at Ollie's wrapped stump.

"Ollie," he said. "You know when you gotta say something—I mean, you just absolutely have to say it or you'll never be able to live with yourself—but you can't figure out how to start it off?"

Ollie shook his head.

"No," he said. "I pretty much say what's on my mind. Hell, sometimes things come out of my mouth that I didn't even know I was thinking."

"Before all this," William said. "I asked the doc, if I were to find my daddy and bring him home and he was to get my mother to a good hospital down in Houston, was there a chance they could save her."

"What did he say?"

"He said there was a better chance of Hoover winning reelection."

"Oh," Ollie said.

He turned and looked away.

"I'm so sorry, bud," William said. "I'm so goddamn sorry."

Ollie scratched at the back of his neck.

"Well," he said. "Don't be."

"But this whole thing," William said. "All of it. It was me just wanting to find him so I could spit in his face. So I could blame him for not being there, even while *I* wasn't. If I had stayed put, none of this would've happened. I can't imagine how hard it's going to be for you now."

"Now?" Ollie asked. "You think things were easy before? And you've had a lot of easy days yourself, have you?"

"You know what I mean."

"I do. Now listen to what *I* mean. There ain't never been such a thing as an easy day," Ollie said. "Two hands or ten. That's lies we tell ourselves about the past or promises we make about the future. Easy days, my ass. I'll tell you something else: There ain't no suggestion box neither. You just play the cards you're dealt. And if it's hard, good. It ought to be. Because the only time things get easy is when you give up fighting. When you lay down and quit. That's your easy days right there. Things being tough? That just means you still care. That's all that means. I've looked easy in the face. Let me tell you. Them cold bodies piled up on that board like spent shells. Like goddamn husks. You think they wouldn't give anything they could for a little bit of hard? For one hand and a beating heart?"

William grabbed the boy and pulled him to him and kissed his forehead before Ollie could push him off.

"I'll be fine," Ollie said, as William grinned at him. "I only need one hand to cover up wrinkles."

"I believe they're called acquired facial markings," William said.

Ollie let himself smile and then turned back to the window where the train's progression sucked away the forest one tree after another until it all just blended together in green.

"A lot prettier country from this side of the glass."

Ollie was soon asleep and William opened his father's journal to the only entry with a title.

Laurie

When my grandfather passed, there was a funeral held at the old country church outside of Huntsville, and there among the mourners was a girl so lovely I thought her heaven sent. And though her beauty was undeniable, it was her weeping that fascinated me the most—this young woman I had not met who was crying for my grandfather so.

"Did you know him?" I asked her as we filed out of the church house after the service. "My grandfather?"

"I did," she told me, and she told me she had visited him some over the years as his health declined. A lonely man, with no family. It saddened her.

"I should hope someone would be Christian enough to do the same for me," she said.

"May I call on you?" I asked her, and before I could even think of the words, they were leaving my mouth.

"You don't mean it," she said. "You're clearly in the throes of grief."

I told her the truth—that I barely knew him.

"Very well," she said. "Then *I* am in the throes of grief."

"Allow me to comfort you," I said.

"Comfort me?" she asked.

"I should hope someone would be Christian enough to do the same for me," I told her.

"Comfort me," she repeated, and I could see she was considering it. "And then what? Off to the big city?"

"No ma'am," I said. "Off to college. Tarleton. I'm gonna learn about agriculture. Be a farmer, like him. That's my dream. A farm. A family. A quiet life."

"That sounds like a lovely dream," she told me.

"Would you like to be in it?"

"Slow down, handsome," she said. "You finish your studies, then look me up."

"What's your name?" I asked.

"Laurie," she told me. "Laurie Dubose."

I did not think she would wait while I got my degree, but she did. Though she surely had many suitors in my absence.

At Tarleton I learned the processes and business of modern farming, but I also studied the classics and theology and philosophy. Each break from school, I went back to Walker County and courted Laurie, quoting for her sonnets and poems and feats of literature. I don't believe she was ever truly impressed, but she listened all the same. She was well balanced. God fearing. She was as fine a woman as I'd ever known.

We married soon after my graduation and purchased a small cotton farm in the southern portion of Angelina County. I built our home, bought a mule and plow, and when Laurie first became pregnant, I thought it the culmination of my life's plan. A farmer and his family, destined for hard work, thoughtful conversation, and the simple happiness brought by each.

But the world had gone too long without war, and now it demanded another bloodletting. Another sacrifice from us, its parasitic guests.

She begged me not to go. I could have claimed deferment for my role in agriculture. I could have gone back to Tarleton as a teacher. She even suggested running, the two of us, such was her desire to avoid the war. She begged me, but I didn't listen. The call of battle was like a siren song to the young and the ignorant. We thought we would be heroes, before we knew there was no such thing. And now nothing is the same, nor will it ever be again. And when I look at her face, all I see is my own regret. My own guilt. I should never have gone.

William held the journal in his lap. *I should never have gone.*

He tried to imagine what his life might have been without the war but strangely he could not. It was as if there was no world, even in his mind, that could exist without it. And he thought of Downtain and a world without trees and how it may be true that men have evolved far beyond a great many things. But war has kept the pace. War is always with us.

The landmarks began to look familiar to the boy and he judged they would be to Huntington soon. He flipped through the journal's pages until he came to the last entry. It was the first one he'd read when the woman in Doucette gave it to him and he read it again now and knew in this moment that he would never see his father again.

> *The horrors do not cease. In the meadow is a tree, and the tree is burning. Soon the grasses will catch. Soon the world will be afire, and the flames will consume all that does not matter. And nothing matters.*

53

When at last he spoke to his mother, he hardly knew where to begin. An apology, but how? What words could convey a fracturing of spirit? What remorse could ever be the equal of regret?

"I'm sorry," he said, and he got down on his knees and then he said it again and he cried and kissed her hand and he went on apologizing for things he might have done differently and apologizing also for a great number of things far beyond his own agency, but he asked her forgiveness all the same.

"I just didn't want to see you like this. I'm sorry. I tried. I tried with the cotton and I failed and I tried to get you to go to Houston but you wouldn't and I tried to find Daddy but I couldn't. And all of it, the good and the bad, was because I couldn't accept what was happening. I was scared of it. Not of him or the farm or anything else—just you. I was scared of seeing you go. I couldn't accept it, so I ran. I left you here alone and maybe one day I'll forgive myself but probably I won't and I guess the dumbest part of all is that it ain't gonna make any difference to you one way or the other."

His sobbing echoed through the empty room like a chorus of mourners.

Mr. Leek opened the door and said it was time and the boy wiped his face and nodded and stood and looked at her once more before Mr. Leek came and closed the lid. Once more and never again.

By late afternoon his mother was buried. She was laid to rest beside her daughter in the little cemetery on a sloping piece of meadow not far from a small pond. The preacher from Shawnee Prairie had moved to Diboll in hopes of a bigger flock, so a young minister from Manning came out for the interment and he spoke of the power of life everlasting and the power it has over death and William looked at the box and frowned.

When the small congregation departed, William stayed behind.

He stood over her grave and was a long time standing.

"The ground does not deserve you. This world did not deserve you. He did not deserve you. I—" He stopped. Turned away from the stone.

He walked through the graveyard toward the pond and he passed by markers and monuments alike and some stood stately and refined and others so eroded it seemed a single gust of wind might scatter them to the elements. There were stones for men who died in the Great War and in the Civil War and in the war against Mexico. Others died by sickness or clumsiness or a single act of passion. But all, in one fashion or another, were taken by time. And in time these tributes would be taken also. Look upon my Works, ye Mighty, and despair.

When the boy reached the water, there was not a man in sight. The sunset was long out over the pond and the pond spoke of it in creased ripplets that rose and fell and ceded swaths of blue-green water to the pink sky reflection. Deer moved in silence through the hardwood forest and down the long-trodden trails of man and beast alike, and all such paths leading to the water's salvation. There they dipped their heads and drank of the pond and there they watched as the light abandoned the earth and their eyes shone metallic in the settling dark. Storm clouds gathered at the lip of the horizon and he ignored them.

He stepped out of his boots and pulled off his socks and left them at the water's edge. He put his bare feet in the pond and closed his eyes and started walking.

He felt the water rising. Knees. Thighs. Waist. It was warm and weightless. Stomach. Chest. Neck. He took a breath and went beneath.

A doe raised her head and looked out at the middle of the pond and when the boy did not resurface the deer looked away with no sort of opinion. As if sooner or later the water would swallow everything anyway.

Below the surface the boy's body turned slowly. His knees came up toward his chest. His chin tucked. The vacuum of silence was roaring all around him. His curled being floated and twisted with the whim of the water.

Pressure in his ears. His head. His heart. His beating heart.

That's what he heard—the pumping of his own blood. His own life playing out in real time and the voices in his head not but a commentary of things imagined. Nothing besides remained.

He rose from the water. Wet hair fell across his forehead and gathering droplets streaked his face, and the pond was still and quiet and gave way to the world of sound what surrounded him—the flutter of doves come down from the prairie lands, the buzzing of bees along the edge of the water, the high-throated chirping from every manner of bird, the industrious thrum of dragonflies, the soft sashay of the wind-tickled leaves, the snap and thud of a falling pecan, the quick splash of a pond fish hunting in the shallow reeds.

And here, he thought, with the interment of what would be wild forever, might the world hold close the divinities of its creation. Here, on the numenless plain, absent of grace and godhead alike, might the world—if it is still the world—watch over and keep them. And in the keeping of its own sanctity might it harrow the stars and bury there an atman among the dust from which all was first born and might be born again, and bloom again that first garden, resown but never reaped. Never sullied. And the world—if it ever was the world—never gone.

William closed his eyes and asked that these things be true, and he knew not to whom or what he prayed, but he prayed all the same. And the sky had darkened in earnest and the birds had gone quiet and when the rain began to fall he lifted his face up to it and kept his eyes closed. It made a dimpled surface of the pond all around him and he was wet from the pond and wet from the rain and wet from his tears and it filled him, this trinity, and it held him and he opened his eyes.

It was well after dark when he arrived home and the notice on the door had tomorrow's date. He took the paper in his hands and held it and stood on the porch and looked out at this place and this part of himself he would never again see outside of tampered memory.

The dead cotton stretched near to the trees and crows lit along the foundering fence and the cold wind came down from the north and he turned his back to it and went inside. He built the last fire in the stove and stood beside it in his wet clothes and after a while he went to his bed and a lizard sat on the windowsill and its pinched head jerked up and wild black eyes stared at him.

"You're not the same lizard," he said, and then he fell asleep.

In between dreams and reality he heard her voice and he could hear it clearly.

I know, she said. *But sometimes it can be so beautiful.*

He kept his eyes closed and there was no other sound save the birds and after a while he got up and dressed and he crept from the room and went quiet across the hall and put his ear to the door but he heard nothing else. He did not open it. He would never open it again.

He stopped in the doorway and the light framed his shape and he turned, a glowing black form, and he looked again at the house his father built and then he left out from it.

A calf came uncertain around the corner of the house and stood there and he stared at it and it at him. After a while it lowed and flicked its tail.

"I ought to just leave you," he said.

A half hour later he was laboring up the Quinns' driveway, leading the calf on a rope.

Mrs. Quinn was on the porch.

"I guess this'un wanted to come down and get one last look at the place," he said.

The woman stayed quiet.

The calf was chomping at dead grass in the yard and William let go of the rope and went up onto the porch.

"You alright, ma'am?" he asked.

"They finally done it," she said, and there was a faraway look to her. "I told them it would kill him and they didn't listen and him just screaming and hollering."

"What's happened? Where's Mr. Quinn?"

She pointed and the boy went in the house and down the hallway and called out to Mr. Quinn and then opened the bedroom door.

The old man was sitting slouched in the bed. He looked up briefly at the boy.

"They say it was a mild heart attack," he said without greeting. "Mild they say."

"You alright?" William asked.

"I was cussing that smug sonofabitch is what I was doing. Him and his goddamn executioners."

"What happened?"

"They've gotta keep the cost of cattle stable. Supply and demand or the like. Five dollars a head they give me. In exchange for my family's legacy."

"They killed your cows," the boy said.

"They took my son," the old man said, and he closed his eyes. "So many good boys. I'd be goddamned if I was gonna sit quiet and let them take from me again."

"But they did."

"Yes," he said, and the boy thought he had never looked older. "They did."

Mr. Quinn coughed and then growled in pain and William moved toward him and the old man shook his head and waved the boy off.

"I guess you didn't find Thomas," he said.

"No," William said, and then they were both quiet.

"You know the silliest thing my daddy ever told me?" Mr. Quinn said, and then he coughed again. "He said there's no such thing as changing times."

William watched him.

"I been thinking about that for fifty years."

"What do you make of it?" the boy asked.

"I don't know yet," he said, and he turned with great effort and reached toward the nightstand and opened a drawer.

"Here," he said, handing the boy fifty dollars. "Them folks looking after Laurie give this to me when she passed. Told me to hold onto it for you. Told me it didn't seem right."

The boy took the money.

"I saw men killed," William said. "Watched them die right in front of me. Watched my friends get hurt. And the whole time I was thinking it was all my fault. Like I set something in motion that caused every bit of it."

The boy was fighting tears.

"Is that how he felt?" he asked. "Is that how he feels?"

The boy was trembling and Mr. Quinn worked to adjust himself and sit up taller against the headboard and he motioned for William to come to his side. The boy did and the old man grabbed him and pulled him in close and kissed him on the cheek and on the head again and again and the boy cried and the old man told him he loved him.

"I love you. I love you. I love you."

William knew Mr. Quinn was speaking to his son—was speaking to Arthur—but he didn't care. They gave one another a thing they each desperately needed and when at last the boy pulled away, the old man touched his face and thanked him.

"You gonna be alright, son?" Mr. Quinn asked.

"I'm not sure," he said. "But I don't think I'm supposed to be sure. I think if we were sure about everything all the time then there'd be something missing from all of this."

"That's an alright thing to think," Mr. Quinn said. "So long as you keep on going, you're never out of it. You understand that? Even if you don't find what you're looking for, you just keep going. You understand?"

"Maybe," William said. "Maybe I do."

The boy went to the door of the room and turned and thanked the old man and the old man nodded and William went back out to the porch and Mrs. Quinn was feeding the calf from a bottle.

"Take care of him," William said, and the woman didn't know if he meant her husband or the calf but she said she would and she meant it.

She watched him go.

He took the money and went to Manning and to the mule barn and bought Clara back for fifty dollars and took her to the funeral home and hitched her out front. No one was in the lobby so he let himself into the back hallway and found Ollie hard at work on a man who'd laughed so hard at an obscene joke he fell out of his chair and fractured his skull.

William watched his friend work, leaned over the body and using his one hand to paint the man's face and his other arm to steady the table.

"Arm feel alright?" William asked.

Ollie nodded.

"Doc says that old woods witch didn't do half bad."

"Good," William said, and then he didn't know what else to say.

The dead man's clothes were in a pile in the corner and he looked at them and looked at the boots and he wondered if anyone would come for them and if not, where would they end up.

"I'm leaving, bud," he said instead.

Ollie paused, briefly, and then continued his process.

"Headed down to New Orleans to win back that girl, are you?"

"No."

"A new lead on your daddy, then," Ollie surmised.

William shook his head.

"No. Just leaving. Headed West."

Ollie paused again.

"Like in the songs?"

"We'll see."

"*You'll* see," Ollie said, putting down his brush. "Not me. It turns out adventuring ain't for everybody. And I'm just fine right here where I've always been."

"I know you are. I'll tell you all about whatever's out there, when I get back."

Ollie shook his head.

"You ain't coming back," he said, and he nodded at his oldest and best friend and William nodded back.

"Then I guess I'll tell you about it some other time," William said, and Ollie smiled.

"Some other time," he said and he picked up his brush and then they were, the both of them, gone from the other's story. And time did toll the bell of their parting.

William stood in the meager thoroughfare of the town and looked at the buildings, smaller now than they'd appeared even one week ago. *Smaller and more fragile*, he thought, *like the world around me.*

But now he would seek that world, to puzzle out its meaning, however delicate, however daunting. He led the mule west, back toward Shawnee Prairie, and he passed by the farm one last time. He told himself not to look but he looked all the same, and in the window his mother and father were drinking their coffee and laughing and this is how he would choose to remember them, and on he went.

Just before the Quinns' driveway, a wagon came from the opposite direction and stopped and Kathy Thurgood leaned down from the driver's bench and asked where he was going.

"Not real sure," he told her. "Where's Katy?"

"She's gone swimming with Caleb Hargrove. Guess you done missed your chance."

William nodded.

"And you?" he asked.

"Headed to see my Oliver."

"Your Oliver?"

"Well somebody has to take care of him, now that you've gone and got him hurt."

William didn't mind the accusation. He smiled.

"I bet he's sure glad that someone is you."

She settled back onto the seat, looking pleased with herself. She popped the reins.

William walked on with the mule and they walked even as the moon rose up behind them. They walked through the night and at dawn they crossed the Neches River into Trinity County and by nightfall they crossed the Trinity into Walker County where the boy's grandfather was buried. On they went until the pine trees quit the land and the Brazos Valley lay out before them and the counties had names the boy did not know. And further still until there was little green to the country and the ground turned to hard rock and the days of yawning plain so stretched before them.

Days passed. The sun's westward retreat, and the boy and the mule trailing after it. And when the moon was full he could see craters and the shadows of craters across its pale face like the footprints of giants. And he listened for the howling of wolves, but he knew such things were no more in this country—would never be again. And no matter his early starts, each day would end the same, the sun beating him to that far horizon, the darkness overtaking his pursuit.

On through the fall and into winter and the cold days found him high in the mountain passes to the west. In the high timbers, him and the mule. Traveling by day and in the evening the boy sat in the failing light like some desperado of old. He sat in the cold dirt, his arms wrapped around his knees. And what colors did appear—put upon by the cold wind and drawn fleeting across the makeshift sky in hues of purple and pink. He put his head in his hands and wept. He wept for the beauty of the world and for the terror of it. He wept for his mother and her faith and her kindness, and he wept for his father and the pain and anger that overwhelmed him. He wept at the sun's setting and in the hours to come wept for its rising, one and the same. And when at last he came down from the mountain, he passed among other travelers on the narrow road and they saw that his face was radiant.

EPILOGUE

It's cold when he finally returns. Fields frozen like a memory.

Not his memory.

Manning is a ghost town. The mill has burned and the people drifted away with the smoke. Shawnee Prairie was never much but it is somehow lesser. He shivers against the winter air.

The cabin is gone. The barn still stands, at least in part. The old roof has gone in on one side and there's vines crawling up the walls like they're reaching out, getting ready to pull the whole thing down into the earth.

He walks on by. Maybe he lifts his head. Maybe he gives some thought to it all. It's early evening and a storm is coming. He can see the black clouds hastening the night.

She's buried there close to the pond. On he comes, pulling his coat tight around him. Old coat with holes in the right pocket but otherwise has held up through the years. The wind blows at it.

He finds her stone among the others and the whole place covered with winter pasture and unmowed.

He stands with flowers in hand. Lenten roses. They're ragged from the cold. So is he. But he lays them there on the cold ground all the same.

He has witnessed many versions of this world. Versions of himself.

The time he spent with her will always be the kindest. This he knows. This he's always known. His regrets are many. Infinite.

The rain is falling now and it's an icy rain and he tells her he's loved her every day and that he'll never stop. He wonders out loud if some men are destined to ruin all that they are a part of. He wonders out loud if men are destined to do anything at all.

"You see," he tells her. "All this time and I haven't learned a goddamn thing."

He walks in the sleet and rain back to the old barn and goes inside for to get dry but there is no getting dry and there is no getting warm and the cold is in his bones. Deeper still. He sits there—shaking, water dripping from his beard—and he watches the road.

He knows it is senseless. He knows he is mad. For two score he has wandered. Through cities he could not imagine and country he did not recognize. Whatever it was he sought in those early days is lost to him now. He cannot even remember its face.

He has taken to mumbling. Speaking to himself of things only he might understand, though in truth he understands little more than those who stop to stare. At times he talks of his life—of some thing that happened half a century ago. Other times he mumbles poetry or holy verses and sometimes he begins to scream and cannot stop.

The ire he held for the world has long ago turned inward, crippling his mind. But still he waits and watches and he imagines the boy out there on the road, passing by on the way to some warmer world. He knows their paths will never cross again. But in his broken vision of the past, he can see him. His son. The old man waves at him.

It is cold and he is tired. So very tired. He lays down and closes his eyes.

The cold is gone.

The boy is waving back.

ACKNOWLEDGMENTS

Thank you to Mark Gottlieb, Trident Media Group, and everyone at Blackstone Publishing. Thank you to my truly brilliant editor, Corinna Barsan, who has now guided me through two novels, and who I hope will be with me for many more. And a huge thank you to Josie Woodbridge who has been my rock since the beginning.

Thanks also to Lucy Griffith, Andy Robinson, William Kent Kreuger, Johnny D. Boggs, Caroline Frost, Kathleen Kent, Owen Egerton, Elizabeth Wetmore, May Cobb, David Joy, Corey Ryan Forrester, Sarah Bird, Christopher Brown, Stacey Swann, Jim Haley, Matt Bondurant, David Heska Wanbli Weiden, Claire Fullerton, Kathy L. Murphy, Mandy Haynes, Robert Gwaltney, Jacob Marquez, Carol Ann Tack, Theresa Bakken, Mark Zvonkovic, Mike McCrary, Oscar Rodriguez, Scott von Doviak, Rudy Ruiz, Scott Semegran, Chris Mullen, Caren Creech, Wes Ferguson, Jacqui Devaney, Cheyanne Clagett, Tucker Cowan, the fellas at the Weather Permitting podcast, and so many others.

Thank you to Becka Oliver, Sarah Beach, J Evan Parks and the Writers' League of Texas, Heather Duncan and the MPIBA, and everyone at the Western Writers of America.

Thanks to Doug Dorst, Jennifer duBois, Lindsay Stern, and the Texas State MFA program.

Special thanks to the Tye Preston Memorial Library.

And thanks as always to my wife, Jordan, whose support is wholly necessary.

Much inspiration was found in the poems of Rabindranath Tagore, W. H. Auden, Percy Bysshe Shelley; the King James and New International Versions of the Bible; the novels of William Gay, Cormac McCarthy, Kent Haruf, William Faulkner, and Thomas Wolfe; and the nonfiction of Jim Harrison, Edward Abbey, and J. Frank Dobie.